DEVIL'S LAIR

MOLOTOV OBSESSION: BOOK 1

ANNA ZAIRES

♠ MOZAIKA PUBLICATIONS ♠

Copyright © 2021 Anna Zaires and Dima Zales
www.annazaires.com

Published by Mozaika Publications, an imprint of Mozaika LLC.
www.mozaikallc.com

Cover by The Book Brander
www.thebookbrander.com

Photography from The Cover Lab
www.thecoverlab.com

e-ISBN: 978-1-63142-619-3
ISBN: 978-1-63142-675-9

1

CHLOE

A CAR BACKFIRES AND THE STOREFRONT WINDOW TO MY left explodes, blasting shards of glass in a wide radius.

I freeze, so stunned I barely feel the glass biting into my bare arm. Then the screams reach me.

"Shots fired! Call 911," someone on the street is yelling, and adrenaline floods my veins as my brain makes the connection between the sound and the glass explosion.

Someone is shooting.

At me.

They found me.

My feet react before the rest of me, propelling me into a jump just as another sharp *pop!* reaches my ears, and the register inside the store explodes into splinters.

The same register I was blocking with my body a second ago.

I taste terror. It's coppery, like blood. Maybe it *is* blood. Maybe I was shot, and I'm dying. But no, I'm running. My heartbeat is roaring in my ears, my lungs pumping for all they're worth as I sprint down the block. I can feel the burn in my legs, so I'm alive.

For now.

Because they found me. Again.

I make a sharp right, sprinting down a narrow side street, and over my shoulder, I catch a glimpse of two men half a block behind me, running after me at full speed.

My lungs are already screaming for air, my legs threatening to give out, but I put on a desperate burst of speed and dash into an alley before they round the corner. A five-foot-tall chain-link fence cuts the alley in half, but I climb up and over it in seconds, adrenaline lending me an athlete's agility and strength.

The back of the alley connects to another street, and a sob of relief bursts from my throat as I realize it's the one where I parked my car before the interview.

Run, Chloe. You can do it.

Desperately sucking in air, I sprint down the street, scanning the curb for a beat-up Toyota Corolla.

Where is it?

Where did I leave the damn car?

Was it behind the blue pickup truck or the white one?

Please let it be there. Please let it be there.

Finally, I spot it, half-hidden behind a white van. Fumbling in my pocket, I extract the keys, and with violently shaking hands, I press the button to unlock the car.

I'm already inside and jamming the key into the ignition when I see my pursuers emerging from the alley a block behind me, each with a gun in his hand.

I'm still shaking five hours later as I pull into a gas station, the first one I've seen on this winding mountain road.

That had been close, much too close.

They're getting bolder, more desperate.

They shot at me on the fucking street.

My legs feel like rubber as I step out of the car, clutching my empty water bottle. I need a bathroom, water, food, and gas, in that order—and ideally a new vehicle, as they might've gotten my Toyota's license plate. That is, assuming they didn't already have it.

I have no idea how they found me in Boise, Idaho, but it might've been through my car.

The problem is, what little I know about evading criminals hellbent on murder comes from books and movies, and I have no idea what my pursuers actually *can* track. Just to be safe, though, I'm not using any of my credit cards, and I ditched my phone the very first day.

Another problem is I have exactly thirty-two dollars and twenty-four cents in my wallet. The waitressing position I interviewed for this morning in Boise would've been a lifesaver, as the café owner was open to paying me cash under the table, but they found me before I could do a single shift.

A few inches to the right, and the bullet would've gone through my head instead of that storefront window.

Blood pooling on the kitchen floor... Pink robe on white tile... Glazed, unseeing stare...

My heart rate spikes and my shaking intensifies, my knees threatening to buckle underneath me. Leaning on the hood of my car, I drag in a shuddering breath, trying to get the mad drumming of my pulse to slow as I shove the memories deep down, where they can't squeeze my throat in a vise.

I can't think about what happened. If I do, I'll fall apart and they'll win.

They might win anyway because I have no money and no clue what I'm doing.

One thing at a time, Chloe. One foot in front of the other.

Mom's voice comes to me, calm and steady, and I force myself to straighten away from the car. So what if my situation has gone from desperate to critical?

I'm still alive, and I intend to stay that way.

I extracted all the glass shards from my arm a couple of hours ago, but the T-shirt I wrapped around it to stop the bleeding looks strange, so I grab my hoodie from the trunk and put the hood up to hide my face from any security cameras that might be inside the gas station. I don't know if the people after me would be able to get access to that footage, but it's better not to risk it.

Again, assuming they're not already tracking my car.

Focus, Chloe. One step at a time.

Taking a steadying breath, I walk into the small convenience store attached to the gas station and, with a small wave at the elderly woman behind the register, go directly to the bathroom in the back. Once my most pressing needs are taken care of, I wash my hands and face, fill up my water bottle from the faucet, and pull out my wallet to count the bills, just in case.

Nope, I didn't miscalculate or miss a stray twenty. Thirty-two dollars and twenty-four cents is all the cash I have left.

The face in the bathroom mirror is that of a stranger, all strained and hollow-cheeked, with dark circles under overly large brown eyes. I've neither eaten nor slept normally since I've been on the run, and it shows. I look older than my twenty-three years, the past month having aged me by a decade.

Suppressing the useless bout of self-pity, I focus on the practical. Step one: decide how to allocate the funds I do have.

The biggest priority is gas for the car. It's got less than a quarter tank, and there's no telling when I'll find another gas station in this area. Filling up all the way will set me back at least thirty dollars, leaving me only a couple of dollars for food to quench the gnawing emptiness in my stomach.

More importantly, the next time I run out of gas, I'm screwed.

Exiting the bathroom, I head to the register and tell the elderly cashier to give me twenty bucks worth of gas. I also grab a hot dog and a banana, and devour the hot dog while she slowly counts out the change. The banana I stash in my hoodie's front pocket for tomorrow's breakfast.

"Here you go, dearie," the cashier says in a croaky voice, handing me the change along with a receipt. With a warm smile, she adds, "You have a nice day now, hear?"

To my shock, my throat constricts, and tears prickle at the back of my eyes, the simple kindness undoing me completely. "Thank you. You too," I say in a choked voice, and stuffing the change into my wallet, I hurry toward the exit before I can alarm the woman by bursting into tears.

I'm almost out the door when a local newspaper catches my eye. It's in a bin labeled "FREE," so I grab it before continuing on to my car.

While the tank is filling up, I get my unruly emotions under control and unfold the newspaper, going straight for the classified section in the back. It's a long shot, but maybe someone around here is hiring for some kind of gig, like washing windows or trimming hedges.

Even fifty bucks could up my chances of survival.

At first, I don't see anything along the lines of what I'm looking for, and I'm about to fold the paper in disappointment when a listing at the bottom of the page catches my attention:

Live-in tutor wanted for four-year-old. Must be well-educated, good with children, and willing to relocate to a remote mountain estate. $3K/week cash. To apply, email resume to tutorcandidates459@gmail.com.

Three grand a week in cash? What the fuck?

Unable to believe my eyes, I reread the ad.

Nope, all the words are still the same, which is insane. Three grand a week for a tutor? In cash?

It's a hoax, it's got to be.

Heart pounding, I finish filling up the tank and get into the car. My mind is racing. I'm the perfect candidate for this position. Not only have I just graduated with an Education Studies major, but I've babysat and tutored kids all through high school and college. And relocation to a remote mountain estate? Sign me up! The more remote, the better.

It's as if the ad was crafted just for me.

Wait a minute. Could this be a trap?

No, that's truly paranoid thinking. Ever since this morning's close call, I've been driving aimlessly with the sole goal of putting as much distance between myself and Boise as possible while staying off the major roads and highways to avoid traffic cameras. My pursuers would've had to have a crystal ball to guess that I'd end up in this remote area, much less pick up this local paper. The only way this could be a trap is if they'd placed similar ads in all the newspapers across the country, as well as on all the major job sites, and even then, it feels like a stretch.

No, this is unlikely to be a trap set specifically for me, but it could be something equally sinister.

I hesitate for a moment, then get out of the car and go back into the store.

"Excuse me, ma'am," I say, approaching the elderly cashier. "Do you live in this area?"

"Why, yes, dearie." A smile brightens her wrinkled face. "Elkwood Creek born and bred."

"Great. In that case"—I unfold the newspaper and place it on the counter—"do you know anything about this?" I point at the ad.

She pulls out a pair of reading glasses and squints at the small text. "Huh. Three grand a week for a tutor—must be even richer than they say."

My pulse jumps in excitement. "You know who placed this ad?"

She looks up, rheumy eyes blinking behind the thick lenses of her glasses. "Well, I can't be certain, dearie, but rumor has it, some wealthy Russian bought out the old Jamieson property, way up in the mountains, and built a brand-new place there. Has been hiring local boys for some random jobs here and there, always paying cash. No one's said anything about a kid, though, so it might not be him—but I can't think of anyone else around these parts with that kind of money, much less anything close to an estate."

Holy shit. This may actually be for real. A rich foreigner—that would explain both the too-high salary and its cash nature. The man—or more likely the couple, since there's a child involved—may not know the going rate for tutors around here, or may not care. When you're wealthy enough, a few grand may be no more meaningful than a few pennies. For me, though, a single week's paycheck could mean the difference between life and death, and if I were to earn that kind of money for a month, I'd be able to buy another used car—and maybe even some fake papers, so I could get out of the country and disappear for good.

Best of all, if the estate is remote enough, it may take a while before my pursuers find me there—if they ever do. With a cash salary, there would be no paper trail, nothing to connect me to the Russian couple.

This job could be the answer to all my prayers… if I get it, that is.

"Is there a public library anywhere around here?" I ask, trying to temper my excitement. I don't want to get my hopes up. Even if my resume is the best they get, the hiring process could take weeks or months, and it's not safe to stick around here that long.

If they found me in Boise, they'll find me here too.

It's only a matter of time.

The cashier beams at me. "Why, yes, dearie. Just drive north about ten miles, and when you see the first buildings, take a left, drive past two intersections, and it'll be on your left, right next to the sheriff's office."

"Wonderful, thank you. Do you have a pen?" When she hands it to me, I jot down the directions on the front of the newspaper.

Not having a smartphone with GPS sucks.

"Have a nice day," I tell the elderly lady, and when I head out this time, there's a definite bounce in my step.

———

The tiny library closes at five p.m., so I hurriedly put together my resume and cover letter on one of the public computers, then email both to the address indicated in the ad. Instead of a phone number and email address, I put only my email on the resume; hopefully, that will suffice.

By the time I'm done, the library is closing, so I get back into my car and drive out of the small town, randomly turning onto narrow, winding roads until I find what I'm looking for.

A clearing in the woods where I can park my Toyota behind the trees, out of sight of anyone driving by.

With the car safely situated, I open the trunk and take out another sweater from the suitcase I was lucky enough to have with me when my life went to pieces. Rolling up the sweater, I stretch out on the backseat, place the makeshift pillow under my head, and close my eyes.

My last thought before sleep drags me under is the hope that I stay alive long enough to hear back about the job.

2

NIKOLAI

A KNOCK ON THE DOOR DISTRACTS ME FROM THE EMAIL I'm reading, and I look up from my laptop as Alina opens the door and gracefully steps into my office.

"We got a promising application tonight," she says, approaching my desk. "Here, take a look." She hands me a thick folder.

I open it. A driver's license photo of a striking young woman stares at me from the front page. Her brown eyes are so big they dominate her small, diamond-shaped face, and even on the grainy printout, her bronzed skin seems to glow, as if lit from within by an invisible candle. But it's her mouth that catches my attention. Small yet perfectly plump, it's a mix between a doll's Cupid-bow pout and something one might find on a porn star.

She's not smiling in this picture; her expression is solemn, her hair pulled back in either a tight ponytail or a bun. The next page, however, has a picture of her laughing, her head thrown back and her face framed by golden-brown waves that disappear below her slender shoulders. She's beautiful in this photo, and so radiant that I feel something inside me go dangerously still and quiet even as my pulse quickens with a primal male response.

Suppressing the bizarre reaction, I flip the page back and read the info on the driver's license.

Chloe Emmons is twenty-three years old, five-foot-four, and resides in Boston, Massachusetts—which means she's a long way from home.

"How did she hear about this position?" I ask, glancing up at Alina. "I thought we only placed the ad in the local papers."

She moves the printouts with the photos aside and taps a glossy red nail on the page underneath. "Read the cover letter."

I turn my attention to the page. It appears Chloe Emmons is on a post-graduation road trip and just happened to be passing through Elkwood Creek when she saw our ad and decided to apply for the position. The cover letter is well written and neatly formatted, as is the resume that follows. I can see why Alina thought it promising. Though the girl has just received her Bachelor's in Education Studies from Middlebury College, she's had more teaching internships and babysitting jobs than the previous three candidates combined.

Konstantin's report on her is next. As usual, he's had his team do a deep dive on her social media, criminal and DMV records, financial statements, school transcripts, medical records, and everything else about her life that had been computerized at any point. It's a longer read, so I look up at Alina. "Any red flags?"

She hesitates. "Maybe. Her mother passed away a month ago—apparent suicide. Since then, Chloe has basically been off the grid: no social media posts, no credit card transactions, no calls on her cell."

"So she's either having trouble coping, or something else is going on."

Alina nods. "My bet is on the first; her mother was the only family she had."

I shut the folder and push it away. "That doesn't explain the lack of credit card transactions. Something's off here. But even if it's what you think, an emotionally disturbed woman is the last thing we need."

A humorless smile touches Alina's jade-green eyes. "Are you sure about that, Kolya? Because I feel like she might fit right in."

And before I can reply, my sister turns around and walks out.

I don't know what makes me pick up the folder again an hour later—morbid curiosity, most likely. Flipping through the thick stack of papers, I find the police report on the mother's suicide. Apparently, Marianna Emmons, waitress, age forty, was found on her kitchen floor, her wrists slit. It was a neighbor who called it in; the daughter, Chloe, was nowhere to be found—and she never showed up to identify or bury the body.

Interesting. Could pretty little Chloe have offed her mom? Is that why she's on her off-the-grid "road trip?"

According to the police report, there was no suspicion of foul play. Marianna had a history of depression, and she'd tried to commit suicide once before, when she was sixteen. But I know how easy it is to stage a murder scene if you know what you're doing.

All it takes is a little foresight and skill.

It's a leap, of course, but I haven't gotten where I am by assuming the best about people. Even if Chloe Emmons isn't guilty of matricide, she's guilty of something. My instincts are telling me there's more to her story, and my instincts are rarely wrong.

The girl is trouble. I know it beyond a shadow of a doubt.

Still, something keeps me from closing the folder. I read through Konstantin's report in its entirety, then go through the screenshots of her social media. Surprisingly, it's not a lot of selfies; for a girl that pretty, Chloe doesn't seem overly focused on her looks. Instead, the majority of her posts consist of videos of baby animals and photos of scenic spots, along with links to blog posts and articles about childhood development and optimal teaching methods.

If not for that police report and her month-long disappearance from the grid, Chloe Emmons would appear to be exactly what she claims: a brand-new college grad with a passion for teaching.

Flipping back to the beginning of the folder, I study the photo of her laughing, trying to understand what it is about the girl that intrigues me. Her pretty face, for sure, but that's only part of it. I've seen—and fucked—women far more classically beautiful than she. Even that porn-doll mouth is nothing special in the grand scheme of things, though no man in his right mind would pass up the chance to feel those plump, soft lips wrapped around his cock.

No, it's something else that exerts that magnetic pull on me, something to do with the radiance of her smile. It's like spotting a ray of sunlight breaking through the clouds on a winter day. I want to touch it, feel its warmth... capture it, so I can have it for my own.

My body hardens at the thought, dark, X-rated images sliding through my mind. A better man—a better father—would shut that folder right away, if only because of the temptation it presents, but I'm not that man.

I'm a Molotov, and we've never done something as prosaic as the right thing.

Drumming my fingers on my desk, I come to a decision.

Chloe Emmons might be too troubled to allow near my son, but I still want to meet her.

I want to feel that ray of sunlight on my skin.

3

CHLOE

THE TWELVE-FOOT-TALL METAL GATE SLIDES APART AS I drive up, my Toyota's motor whining at the steep incline of the unpaved road leading up the mountain to the estate. Gripping the wheel tightly, I drive through the open gate, my nervousness intensifying with each second.

I still can't believe I'm here. I was almost certain I would have nothing in my inbox when I went to the library this morning. It was way too soon to expect a response. Just in case, though, I wanted to check my email and then spend a few hours looking online for other gigs within a half-tank's driving distance. But the email was already there when I logged in; it had arrived at ten p.m. yesterday.

They want to interview me.

At noon today.

My palms are slippery with sweat, so I wipe first

one hand, then the other on my jeans. I have nothing resembling an interview-appropriate outfit, so I'm wearing my only pair of clean jeans and a plain long-sleeved T-shirt—I need the sleeves to cover the scratches and scabs the glass shards left on my arm. Hopefully, my potential employers won't hold the casual attire against me; after all, I'm interviewing for a tutor position in the middle of nowhere.

Please let me get the job. Please let me get it.

The sleek metal gate I just drove through is part of a metal wall of the same height that extends into the rugged mountain forest on each side of the road. I wonder if that means the wall loops around the entire estate. It's hard to imagine—according to the librarian who gave me directions, the property consists of over a thousand acres of wild mountainous terrain—but I couldn't see where the wall ended, so it's possible. And since the gate opened on its own at my approach, there must be cameras in place as well—which, while somewhat alarming, is also reassuring.

I have no idea why these people need so much security, but if I get this job, I'll be safe inside their compound as well.

The winding dirt road I'm on seems to go on forever, but finally, after about a mile, the forest on the sides begins to thin and the terrain flattens out. I must be approaching the peak of the mountain.

Sure enough, as I round the next bend, the sleek two-story mansion comes into view.

An ultra-modern marvel of glass and steel, it should stand out like a sore thumb among all this untamed nature, but instead, it's skillfully integrated into its surroundings, with a portion of the house built into a rocky outcropping. As I pull up in front of it, I see an all-glass terrace wrapping around the back and realize that the house is perched on a cliff overlooking a deep ravine.

The views inside must be to kill for.

Deep breath, Chloe. You can do it.

Turning off the car, I smooth my sweaty palms over my jeans, straighten my shirt, make sure my hair is still in a neat bun, and grab the resume I printed out at the library. I usually interview well, but I've never had so much at stake before. Every nerve in my body is on edge, my heart pounding so fast I feel dizzy. Of course, I could also be dizzy because all I've had to eat today is the banana, but I don't want to think about that and the fact that if I don't get the job, hunger may be the least of my problems.

Resume in hand, I step out of the car. I'm about a half hour early, which is better than being late but not optimal. I was afraid I'd get lost without a GPS, so I left the library and headed over here as soon as the librarian explained where to go and gave me a local map. I didn't get lost, though, so now all I need is to walk over to that sleek, futuristic-looking front door and ring the doorbell.

Steeling my spine, I prepare to do exactly that when

the door swings open, revealing a tall, broad-shouldered man clad in a pair of dark jeans and a white button-up shirt with the sleeves rolled up to his elbows.

"Hi," I say, putting on a bright smile as I walk toward him. "I'm Chloe Emmons, here to interview for the..." I stop, my breath catching in my lungs as he steps out into the light and a pair of stunning hazel eyes meets mine.

Except "hazel" is too generic a term for them. I've never seen eyes like that. A rich, dark amber mixed with forest green, they're surrounded by thick black lashes and glitter with a peculiar fierceness, an intensity that wouldn't look out of place on a jungle predator. Tiger eyes, belonging to a man who himself is power and danger personified—a man so cruelly handsome my already-elevated heart rate goes supersonic.

High, wide cheekbones, a straight blade of a nose, jaw sharp enough to cut marble—the sheer symmetry of those striking features would've been enough for them to grace the covers of magazines, but when combined with that full, cynically curved mouth, the effect is absolutely devastating. Like his lashes, his eyebrows are thick and black, as is his hair, which is long enough to cover his ears and so straight it looks like a raven's wing.

Closing the distance between us with long, smooth strides, he extends his hand toward me. "Nikolai

Molotov," he says, pronouncing the name as a Russian native would—though there's no trace of accent in his deep, rough-silk voice. "It's a pleasure to make your acquaintance."

4

CHLOE

Dumbstruck, I shake his hand. It's big and strong, his lightly tanned skin warm as his long fingers wrap around mine and squeeze with carefully restrained power. A shiver ripples down my spine at the sensation, my body heating all over, and it takes everything I have not to sway toward him as my knees turn to jelly underneath me.

Get a grip, Chloe. This is a potential employer. Get a fucking grip.

With a herculean effort, I pull my hand away and reach for what remains of my composure. "It's nice to meet you, Mr. Molotov." To my relief, my voice comes out steady, my tone calm and friendly, as befits a person interviewing for a job. Taking a half-step back, I smile up at my host. "I'm sorry I'm a bit early."

His tiger eyes gleam brighter. "No problem. I've been looking forward to meeting you, Chloe. And please, call me Nikolai."

"Nikolai," I repeat, my stupid heartbeat accelerating further. I don't understand what's happening to me, why I'm having this reaction to this man. I've never been one to lose my mind over a chiseled jaw and washboard abs, not even when I was a hormonal teenager. While my friends were crushing on football players and movie stars, I dated boys whose personalities I liked, whose minds attracted me more than their bodies. For me, sexual chemistry has always been something that develops over time rather than being there from the start.

Then again, I've never met a man who exudes such raw animal magnetism.

I didn't know men like this existed.

Focus, Chloe. He's most likely married.

The thought is like a splash of cold water in my face, jerking me back to the reality of my situation. What the fuck am I doing, drooling over some kid's father? I need this job to *survive*. The forty-mile drive here ate more than a quarter tank of gas, and if I don't earn some money soon, I'll be stranded, a sitting duck for the killers coming after me.

The heat inside me cools at the thought, and when Nikolai says, "Follow me," and walks back into the house, my nerves jangle with anxiety instead of whatever it was that came over me at the sight of him.

Inside, the house is as ultra modern as it is on the outside. All around me are floor-to-ceiling windows with stunning views, modern-art-museum-worthy decorations, and sleek furniture that looks like it came straight out of some interior designer's showroom. Everything is done in shades of gray and white, softened in a few places by natural wood and stone accents. It's beautiful and more than a little intimidating, just like the man in front of me, and as he leads me through an open-layout living room to a spiral wood-and-glass staircase in the back, I can't help feeling like a mangy pigeon that's accidentally flown into a gilded concert hall.

Tamping down on the unsettling sensation, I say, "You have a beautiful house. Have you been living here long?"

"A few months," he replies as we go up the stairs. He glances at me. "What about you? You said in your cover letter you're on a road trip?"

"That's right." Feeling on firmer ground, I explain that I graduated from Middlebury College in June and decided to see the country before diving into the working world. "But then of course, I saw your listing," I conclude, "and it sounded too perfect to pass up, so here I am."

"Yes, indeed," he says softly as we stop in front of a closed door. "Here you are."

My breath hitches again, my pulse speeding up uncontrollably. There's something unnerving in the darkly sensual curve of his mouth, something almost… *dangerous* in the intensity of his stare. Maybe it's the unusual color of his eyes, but I feel distinctly uneasy when he presses his palm to an unobtrusive panel on the wall and the door swings open in front of us, spy-movie style.

"Please," he murmurs, motioning for me to enter, and I do so, doing my best to ignore the unsettling sensation that I'm entering a predator's lair.

The "lair" turns out to be a large, sunlit office. Two of the walls are made entirely of glass, revealing breathtaking mountain vistas, while a sleek L-shaped desk in the middle holds several computer monitors. To the side is a small round table with two chairs, and that's where Nikolai leads me.

Hiding a relieved exhale, I take a seat and lay my resume on the table in front of him. Clearly, I'm on edge, my nerves so frayed after the past month that I'm seeing danger everywhere. This is an interview for a tutor position, nothing more, and I need to get a hold of myself before I blow it.

Despite the admonition, my pulse spikes again as Nikolai leans back in his chair and regards me with those unsettlingly beautiful eyes. I can feel the growing dampness of my palms, and it's all I can do not to wipe them again on my jeans. As ridiculous as it is, I feel stripped bare by that gaze, all my secrets and fears exposed.

Stop it, Chloe. He knows nothing. You're interviewing to be a tutor, nothing more.

"So," I say brightly to hide my anxiety, "may I ask about the child I'd be tutoring? Is it your son or daughter?"

His face takes on an indecipherable expression. "My son. Miroslav. We call him Slava."

"That's a great name. Is he—"

"Tell me about yourself, Chloe." Leaning forward, he picks up my resume but doesn't look at it. Instead, his eyes are trained on my face, making me feel like a butterfly pinned under a microscope. "What is it about this position that intrigues you?"

"Oh, everything." Taking a breath to steady my voice, I describe all the babysitting and tutoring I've done throughout the years, and then I go over my internships, including my last summer job at a special-needs camp, where I worked with children of all ages. "It was a great experience," I conclude, "both challenging and rewarding. My favorite part of it, though, was teaching math and reading to the younger kids—which is why I think I'd be perfect for this role. Teaching is my passion, and I'd love a chance to work with a child one-on-one, to tailor the curriculum to his or her interests and abilities."

He sets the resume down, still without bothering to look at it. "And how do you feel about living in a place that's so removed from civilization? Where there's nothing but wilderness for dozens of miles around and only minimal contact with the outside world?"

"That sounds…" *Like a haven.* "…amazing." I beam at him, my excitement unfeigned. "I'm a big fan of the wilderness, and nature in general. In fact, my alma mater—Middlebury College—was chosen partly because of its rural location. I love hiking and fishing, and I know my way around a campfire. Living here would be a dream come true." Especially given all the security measures I spotted on the way in—but I don't say that, of course.

I can't appear to be anything other than a brand-new college grad looking for adventure.

He arches his eyebrows. "You won't miss your friends? Or family?"

"No, I—" To my dismay, my throat constricts with a sudden rush of grief. Swallowing, I try again. "I'm very independent. I've been traveling around the country on my own for the past month, and besides, there are always phones, videoconferencing apps, and social media."

He cocks his head. "Yet you haven't been posting on your social media profiles for the past month. Why's that?"

I stare at him, my heartbeat skyrocketing. He's looked at my social media? How? When? I have the highest privacy settings in place; he should be unable to see anything about me other than the fact that I exist and use social media like a normal person. Has he had me investigated? Hacked into my accounts somehow?

Who is this man?

"I actually don't have a phone right now." A trickle of sweat runs down my spine, but I succeed in keeping my tone level. "I got rid of it because I wanted to see if I could function on this road trip without all the electronics. A personal challenge of sorts."

"I see." His eyes are more green than amber in this light. "So how do you keep in touch with family and friends?"

"Email, mostly," I lie. There's no way I can admit that I haven't kept in touch with anyone and have no plans to do so. "I've been visiting public libraries and using the computers there once in a while." Realizing my fingers are laced tightly together, I unclench my hands and force a smile to my lips. "It's quite liberating, not being tied to a phone, you see. Extreme connectivity is both a blessing and a curse, and I'm enjoying the freedom of traveling around the country as people have done in the past, with only a paper map to guide me."

"A Gen Z luddite. How refreshing."

I flush at the gentle mockery in his tone. I know how my explanation sounds, but it's the only thing I can come up with to justify my lack of recent social media activity and, in case he looks at my resume closely, absence of a cell phone number. In fact, it's a good excuse for everything, so I might as well roll with it.

"You're right. I'm a bit of a luddite," I say. "That's probably why city life holds so little appeal for me, and why I found your job posting so intriguing. Living out here"—I motion at the gorgeous views outside—"and tutoring your son is the kind of job I've always wanted, and if you hire me, I will dedicate myself to it completely."

A slow, dark smile curves his lips. "Is that right?"

"Yes." I hold his gaze, even as my breath turns shallow and prickles of heat run over my skin. I really don't get my reaction to this man, don't understand how I can find him so magnetic even as he sets off all kinds of alarms in my mind. Paranoia or not, my instincts are screaming that he's dangerous, yet my finger itches to reach out and trace the clearly defined edges of his full, soft-looking lips. Swallowing, I wrench my thoughts away from that treacherous territory and say with as much earnestness as I can manage, "I'll be the most perfect tutor you can imagine."

He regards me without blinking, the silence stretching into several long seconds, and just when I feel like my nerves might snap like an overextended rubber band, he stands up and says, "Follow me."

He leads me out of the office and down a long hallway until we reach another closed door. This one must not have any biometric security, since he just knocks on the door and, without waiting for an answer, goes in.

Inside, another floor-to-ceiling window provides more breathtaking views. However, there's nothing sleek and modern about this room. Instead, it looks like the aftermath of a toy factory explosion. Colorful chaos is everywhere I look, with piles of toys, children's books, and LEGO pieces scattered all over the floor, and a child-sized bed covered by a Superman-themed sheet in the corner. The Superman-themed pillows and blanket from the bed are piled high in another corner, and it's not until my host says in a commanding tone, "Slava!" that I realize there's a little boy building a LEGO castle next to that pile.

At his father's voice, the boy's head jerks up, revealing a pair of huge amber-green eyes—the same mesmerizing eyes the man next to me possesses. In general, the boy is Nikolai in miniature, his black hair falling around his ears in a straight, glossy curtain and his child-round face already showing a hint of those striking cheekbones. Even the mouth is the same, lacking only the cynical, knowing curve of his father's lips.

"Slava, *idi syuda*," Nikolai orders, and the boy gets up and cautiously approaches us. As he stops in front of us, I notice he's wearing a pair of jeans and a T-shirt with a picture of Spider-Man on the front.

Looking down at his son, Nikolai starts speaking to him in rapid-fire Russian. I have no idea what he's saying, but it must have something to do with me because the boy keeps glancing at me, his expression both curious and fearful.

As soon as Nikolai is done speaking, I smile at the child and kneel on the floor, so we're on the same eye level. "Hi, Slava," I say gently. "I'm Chloe. It's nice to meet you."

The boy looks at me blankly.

"He doesn't speak English," Nikolai says, his voice

hard. "Alina and I have tried to teach him, but he knows we speak Russian, and he refuses to learn it from us. So that would be your job: teaching him English, along with anything else a child his age should know."

"I see." I keep my gaze on the boy, smiling at him warmly even as more alarms go off in my mind. There's something odd in the way Nikolai talks to and about the child. It's as if his son is a stranger to him. And if Alina—who I assume is his wife and the mother of the child—knows English as well as my host, why doesn't Slava speak at least a few words? Why would he refuse to learn the language from his parents?

In general, why doesn't Nikolai pick up the boy and hug him? Or playfully ruffle his hair?

Where's the warm ease with which parents usually communicate with their children?

"Slava," I say to the boy softly, "I'm Chloe." I point at myself. "Chloe."

He regards me with his father's unblinking stare for several long moments. Then his mouth moves, shaping the syllables. "Klo-ee."

I beam at him. "That's right. Chloe." I tap my chest. "And you're Slava." I point at him. "Miroslav, right?"

He nods solemnly. "Slava."

"Do you like comic books, Slava?" I gently touch the picture on his T-shirt. "This is Spider-Man, isn't it?"

His eyes brighten. "*Da*, Spider-Man." He pronounces it with a Russian accent. "*Ti znayesh o nyom?*"

I glance up at Nikolai, only to find him watching me with a dark, indecipherable expression. A tingle of unwelcome awareness zips down my spine, my breath hitching at a sudden feeling of vulnerability. On my knees is not where I want to be with this man.

It feels a lot like baring my throat to a beautiful, wild wolf.

"My son is asking if you know about Spider-Man," he says after a tension-filled moment. "I assume the answer is yes."

With effort, I tear my gaze away from him and focus on the boy. "Yes, I know about Spider-Man," I say, smiling. "I loved Spider-Man when I was your age. Also Superman and Batman and Wonder Woman and Aquaman."

The child's face brightens more with every superhero I name, and when I get to Aquaman, a mischievous grin appears on his face. "Aquaman?" He wrinkles his small nose. "*Nyet, nye* Aquaman."

"No Aquaman?" I widen my eyes exaggeratedly. "Why not? What's wrong with Aquaman?"

That draws a giggle. "*Nye* Aquaman."

"Okay, you win. Not Aquaman." I let out a sad sigh. "Poor Aquaman. So few kids like him."

The boy giggles again and runs over to a pile of comic books next to the bed. Grabbing one, he brings it back and points at the picture on the front. "Superman *samiy sil'niy*," he declares.

"Superman is the best?" I guess. "Your favorite?"

"He said he's the strongest," Nikolai says evenly,

then switches over to Russian, his voice taking on the same commanding tone.

The boy's face falls, and he lowers the book, his posture dejected.

"Let's go back to my office," Nikolai says to me, and without another word to his son, he heads for the door.

5

NIKOLAI

As I step out of the room, I can hear her saying goodbye to my son, her voice sweet and bright, and the painful thudding in my chest intensifies, anger mixing with the strongest lust I've ever felt.

Six months.

Six months, and I haven't gotten so much as a smile out of the boy. Alina has, though, and now so has this girl, this total stranger.

Slava laughed with her.

He showed her his favorite book.

He let her touch his shirt.

And the entire time I watched her with my son, all I could think about was how she'd look spread out naked underneath me, her sun-streaked hair freed from the tight bun confining it and her big brown eyes trained on me as I bury myself in her silky flesh, over and over again.

If I needed further proof that I'm unfit to be a father, here it is, in spades.

"Sit, please," I tell Chloe when we're back in my office. Despite my best efforts, my voice is tight, the roiling cauldron of emotions inside me too powerful to be contained. I want to grab the girl and fuck her on the spot, and at the same time, I want to shake her and demand she tell me how she worked her magic on Slava so quickly... why my son responded to her within minutes while I've been unable to get more than a few words out of him for months.

She sits down in the same chair as before, perching on the edge of the seat as delicately as a butterfly on a flower. Her eyes are locked inquisitively on my face, her expression perfectly composed, and if not for her small hands knotting together on the table, I would've thought she's as cool as she appears. But she's nervous, this pretty mystery of a girl, nervous and more than a little desperate.

I don't know why that is, but I'm going to find out.

"What did you think of my son?" I ask, my tone smoothing out as I lean back in my chair. Now that we're away from Slava, the strange tightness I often get in my ribcage around him is easing, the irrational anger and jealousy fading until it's only a faint pulse at the back of my mind.

So what if the boy likes this stranger better?

That means she might actually be able to do the job I'm about to hire her for.

I don't know when exactly I reached this decision,

at what point I decided my fascination with Chloe Emmons justifies the danger she might pose to my family. Maybe it was when she was glibly lying about why she stopped using social media, or as she was fearlessly holding my gaze after vowing to devote herself to the job. Or maybe it was when I came out of the house and those soft brown eyes landed on me for the first time, making every hair on my body stand on end with scorching awareness.

Attraction is too weak a word to describe the pull I feel toward her. My hands are literally twitching with the urge to touch her, to trail my fingers over her finely molded jaw and see if her bronzed skin is as baby soft as it appears. In pictures, she was bright and pretty, her radiance shining off the page. In person, she's all that and more, her smile full of unselfconscious warmth, her unflinching gaze speaking of both vulnerability and strength.

And underneath it all is desperation. I can see it, feel it... smell it. Fear, hopelessness—it has a scent, like blood. And like blood, it calls to the darkest parts of me, to the beast that I've been keeping carefully leashed. Worse yet, this inconvenient attraction isn't one-sided.

Chloe Emmons is drawn to me.

Masked by her bright, friendly smile is a purely feminine interest, a response as primal as my reaction to her. When I shook her hand, I felt a tremor run over her skin, saw her lips part on a shallow exhale as her delicate fingers twitched in my grip.

No, the girl is not indifferent to me at all, and that makes her fair game.

"I thought Slava was very bright," she answers, and my gaze falls to the tempting shape of her mouth. Her upper lip is a bit fuller than the lower, giving the impression of a slight overbite when she's not smiling. "I'm not sure why he refuses to learn English from you, but I'm confident I'll be able to teach him," she continues as I ponder if that small imperfection makes her features more or less appealing. More, I decide as she explains the teaching methods she intends to use. Definitely more, because all I can think about is how much I want to taste the plush softness of those lips and feel them on my body.

With effort, I refocus on her words.

"—and so we'll start with the—"

"What's your take on corporal discipline for children?" I interrupt, leaning forward. I've heard enough to know that she's capable of doing the job. There's only one other thing I need to know now. "Do you believe in spanking and such?"

She gives me an appalled look. "Of course not! That's the last thing—No, I would never condone that." Her eyes narrow fiercely as she leans in, slender hands balling into fists on the table. "Do *you*?"

"No. I don't."

She visibly relaxes, and I conceal a satisfied smile. For a second there, she looked like she was going to punch me with those tiny fists. And that reaction wasn't faked; every muscle in her body tensed at once, as if she'd been about to launch herself into battle. The mere possibility of my son getting spanked made her forget whatever is behind her desperation and ready to rip into me like a mama bear.

That's not the reaction of a woman who'd ever hurt a child. Whatever danger Chloe Emmons poses, it's not one of violent tendencies—at least none that would be directed at Slava.

The jury is still out about the true cause of her mother's death.

It's probably yet another sign that I'm unfit to be a parent, but a part of me is looking forward to the trouble she might bring. It's quiet here, in this remote corner of Idaho—beautiful and way too fucking quiet. The life I left behind is nothing like the one I've been leading for the past six months, and I can't deny that I miss the adrenaline rush of being at the helm of one of the most powerful families in Russia.

This girl with her intriguing lies and porn-doll mouth won't replace that for me, but one way or another, she'll provide some entertainment.

Leaning back, I lace my fingers over my ribcage and smile at her. "So, Chloe... when can you begin?"

6

CHLOE

I almost jump up and shout, "Now! This minute. This second." Only that would betray my desperation and ruin the whole thing, so I stay in my seat and say with some semblance of composure, "Whatever works best for you. I'm available right away."

Nikolai's eyes glint dark gold. "Excellent. I'd like you to start today. I assume you're okay with the salary stated in the ad?"

"Yes, thank you. It's adequate." By which I mean it's more money than I could've hoped to earn anywhere else, but all the interview books tell you not to appear too eager and to negotiate. I don't have the balls to do the latter, but I can attempt the former. Striving for a casual tone, I ask, "How often will I be paid?"

"Weekly. We'll count today as your first day, so you'll get the first paycheck next Tuesday. Does that work?"

I nod, too excited to speak. One week—or rather,

six and a half days—from now, I'll have money. Actual, real, substantial money, the kind that would provide me with food and gas for months if I have to run again.

"Excellent." He rises to his feet. "Come, I'll show you to your room."

I follow him, doing my best not to notice the way his designer jeans hug his muscled thighs and how his well-fitted shirt stretches over his powerful shoulders. The last thing I need is to lust after my employer, a man who's most likely married to a woman I have yet to meet. Which, come to think of it, is strange.

Why wasn't Slava's mother involved in this hiring decision?

Catching up to Nikolai, I clear my throat to get his attention. "Will I get to meet Alina soon?" I ask when his gaze lands on me. "Or is she away?"

He raises his eyebrows. "She's—"

"Right here." A stunning young woman steps out of the room we were about to enter. Tall and slim, she's wearing a red dress that could've come straight from a runway in Paris. On her feet is an elegant pair of nude-colored heels, and her long, straight, jet-black hair frames a strikingly beautiful face. Her full lips are painted red to match her dress, and a skillful application of black eyeliner emphasizes the cat-like tilt of her jade-green eyes.

Extending a perfectly groomed hand toward me, she says smoothly, "Alina Molotova. I take it the interview went well?" Like her husband, she speaks flawless American English, with only her pronunciation of her name betraying her foreign origins.

Recovering from the shock of her appearance, I shake her hand. "It's a pleasure to meet you, Mrs. Molotova." I say her name the way she did, with an "a" at the end; I remember from my Russian Lit course that Russian surnames are gendered. "I'm—"

"Chloe Emmons, I know. And please, call me Alina." She smiles, revealing a tiny gap between her front teeth —an imperfection that only enhances her striking beauty.

"Thank you, Alina." I smile back, even as an unpleasant ache tightens my chest.

Nikolai's wife is beyond gorgeous, and for some reason, I hate that fact.

Strangely, Nikolai doesn't look pleased with her either. "What are you doing here?" His tone is hard, his dark eyebrows knitting together in a frown.

Alina's smile turns catlike. "I was preparing Chloe's room, of course. What else?"

His response in Russian is swift and sharp, but she just laughs—a pretty, bell-like sound—and says to me, "Welcome to the household, Chloe."

With that, she walks away, her stride as graceful as a model's on a catwalk.

Exhaling a breath, I turn back to Nikolai, only to see him entering the room. I follow him in and find myself in a spacious, ultra-modern bedroom with a floor-to-ceiling window showcasing more breathtaking views.

"Wow." I walk over to the window and stare out at the snow-capped peaks of distant mountains veiled by a blueish haze. "This is... just wow."

"Beautiful, isn't it?" he says, and my pulse jumps as I realize he's come up to stand next to me, his gaze on the magnificent vista outside. In profile, he's even more stunning, his features as hard and perfect as if they'd been carved from the cliff we're perched on, his powerful body as much a force of nature as the unforgiving wilderness around us.

Dangerous.

The word whispers across my mind, and this time, I can't convince myself it's simply paranoia. He's dangerous, this mysterious employer of mine. I don't know how, I don't know why, but I can feel it. A month ago, the blinders I'd worn my whole life—the ones all normal people wear—were violently ripped away, and I can't unsee the darkness in the world, can't pretend it isn't there. And I see the darkness in Nikolai.

Underneath that stunning male beauty and those smooth manners lurks something savage... something terrifying.

He turns to face me, and it takes all my courage to remain in place and meet his tiger-bright gaze. My heart is thumping heavily in my chest, yet a white-hot current seems to leap between us, the air particles taking on an electric charge. My nerve endings sizzle with it, heating my skin and turning my breath shallow and uneven.

Run, Chloe.

Swallowing hard, I step back, Mom's voice ringing in my head as clearly as if she were here. And I desperately want to listen to it, but I'm down to a few dollars in my wallet and a quarter-tank of gas in my ancient clunker of a car. This man, who both attracts and terrifies me, is my only hope of survival, and whatever danger I face here can't be worse than what's waiting for me if I leave.

His eyes gleam with dark amusement as I take another step back and then another, and I again get the unsettling sensation that he's seeing right through me, that he somehow senses both my fear and my shameful attraction to him.

Forcing myself to turn away, I look around, feigning interest in my surroundings—as if anything around here could be as fascinating as he is. "So this will be my room?"

"Yes. Do you like it?"

"I love it." I look up at a large TV hanging from the ceiling over the bed, then walk over to a door across from the one opening into the hallway. It leads to a sleek white bathroom with a glass shower stall large enough to accommodate five people. Another door turns out to hide a walk-in closet the size of my college dorm room, all empty and waiting for my meager belongings.

It's luxury of the kind I've only seen in movies, and it adds to my unease.

Who are these people? Where did they get their

wealth? How did Nikolai know about my absence from social media when all my profiles are private?

Why do they need so much security in a place so remote?

I didn't want to think too deeply about any of this before—my focus was on getting the job—but now that I'm here, now that this is real, I can't help wondering what I've gotten myself into. Because there's one easy answer to all my questions, one word that, thanks to Hollywood, comes to mind when I think about wealthy Russians.

Mafia.

Is that what my new employers are?

7

CHLOE

Heart hammering, I turn to look at Nikolai. He's watching me with the same unsettling amusement, and I suddenly feel like a mouse being played with by a big, gorgeous cat.

Who may be in the mafia.

"So," I begin uncomfortably, "I should probably—"

"Give me your car keys." He walks up to me. "I'll have your things brought up."

"That's okay. I can do that myself. I'll just—" I shut my mouth because he extends his hand palm up, his expression uncompromising.

Fumbling in my pocket, I extract the keys and drop them onto his broad palm. "Here you go."

"Thank you." He pockets the keys. "Settle in and make yourself comfortable. Pavel will bring your bags in a minute."

"There's just one—a small suitcase in the trunk," I say, but he's already walking out.

Exhaling a breath I didn't realize I was holding, I collapse onto the bed. Now that the interview is over, the adrenaline that sustained me is dropping, and I feel wrung out, so completely drained that all I can do is lie there and stare blankly at the high ceiling. After a while, I recover enough to register the fact that the white coverlet underneath me is made of some soft, fuzzy material, and I spread my palms over it, stroking it as I would a pet.

A knock on the door jolts me out of my semi-catatonic state. Sitting up, I call out, "Come in!"

A man the size of a cave bear enters, carrying my suitcase, which looks more like a handbag in his enormous hand. Tattoos run up the sides of his thick neck, and his weathered face reminds me of a brick—hard, ruddy, and uncompromisingly square. His military-short hair is an indeterminate shade of brown liberally sprinkled with gray, and his hard gray eyes remind me of melted bullets.

"Hi," I say, mustering a smile as I get to my feet. "You must be Pavel."

He nods, his expression unchanged. "Where do you want this?" he asks in a deep, thickly accented growl.

"Right here is fine, thank you. I got this." I walk over to take the suitcase from him, and as I approach, I realize he must be the biggest man I've ever met, both in terms of height and width. More tattoos decorate the backs of his hands and peek out from the v-neck of the sweater that stretches tightly over his prominent pecs.

Trying not to gulp nervously, I stop in front of him and clasp the handle of the suitcase he's just set on the floor. "Thank you." I smile brighter, looking up. Very far up—my neck actually hurts from how far I have to bend it back.

He nods again, his thick jaw stiff, then turns and walks out.

Okay then. So much for befriending other staff members. What's the man-bear's job here, anyway? Bodyguard?

Mafia enforcer, maybe?

I push the thought away. Even though the guy fits the stereotype to a T, I refuse to dwell on this possibility. What would be the point? Even if my new employers are mafia, I'm safer here than out there.

I hope.

Shutting the door behind Pavel, I unpack—a process that takes all of ten minutes—and gaze longingly at the bed with its fuzzy white coverlet. I'm exhausted and not only from the interview. Between the nightmares that haunt me at night and the constant worry during the day, I haven't had more than four hours of sleep in weeks. But I can't just sleep the afternoon away.

I was hired to do a job, and I intend to do it.

To perk myself up, I take a quick shower in the enormous bathroom and change into a fresh T-shirt— my last one. I have to inquire about where to do laundry ASAP, but first things first.

It's time I got to know my young student.

The door to Slava's room is open as I approach, and I see Alina inside, talking to the boy in melodious Russian. Hearing my footsteps, she glances over at me and arches her eyebrows in a way that reminds me of her husband.

"Eager to start?"

I smile at her. "If you don't mind, I was thinking Slava and I could get to know each other this afternoon." I catch the child's gaze and give him a wink, earning myself a huge smile.

Alina's expression warms at her son's reaction. "Of course I don't mind. I was just explaining to him that you'll be living here and teaching him. He's quite excited about the idea."

"So am I." I crouch in front of the boy. "We'll have a great time, won't we, Slava?"

He clearly doesn't understand what I'm saying, but he grins regardless and rattles off something in Russian.

"He's asking if you like castles," Alina says.

"Yes, I do," I tell Slava. "Show me what you've got there. Is this your fortress?" I gesture at the partially built LEGO project.

The boy giggles and plops down among the LEGO pieces. Picking up two, he attaches them to the walls of the castle, and I help him by attaching two more. Only I apparently did it wrong because he shakes his head and takes off my pieces, then places them right next to where I attached them.

"Oh, I see. You're leaving room for windows. Windows, right?" I point at the giant window in his room.

He bobs his head. *"Da, okna. Bol'shiye okna."* Grabbing my wrist, he places another piece in my palm and guides my hand to the proper place on the wall. *"Nado syuda."*

"Got it." Grinning, I attach the next piece. "Like so, right?"

"Da," he says excitedly and grabs more pieces. We proceed in that vein, with him guiding me in castle assembly until Alina clears her throat.

"Seems like you two are on the same page, so I'll leave you to it," she says when I look up. "You have a half hour before Slava's snack time. Are you hungry by any chance, Chloe?"

My stomach responds before I can, emitting a loud growl, and Alina laughs, her green eyes lighting with amusement.

"I'm guessing that's a yes. Any food preferences or allergies?"

"I'm good with anything," I say, grateful that my darker skin tone conceals my embarrassed flush. I can't imagine Alina's elegant, long-limbed body ever emitting such an indiscreet noise—though, if she's human, it must upon occasion. Of course, jury's still out on the human part.

In those high heels and that stunning dress, Nikolai's wife looks too glamorous to be real.

Some of my embarrassment must show because her amusement deepens, her lips curving in a way that again reminds me disconcertingly of her husband. "How very accommodating of you. I'll let Pavel know."

Pavel? Is the man-bear their cook or something? Before I can ask, Alina turns to her son and says something in Russian, then strolls out, leaving me alone with my charge.

8

NIKOLAI

"So, tell me, brother... Did you acquire her for Slava or yourself?"

I pause in the middle of putting on my cufflinks and turn around to meet Alina's coolly mocking gaze. "Does it matter?" I have no idea how she sniffed out my interest in our new hire, but I'm not surprised.

My sister has always been able to read me better than anyone.

She leans against the doorframe of my walk-in closet, where I'm changing for dinner. "I guess I should've expected it. She's pretty, isn't she?"

"Very." I deliberately turn my back to her. Alina lives to get a rise out of me, but she's not going to succeed tonight. Nor is she going to shame me into staying away from Chloe.

The girl intrigues me too much for that.

"You know she spent the entire afternoon with Slava, right?" Alina strolls deeper into my closet and picks up my skinny black tie, the one I was just about to put on.

Resisting the impulse to reach for a different one just to spite her, I take the tie from her and put it on with practiced motions. "Yes, I do."

There are cameras in my son's room, and I spent *my* afternoon watching him play with his new tutor. They finished building the castle Slava was working on, ate the fruit-and-cheese platter Pavel brought, then played a game of tag, where Chloe chased him around his room and down the hallway, making him laugh so hard he was giggle-snorting. Afterward, Chloe read to him from some of his favorite comic books—the English-language ones, not the Russian translations Alina smuggled in to worm her way into the boy's good graces. As she spoke, Slava looked fascinated with his beautiful young teacher, something I can't blame him for.

I'd kill for her to sit next to me and read to me in that soft, slightly husky voice, to feel her hand play with my hair the way it so casually played with my son's when he snuggled up to her as if he's known her all his life.

"She's good with him," Alina continues as I finish buckling my belt and reach for my suit jacket. "Really good."

"I noticed."

"Yet you're still going to fuck her. Just like *he* would have."

I keep my tone level. "I never claimed to be any different."

"But you can be. Kolya…" She lays her hand on my arm, and when I meet her gaze, she says quietly, "We left. We came here. This is our chance to start over, to make ourselves into whoever we want to be. Forget our father. Forget all of it. You've put in your time; now it's Valery and Konstantin's turn."

A dry chuckle escapes my throat. "What makes you think I want to start over? Or be anything other than who I am?"

"The fact that you left. The fact that we're here, having this discussion." Her expression is earnest, open for once. "Let the girl be Slava's tutor and nothing more. Amuse yourself elsewhere. She's too young for you. Too innocent."

"She's twenty-three, not twelve. And I've just turned thirty-one—hardly an insurmountable age difference."

"I'm not talking about age. She's not like us. She's soft. Vulnerable."

"Exactly. And you brought her to my attention." I smile cruelly. "What did you think would happen?"

Alina's face hardens. "You're going to destroy her. But then again"—her lips twist in a bitter smile as she steps back—"that's the Molotov way, isn't it? Enjoy your new toy, Kolya. I can't wait to see you play with her at dinner."

And without another word, she walks out.

9

CHLOE

HOLDING SLAVA'S HAND, I APPROACH THE DINING ROOM, my knees all but knocking together. I don't know why I'm so nervous, but I am. Just the thought of seeing Nikolai again makes me feel like a rabid honey badger has taken up residence in my stomach.

It's the mafia question, I tell myself. Now that the idea has occurred to me, I can't get it out of my mind, no matter how hard I try. That's why my breath quickens and my palms grow damp each time I picture the cynical curve of my employer's lips. Because he might be a criminal. Because I sense a dark, ruthless edge in him. It has nothing to do with his looks and the heat that flows through my veins whenever his intense green-gold gaze lands on me.

It can't have anything to do with that because he's married, and I would never poach another woman's husband, especially when a child is involved.

Still, I can't help wondering how long Nikolai and

his wife have been together... whether he loves her. So far, I've only seen them together briefly, so it's impossible to tell—though I did sense a certain lack of intimacy between them. But I'm sure that was just wishful thinking on my part. Why wouldn't my employer love his wife? Alina is as gorgeous as he is, so much so they almost look alike. No wonder Slava is such a beautiful child; with parents like that, he's won the genetic lottery, big time.

I glance down at the boy in question, and he looks up at me, his huge eyes eerily like his father's. His expression is solemn, the exuberance he displayed when we played together gone. Like me, he seems anxious about our upcoming meal, so I give him a reassuring smile.

"Dinner," I say, nodding toward the table we're approaching. "We're about to have dinner."

He blinks up at me, saying nothing, but I know he's filing away the word, along with everything else I've said to him today. Young children are like sponges, absorbing everything adults say and do, their brains forming connections at dazzling speed. When I was in high school, I babysat for a Chinese couple. Their five-year-old spoke zero English when I met her, but after a few weeks of kindergarten and a dozen evenings with me, she was almost fluent. The same thing will happen to Slava, I have no doubt.

Already, by the end of this afternoon, he was repeating a few words after me.

No one's in the dining room yet, though Pavel

gruffly told me to be down here at six when he brought the fruit-and-cheese tray to Slava's room. However, the table is already set with all manner of salads and appetizers, and my mouth waters at the deliciousness waiting for us. While the afternoon snack quenched the worst of my gnawing hunger, I'm still starving, and it takes all of my willpower not to fall ravenously on the artfully arranged platters of open-faced caviar sandwiches, smoked fish, roasted vegetables, and leafy green salads. Instead, I help Slava climb up onto a chair that has a child's booster seat on it, and then I begin pointing out the names of the different foods in English. "We call this dish *salad*, and the green thing inside it is *lettuce*," I'm saying as the *click-clack* of high heels announces Alina's arrival.

I look up at her with a smile. "Hello. Slava and I were just—"

"Why hasn't he changed?" Her dark eyebrows pull together as she takes in the child's appearance. "He knows we change for dinner."

I blink. "Oh, I—"

She interrupts with a stream of rapid-fire Russian, and I see the boy's shoulders tighten as he slinks down in his seat, as if wanting to disappear. Apparently realizing she's upsetting her son, Alina softens her tone and eventually gets what sounds like a chastised apology out of the child.

She faces me. "Sorry about that. Slava knows better than to come down like this, but he forgot in all the excitement."

My face burns as I realize that "like this" means his normal casual clothes, which are no different from the jeans and long-sleeved T-shirt I'm wearing. Nikolai's wife, on the other hand, has changed into an even more glamorous dress—a silver-blue ankle-length gown—and looks like she's on her way to a Hollywood premiere.

"I'm sorry," I say, feeling like a fanny-pack-wearing tourist who's stumbled into a Parisian fashion show. "I didn't realize there was a dress code."

"Oh, you're fine." Alina waves an elegant hand. "It's not a requirement for *you*. But Slava is a Molotov, and it's important that he learn the family traditions."

"I see." I don't see, actually, but it's not my place to argue with family traditions, however absurd they may be.

"And don't worry," Alina adds, taking a seat across from Slava. "If you wish to dress properly as well, I'm sure Kolya will buy you some appropriate clothing."

Kolya? Is that what she calls her husband?

"That's not necessary, thank you—" I begin, only to fall into a stunned silence as I catch sight of Nikolai approaching the table. Like his wife, he's changed for dinner, his high-end designer jeans and button-up shirt replaced by a sharply tailored black suit, crisp white shirt, and skinny black tie—an outfit that wouldn't look out of place at a high-society wedding... or the same movie premiere Alina's planning to attend. And while an average-looking man could easily pass for handsome in a suit like this, Nikolai's dark, masculine beauty is heightened to an almost unbearable degree. As I take in his appearance, my pulse goes through the roof and my lungs constrict, along with lower regions of my—

Married, Chloe. He's married.

The reminder is like a slap in the face, yanking me out of my dazzled trance. Forcing a breath into my oxygen-deprived lungs, I give my employer a carefully restrained smile, one that *doesn't* say that my heart is racing in my chest and that I'm wishing like hell Alina didn't exist. Especially since his striking gaze is trained on me instead of his gorgeous wife.

"You're late," she says as he pulls out a chair and sits next to her. "It's already—"

"I know what time it is." He doesn't take his eyes off me as he responds to her, his tone coolly dismissive. Then his gaze flicks to the boy at my side and his features tighten as he takes in his casual appearance.

"I'm sorry, it's my fault," I say before he can also reprimand the child. "I didn't realize we needed to get dressed up for dinner."

Nikolai's attention returns to me. "Of course you didn't." His gaze travels over my shoulders and chest, making me acutely conscious of my plain long-sleeved T-shirt and the thin cotton bra underneath that's doing nothing to hide my inexplicably erect nipples. "Alina is right. I need to buy you some proper clothes."

"No, really, that's—"

He holds up his palm. "House rules." His voice is soft, but his face could've been laid in stone. "Now that you're a member of this household, you must abide by them."

"I… all right." If he and his wife want to see me in fancy clothes at dinner and don't mind spending the money to make it happen, so be it.

Like he said, their house, their rules.

"Good." His sensual lips curve. "I'm glad you're so accommodating."

My breath quickens, my face warming again, and I look away to hide my reaction. All the man did was smile, for fuck's sake, and I'm blushing like a fifteen-year-old virgin. And in front of his wife, no less.

If I don't get a handle on this ridiculous crush, I'll be fired before the end of the meal.

"Would you like some salad?" Alina asks, as if to remind me of her existence, and I shift my attention to her, grateful for the distraction.

"Yes, please."

She gracefully ladles a serving of leafy green salad onto my plate, then does the same for her husband and son. In the meantime, Nikolai extends the platter with caviar sandwiches toward me, and I take one, both because I'm hungry enough to eat anything residing on bread and because I'm curious about the notorious Russian delicacy. I've had this type of fish roe—the big orange kind—in sushi restaurants a couple of times, but I imagine it's different like this, served on a slice of French baguette with a thick layer of butter underneath.

Sure enough, when I bite into it, the rich umami

flavor explodes on my tongue. Unlike the fish roe I've tasted, Russian caviar appears to be preserved with liberal amounts of salt. It would be too salty on its own, but the crusty white bread and mellow butter balance it perfectly, and I devour the rest of the small sandwich in two bites.

Eyes gleaming with amusement, Nikolai offers me the platter again. "More?"

"I'm good, thank you." I'd love another caviar sandwich—or twenty—but I don't want to seem greedy. Instead, I dig into my salad, which is also delicious, with a sweet, tangy dressing that makes my taste buds tingle. Then I try a bite of everything on the table, from the smoked fish to some kind of potato salad to grilled eggplant drizzled with a cucumber-dill yogurt sauce.

As I eat, I keep an eye on my charge, who's eating quietly beside me. Alina has given Slava a small portion of everything the adults are having, the caviar sandwich included, and the boy seems to have no problem with that. There are no demands for chicken fingers or French fries, no sign of the typical pickiness of a four-year-old. Even his table manners are those of a much older child, with only a couple of instances of him grabbing a piece of food with his fingers instead of his fork.

"Your son is very well-behaved," I tell Alina and Nikolai, and Nikolai lifts his eyebrows, as if hearing it for the first time.

"Well-behaved? Slava?"

"Of course." I frown at him. "You don't think so?"

"I haven't given it much thought," he says, glancing at the boy, who's diligently spearing a piece of lettuce with his adult-sized fork. "I suppose he conducts himself reasonably well."

Reasonably well? A four-year-old who sits calmly and eats everything served to him with zero whining or interruptions of adult conversation? Who handles utensils like a pro? Maybe this is a thing in Europe, but I've certainly never seen it in America.

Also, why hasn't my employer given his son's behavior much thought? Aren't parents supposed to worry about things like that?

"Have you been around many other children his age?" I ask Nikolai on a hunch, and catch his mouth flattening for a second.

"No," he says curtly. "I haven't."

Alina shoots him an indecipherable look, then turns to me. "I don't know if my brother has told you this," she says in a measured tone, "but we only learned of Slava's existence eight months ago."

I choke on a pickled tomato I've just bitten into and break into a coughing fit, the spicy, vinegary juices having gone down the wrong pipe. "Wait, what?" I gasp out when I can speak.

Eight months ago?

And did she just call Nikolai her *brother*?

"I see this is news to you," Alina says, handing me a glass of water, which I gratefully gulp down. "Kolya"— she glances at Nikolai, who's wearing a hard, closed-off expression—"hasn't told you much about us, has he?"

"Um, no." I set the glass down and cough again to clear the hoarseness from my voice. "Not really." My new employer hasn't said much at all, but I've made all sorts of assumptions, and wrong ones at that.

Alina is Nikolai's sister, not his wife. Which means the boy is not her son.

They didn't know he existed until eight months ago.

God, that explains so much. No wonder father and son act like they're strangers to each other—they *are*, for all intents and purposes. And I was right when I sensed a lack of lover-like intimacy between Nikolai and Alina.

They aren't lovers.

They're siblings.

Looking at the two of them now, I don't understand how I could've missed the resemblance—or rather, why the resemblance I did notice didn't clue me in to their familial relationship. Alina's features are a softer, more delicate version of the man sitting in front of me, and though her green eyes lack the deep amber undertones of Nikolai's stunning gaze, the shape of her eyes and eyebrows is the same.

They're clearly, unmistakably siblings.

Which means Nikolai is not married.

Or at least not married to Alina.

"Where is Slava's mother?" I ask, striving for a casual tone. "Is she—"

"She's dead." Nikolai's voice is cold enough to give

frostbite, as is the look he levels at Alina. Turning back to face me, he says evenly, "We had a one-night stand five years ago, and she didn't tell me she was pregnant. I had no idea I had a son until she was killed in a car accident eight months ago, and a friend of hers found a diary naming me as the father."

"Oh, that's…" I swallow. "That must've been very difficult. For you, and especially for Slava." I look at the boy at my side, who's still eating calmly, as if he has no care in the world. But that's not the case at all, I know that now. Nikolai's son has survived one of the biggest tragedies that can befall a child, and however well-adjusted he seems, I have no doubt the loss of his mother has left deep scars on his psyche.

I'm an adult, and I'm having trouble coping with my grief. I can't imagine what it's like for a little boy.

"It was," Alina agrees softly. "In fact, my brother—"

"That's enough." Nikolai's tone is still perfectly level, but I can see the tension in his jaw and shoulders. The topic is an unpleasant one for him, and no wonder. I can't imagine what it must be like to find out you have a child you've never met, to know you've missed the first years of his life.

I have a million questions I want to ask, but I can tell now's not the time to indulge my curiosity. Instead, I reach for more food and spend the next few minutes complimenting the chef—who, it turns out, is indeed the gruff, bear-like Russian.

"Pavel and his wife, Lyudmila, came with us from Moscow," Alina explains as the man-bear himself appears from the kitchen, carrying a large platter of lamb chops surrounded by roasted potatoes with mushrooms. With a grunt, he sets the food on the table, grabs a couple of empty appetizer plates, and disappears back into the kitchen as Alina continues. "Lyudmila is under the weather today, so Pavel is doing all the work. Normally, he does most of the cooking and cleaning, while she serves the food. Her main job, though, is looking after Slava."

"Are they the only two people living here besides your family?" I ask, accepting a lamb chop and a scoop of potatoes with mushrooms when she extends the platter toward me after giving a decent-sized portion to Slava—who again digs in without fuss.

"They're the only people residing in the house with us," Nikolai answers. "The guards have a separate bunker on the north side of the estate."

My heart jumps. "Guards?"

"We have a few men securing the compound," Alina says. "Since we're so isolated out here and all."

I do my best to conceal my reaction. "Yes, of course, that makes sense." Except it doesn't. If anything, the remote location should make it safer. From what I could see on the map, only one road leads up the mountain, and there's already an impenetrable-looking gate there, not to mention that ridiculously tall metal wall.

Only people with powerful, dangerous enemies would think it necessary to hire guards on top of all those measures.

Russian mafia.

The words whisper through my mind again, and my heartbeat intensifies. Lowering my gaze to my plate, I cut into my lamb chop, doing my best to keep my hand steady despite the anxious whirling of my thoughts.

Am I in danger here? Did I jump from the frying pan into the fire? Should I—

"Tell us more about yourself, Chloe."

Nikolai's deep voice cuts into my nervous contemplation, and I look up to find his tiger eyes on me, his lips curved in a sardonic smile. Once again, I have the disconcerting sensation that he's seeing straight into my head, that he knows exactly what I'm thinking and fearing.

Pushing the unsettling feeling away, I smile back. "What would you like to know?"

"Your driver's license says you reside in Boston. Is that where you grew up?"

I nod, spearing a piece of lamb chop. "My mom moved us there from California when I was a baby, and I grew up in and around the Boston area." I bite into the tender, perfectly seasoned meat and again have to give props to Pavel—it's the best lamb chop I've ever had. The potatoes with mushrooms are amazing too, all garlicky and buttery, so good I could eat a pound in a sitting.

"What about your father?" Alina asks when I'm halfway through the lamb chop. "Where is he?"

"I don't know," I say, patting my lips with a napkin. "My mom never told me who he is."

"Why not?" Nikolai's voice sharpens. "Why didn't she tell you?"

I blink, taken aback, until it dawns on me what he must be thinking. "Oh, she didn't hide the pregnancy from him. He knew she was pregnant and chose to walk away." Or at least that's what I've gathered based on the few hints my mom had dropped over the years. For whatever reason, she hated this topic, so much so that whenever I pushed for answers, she'd take to bed with a migraine.

Nikolai's tone softens a fraction. "I see."

"I think he wasn't ready for that kind of responsibility," I say, feeling the need to explain. "My mom was only seventeen when she had me, so I'm guessing he was very young as well."

"You're guessing?" Alina lifts her perfectly shaped eyebrows. "Your mom didn't even tell you his age?"

"She didn't like to talk about it. It was a difficult time in her life." My voice tightens as another wave of grief washes over me, my chest squeezing with an ache so intense I can barely breathe through it.

I miss my mom. I miss her so much it hurts. Though I saw her body with my own eyes, a part of me still can't believe she's dead, can't process the fact that a woman so beautiful and vibrant is gone forever from this world.

"Are you okay, Chloe?" Alina asks softly, and I nod, blinking rapidly to hold back the tears stinging my eyes.

"Are you sure?" she presses, her green gaze filled

with pity, and in a flash of intuition, I realize that she knows—and so does Nikolai, who's watching me with an unreadable expression.

Somehow, they both know my mom is dead.

A rush of adrenaline chases away the grief as my mind leaps into overdrive. There's little doubt now: They had me investigated prior to our interview. That's how Nikolai knew about my lack of posts on social media, and why Alina is looking at me this way.

They know all sorts of things about me, including the fact that I lied to them by omission.

Thinking fast, I give a visible swallow and look down at my plate. "My mom…" I let my voice break, like it wants to. "She died a month ago." Allowing the tears to flood my eyes, I look up, meeting Nikolai's gaze. "That's another reason I decided to go on the road trip. I needed some time to process things."

His eyes glint a darker shade of gold. "My deepest condolences for your loss."

"Thank you." I wipe away the moisture on my cheeks. "I'm sorry I didn't mention it earlier. It's not something I felt comfortable casually bringing up in an interview." Especially since my mom was killed and the men who did it are after me. I really hope Nikolai doesn't know about *that*.

Then again, he wouldn't have hired me if he did. It's not the sort of thing you want around your family.

"I'm very sorry for your loss," Alina says, a genuine expression of sympathy on her face. "That must've been difficult for you, losing your only parent. Do

66

you have any other family? Grandparents, aunts, cousins?"

"No. My mom was adopted from an orphanage in Cambodia by an American missionary couple. They were killed in a car accident when she was ten, and none of their family wanted her, so she grew up in foster care."

"So you're all alone now," Nikolai murmurs, and I nod, the squeezing ache in my chest returning.

Growing up, I'd never minded the lack of extended family. Mom had given me all the love and support I could've wished for. But now that she's gone, now that it's no longer the two of us against the world, I'm painfully aware that I don't have anyone to rely on.

The friends I'd made in school and college are busy with their own, infinitely less fucked-up lives.

Realizing I'm drifting dangerously close to self-pity, I pull my gaze away from Nikolai's probing stare and turn my attention to the child at my side. He's finished his potatoes and is now industriously working on his lamb chop, his little face the very picture of concentration as he struggles to cut a bite-sized piece of meat using a fork and knife that someone left by his plate. Not a dull bread knife, either, I realize with a jolt.

An actual sharp steak knife.

"Here, darling, let me," I say, grabbing it from him before he can slice off his fingers. "This is—"

"Something he needs to learn how to handle," Nikolai says, reaching across the table to take the knife from me. His fingers brush over mine as he clasps the handle, and I feel it like an electric shock, the warmth of his skin igniting an answering furnace inside me. My insides tighten, my breath quickening, and it's all I can do not to yank back my hand as if scalded.

At least he's not married, an insidious little voice whispers in my head, and I shush it with vengeance.

Married or not, he's still my employer and thus strictly off-limits.

Biting my lip, I watch him hand the knife back to the child, who resumes his dangerous task.

"You're not worried he'll cut himself?" I can't keep the judgment out of my voice as I stare at the little fingers wrapped around a potentially lethal weapon. Slava is handling the knife with a reasonable degree of skill and dexterity, but he's still too young to be dealing with something so sharp.

"If he does, he'll know better next time," Nikolai says. "Life doesn't come with a safety lock."

"But he's only *four*."

"Four and eight months," Alina says as the boy succeeds in cutting a piece of lamb chop and, looking pleased with himself, forks it into his mouth. "His birthday's in November."

I'm tempted to keep arguing with them, but it's my first day and I've already pushed the envelope more than is wise. So I keep my mouth shut and focus on my food to avoid looking at the child wielding a knife next to me... or his callous, yet dangerously attractive father.

Unfortunately, said father keeps looking at me.

Each time I lift my gaze from my plate, I find his mesmerizing eyes on me and my heartbeat jumps, my hand tingling at the recollection of what it felt like to have his fingers brush against mine.

This is bad.

So bad.

Why is he looking at me like that?

He can't be attracted to me as well... can he?

NIKOLAI

IF THERE WAS ANY DOUBT IN MY MIND THAT I'M GOING to enjoy unraveling the mystery that is Chloe, it's gone by the time Pavel brings out dessert. Everything about her fascinates me, from the mixture of truth and lies falling so easily from her lips to the way she delicately and politely devours enough food to feed two NFL linebackers. And underneath my fascination is a primal attraction more powerful than anything I've experienced. I've never wanted a woman this much, and with so little provocation. She's not flirting, not doing anything to get my attention, yet from the moment I took my seat across from her, I've been hard, the sight of her plush lips closing around a fork turning me on more than the most erotic strip show in Moscow.

Even talking about Ksenia and the way she fucked me over with Slava couldn't cool the fire burning inside me.

"This has to be the most delicious thing I've ever had," Chloe says after trying a forkful of the Napoleon dessert, and I murmur my agreement, though I can barely taste the multilayered puff-pastry cake. My mind is occupied by how *she* will taste and feel when I take her to bed.

I have a feeling my son's new tutor will be the most delicious thing *I've* ever had.

"Don't, Kolya," Alina says quietly in Russian when Chloe turns to Slava and begins teaching him the English word for *cake*. "Please, I beg you, leave her be."

I glance at my sister in irritation. "I'm not going to force her." That's not my MO, and besides, after watching the girl sneak glances at me for the past hour, I'm even more sure this attraction goes both ways.

She'll be mine. It's only a matter of time.

"I'm beginning to think you may be worse than he was," Alina says in a low voice. "At least he tried to justify it with bullshit excuses. But you don't even try, do you? You just do whatever the fuck you want, regardless of who gets hurt in the process."

"That's right." I give her a hard smile. "And you'll do well to remember that."

If my sister thinks that comparing me to our father is going to change anything, she couldn't be more wrong. I know I'm like him. I always have been—which is why I never intended to have children.

Our little exchange in Russian catches Chloe's attention, and her eyes meet mine as she glances over at me. Immediately, she looks away, but not before I see her smooth throat move in a nervous swallow as her tongue flicks out to moisten her bottom lip.

Oh, yes, she's attracted to me. Attracted and worried about that fact.

I push away my half-eaten dessert and pick up my cup of tea to take a long sip. Catching her gaze again, I set the cup down and give her a slow, deliberate smile. "So, what did you think of your first Russian meal, Chloe?"

"It was amazing." Her voice is a touch breathless. "Pavel is a wonderful cook."

I let my smile deepen. "He is, isn't he?" He's even more skilled at other things, like knifework, but I'm not about to tell her that. She's already putting two and two together and coming up with four. I could see the way she reacted when I mentioned the guards. She suspects we're not just a wealthy family, and that makes her almost as nervous as her attraction to me.

I wonder if it's the natural wariness of a sheltered civilian, or if there's something more to it... like whatever secrets she's trying to hide.

The smart thing, the prudent thing, would've been to uncover those secrets before hiring her, but that would've taken time, and I didn't want to chance her slipping away and disappearing. Besides, after observing her throughout the meal, I'm even more convinced she doesn't pose a physical threat to my family. The way she snatched the knife from Slava betrayed not only her overprotectiveness of the boy but also her lack of skill with a blade. She held the knife like someone who's never used it as a weapon, either of the offensive or defensive variety, and I doubt that was an act—not when her fear for Slava was entirely real.

She thinks my son, a Molotov, needs to be protected from something as innocuous as a sharp blade.

The inexplicable tightness in my chest returns, and it takes all my strength not to glance at the boy. If I do, it'll only get worse. Instead, I keep my focus on Chloe and the way her lashes lower in response to my smile, her chest rising and falling in a faster rhythm. Her nipples are hard again, I note with savage satisfaction; whatever bra she's wearing under her shirt, if any, is quite revealing.

I can't wait to see her in a nice designer dress, her slender shoulders bared. Something slinky and cream-colored, to highlight the warm hue of her skin. She'll put it on for me before dinner, and I'll spend the entire meal fantasizing how I'll rip it off her later that night—not that I need her dressed in any particular way for those fantasies to manifest in my mind.

The cheap T-shirt and jeans she's wearing work for that purpose just fine.

"You should feel free to go to bed, Chloe," Alina says when Pavel brings out a tray with digestifs, then helps Slava out of his chair and takes him upstairs to get him ready for bed. "Don't feel compelled to stay here with us. I'm sure you're tired after such a long day."

"And I'm sure she can stay for a drink," I say before

Chloe can do more than give Alina a grateful smile. There's no way I'm letting the girl escape so quickly. "In fact," I continue, giving my sister a hard look, "weren't you saying *you're* tired? Maybe you should join Pavel in reading Slava a bedtime story and head to bed early yourself."

Alina wants to argue with me, I can see it, but even she knows it's not a good idea to push me further right now. She's become bolder since we left Moscow, freer with her sharp tongue. She thinks that because I temporarily handed over the reins to our brothers, I've softened, but she couldn't be more wrong.

The beast inside me is alive and well... and focused on a sweet new quarry.

"All right," she says after a tense moment. "In that case, good night. Enjoy your drink."

She gets up, and Chloe follows her example. "I think I will—"

"Sit," I say with a commanding gesture, and the girl sinks back down, blinking like a startled fawn as Alina strolls away with one final glare in my direction.

I wait until she's gone before gracing my quarry with a smile. "So tell me, Chloe..." I reach for the decanters on the tray. "Do you prefer cognac, brandy, or whiskey for your digestif?"

11

CHLOE

I stare at Nikolai, my heart thudding heavily. Am I misreading the situation, or did he engineer it so we'd end up alone at the table?

"I... don't really drink," I say, my throat dry. The look in his richly colored eyes again makes me feel like a mouse trapped by a very large cat—except no mouse would feel such a pull toward a predatory feline.

I want to touch him almost as much as I want to run away.

He arches his dark eyebrows. "No alcohol ever? I find that hard to believe."

"That's not what I meant. It's just, you know, usually beer or wine at a party..." My voice trails off as he lifts one of the crystal decanters and pours two fingers' worth of amber-colored liquid into a whiskey glass, then slides it toward me.

"Try this. It's one of the finest cognacs in the world."

I hesitantly lift the glass and sniff its contents. I've

never actually had cognac. Vodka shots a bunch of times, yes. Tequila on a few memorable occasions, for sure. But not cognac—and judging by the strong liquor fumes hitting my nostrils, it's not something I should drink around Nikolai tonight or on any other night.

Not when I'm so confused about what's happening between us.

He pours himself a glass as well. "To our new partnership." He lifts the drink in a toast, and I have no choice but to clink my glass against his. Bringing it to my lips, I take a sip—and break into a coughing fit, my eyes watering as my throat and chest ignite with fire.

Damn, this stuff is *strong*.

Nikolai watches me, dark amusement glimmering in his gaze. "You really aren't much of a drinker," he says when I've finally caught my breath. "Try it again, but slower this time. Let it sit in your mouth for a few seconds before you swallow it. Absorb the taste, the texture... the burn."

This is a bad idea, I know, but I follow his instructions, taking another sip and holding it for a bit before letting it go down my throat. It still scorches my esophagus, but not as much as the first time, and in the wake of the fiery sensation, a pleasant warmth spreads through my limbs.

"Better?" he inquires softly, and I nod, unable to tear my gaze away from his hypnotic stare. Maybe it's the alcohol already messing with my inhibitions, or the fact that we're all alone, but this feels oddly like a date... like there's a sense of intimacy building between us. I want to reach across the table and trace the sensual curve of his lips, to lay my hand on top of his broad palm and feel its strength and warmth.

I want him to kiss me, and if I'm not misjudging the simmering heat in his eyes, that may be what he wants as well.

"Why did you ask me to stay for a drink?"

I want to take the words back as soon as they leave my mouth, but it's too late. A sardonic smile appears on his face, and he tips his head to one side, indolently swirling the cognac inside his glass. "Why do you think?"

"I don't…" I wet my lips. "I don't know."

"But if you had to venture a guess?"

My heartbeat kicks up higher. There's no way I can say what I'm thinking. If I'm wrong, this will go very poorly for me. In fact, I don't see how this could go well for me. If I'm right and he's attracted to me, that opens an enormous can of worms. And if I imagined it—

"Don't overthink it, *zaychik*." His voice is deceptively gentle. "This isn't one of your school exams."

Right. And I'd much rather it were—because then the only thing I'd have to worry about is a failing grade. The stakes are infinitely higher here. If I get this wrong, if I upset him, I could lose the job, and with it, any hope of safety.

Out there, beyond the confines of this estate, are monsters hunting me, and in here is a man who may be just as dangerous... and not just because he seems to enjoy playing this sadistic little game with me.

"What does that mean?" I ask cautiously. "Zay-something?"

"Zaychik?" Darkness glimmers in his smile. "It means *little hare*. A Russian endearment of sorts."

My face heats, my pulse taking on an uneven rhythm. The odds that I'm wrong are decreasing by the moment, and that makes me even more nervous. I'm no virgin, but I've never dated anyone remotely like this man. My boyfriends in college were precisely that —boys who started off as my friends—and I have no idea how to handle this dangerously magnetic stranger who's also my boss.

And who may be in the mafia.

It's the last thought that brings much needed clarity to the contradictory tangle of emotions in my head.

Steadying my jangling nerves, I rise to my feet. "Thank you for the dinner and the drink. If you don't mind, I'll go to bed now. Alina's right—it's been a long day."

For two long heartbeats, he doesn't say anything, just watches me with that mocking smile, and my anxiety spikes, my stomach tying itself into knots. But then he sets down his glass and says softly, "Sleep well, Chloe. I'll see you tomorrow morning."

And just like that, I'm free—and equal parts relieved and disappointed.

1 2

NIKOLAI

I TOSS AND TURN FOR TWO HOURS, TRYING TO FALL asleep, but nothing happens. Finally, I give up and just lie there, staring at the dark ceiling, my muscles tight and my cock hard and aching despite the relief I gave it with my fist.

What is it about this girl that's getting to me? Her looks? The mystery she represents? It was all I could do to let her go this evening, to back off and allow her to go to bed instead of reaching across the table to pull her to me.

What would she have done if I'd acted on that impulse?

Would she have stiffened, screamed... or would she have melted against me, her brown eyes turning soft and hazy, her lips parting for my kiss?

Swearing under my breath, I get up, throw on a robe, and walk over to my computer. It's late morning in Moscow, so I might as well catch up with my brothers on some business.

Anything is better than dwelling on Chloe and the frustrating ache in my balls.

Konstantin doesn't pick up my video call, so I try Valery. My younger brother answers right away, his face as smooth and expressionless as always. Despite the four-year difference between us, we look enough alike to be mistaken for twins—and often are, along with our older brother, Konstantin, and our cousin, Roman.

Molotov genes are a potent, toxic thing.

"Missing us already?" Valery's tone betrays nothing of his emotions—if he has any, that is. It's possible my brother feels as little as he shows. I've never seen him lose his temper, even as a child, and I've certainly never seen him cry. Then again, I was away at boarding school throughout most of his childhood, so I can't claim to be a Valery expert.

We're not close, my brothers and I; our father had ensured that.

"Did you get the sign-off on the manufacturing plant?" I ask in lieu of a reply. "Or is that still pending?"

Valery regards me with an unblinking stare. "It's on the President's desk as we speak. He promised to get it back to me by tomorrow."

"Good." It's a deal I worked on for several months before leaving Moscow, and I want to make sure it goes through. "What about the tax credit bill?"

"Progressing as hoped." My brother tilts his head.

"Why the late-night call? All this could've waited until tomorrow."

I shrug. "Just having some trouble sleeping."

Valery's gaze sharpens. "Something to do with Slava?"

"No." At least not in the way he thinks. "Where's Konstantin?" I want his team to do a deeper dive on Chloe Emmons, with a specific focus on the past month.

I need to know what she did and where she went while she was off the grid.

"Berlin," Valery answers. "Acquiring more servers."

"Again?"

It's his turn to shrug. In my absence, my brothers have divided up the responsibilities according to their interests and strengths, with technology falling squarely into Konstantin's domain. Not that it had ever been otherwise; even when we were in elementary school, our older brother could run circles around the nation's top programmers. The main difference now is Valery stays out of Konstantin's business, letting him do as he will, whereas when I headed up the family organization, I oversaw everything, Konstantin's dark web ventures included.

"Fine," I say. "I'll get in touch with him there. Now fill me in on the rest of it."

And Valery does. By the time we end the call, I feel like I'm back in the loop—or at least as much in the loop as I can be while being half a world away. So much of our business takes place in person, at the galas and opera houses and high-end restaurants frequented by the power brokers of Eastern Europe. You can't subtly bribe a politician over email, can't intimidate a supplier into giving you a discount over Skype. It's all about rubbing elbows with the right people, being in the right place at the right time—and not leaving traces, digital or otherwise, if you have to cross a line to get things done.

Shutting down my laptop, I throw off the robe and stride over to the window, where a half-moon caught partially behind a cloud provides just enough illumination to make out the tops of the trees on the mountainside. I'm still tense, every muscle in my body coiled tight. The call distracted me, as hoped, but now that it's over, I'm thinking about Chloe again. Wanting her again.

Fuck.

Maybe I shouldn't have let her leave the table. I enjoyed her nervousness, the wariness in her pretty brown eyes. She reminded me of a wild hare, ready to flee at the first sign of danger, and I wanted to chase her if she did.

But I didn't. I let her go. She looked tired, and not the kind of tired one gets from undersleeping for a night or two. It was exhaustion, deep-seated and total. Her clothes were loose on her, as if she's recently lost weight, and her delicate features were sharper than in the pictures, her eyes ringed by deep shadows. Whatever happened to her has brought her to the brink of a collapse, and at that moment, when she stood up from her seat, so fragile and brave, I felt a strange urge to comfort her... to protect her from whatever demons had etched those signs of strain into her face.

No, that's idiotic. I hardly know the girl. I didn't want to push her to the breaking point, that's all.

Walking over to my closet, I pull on a pair of running shorts and sneakers and head out of the room. Maybe it's just as well that I let her be tonight. Tomorrow, I'll get in touch with Konstantin and begin the process of uncovering her secrets. In the meantime, it doesn't hurt to let her rest, get her bearings... acclimate to the idea that I want her.

No matter what my cock thinks, there's no rush.

After all, she's here now, and she's not going anywhere.

13

CHLOE

"No!"

I land on all fours, panting, my entire body trembling and covered in sweat. It's dark and I'm naked, and I have no idea where I am or what's happening. Then I register the feel of the hardwood floor under my palms and the faint moonlight pouring in through the wall-sized window, and it all clicks into place.

I'm in my room at the Molotov estate, and none of what I saw is real.

It was another nightmare.

Wincing, I push up to my knees—which immediately scream in protest. I must've bruised them when I threw myself off the bed.

Slender brown arm in a pool of blood... Gun in a black-gloved hand... Huge pickup truck barreling toward me...

A fresh surge of adrenaline propels me to my feet

despite the pain. Sucking in air, I fumble in the darkness for a lamp switch. My hand lands on the bed, and I feel my way over to the nightstand.

The bedside lamp comes on at my touch, illuminating the room with a soft golden glow. My knees buckle with relief, and I sink onto the mattress, letting the light push away the lingering bits and pieces of the nightmare.

It was just a dream.

I'm safe.

They can't get to me here.

After a couple of minutes, I feel steady enough to stand, and I walk over to the bathroom to rinse off the sweat drying on my skin. Before doing so, I flick off the lamp, as I ran out of clean clothes to sleep in but couldn't figure out how to work the blinds on the window. There's probably a button hidden somewhere, but I was too tired to find it last night. As soon as I got to my room, I stripped off my clothes, hand-washed my shirt and underwear in the sink so I'd have something clean to wear in the morning, and passed out the second my head hit the pillow.

Even worries about my disturbingly attractive employer couldn't keep me awake.

Now, though, as I stand in the shower, my mind turns to him, and my heartbeat revs up, my breath quickening with a mixture of anxiety and excitement.

Nikolai wants me.

I think.

Maybe.

I could be wrong.

Or... not.

Heat pools low in my belly, my breasts tightening as I picture the darkly intent look in his eyes and replay the things he said... and how he said them. No, I'm not wrong. At least not about his attraction to me. It's possible he was just toying with me and has no intention of acting on said attraction, but I don't think so.

I think he intends to fuck me, and I have no idea how I feel about that.

Actually, that's a lie. My mind might be torn, but my body is very straightforward in its feelings. The heat inside me intensifies, an aching tightness coiling deep inside my core as I imagine what it would be like if he came up to my room at this very moment and knocked on my door... then, not getting a response, opened it and walked in.

If he was sitting on the bed, waiting, when I came out of the bathroom naked.

My eyes drift shut, my hands cupping my breasts, then sliding down my body as I picture him standing up and walking toward me... reaching out to touch me. My fingers slip between my thighs, where I'm slick and aching, and I imagine it's his hand, his cruelly sensual mouth down there. My breath hitches as the ache transforms into a heated throb, my leg muscles quivering with rising tension, and with a sudden burst of sensation, I come, my toes curling on the wet tiles as I lean against the glass wall of the stall, gasping for air.

Stunned, I open my eyes and pull my hand away, my heart racing madly in my chest.

I can't believe what's just happened. I've never been able to orgasm this way before, with only my fingers. Normally, I need a minimum of fifteen minutes with my vibrator—or for a guy to go down on me for a half hour—and even then, it's hit or miss, depending on how stressed or tired I am. Arousal is very much a mental thing for me, which is why I've never gone for casual hookups.

I have to know a man to get intimate with him.

I have to like and trust him.

Or at least that's what I'd always thought. I have no idea if I like Nikolai, and I certainly don't trust him.

So why does the mere thought of him bring me to the brink of orgasm?

Why am I drawn to a man who makes me feel like hunted prey?

———

The light falling on my face pulls me out of a sound sleep, and I groan, rolling over to escape it. But it's everywhere, bright and warm, and it dawns on me that it must be morning, even if it doesn't feel like it.

Forcing open my heavy eyelids, I sit up and rub my face. Though I went right back to sleep after my impromptu masturbation session, I still feel tired, as if

I've gotten only a few hours of shut-eye instead of the nine or ten I must've actually snoozed for. I have no idea what time it is now, but I'm pretty sure I went to bed before ten.

Must be all those sleepless weeks catching up with me.

Swinging my legs to the floor, I take in the gorgeous view outside the window. Despite the bright sunlight, traces of fog envelop the distant mountain peaks, and the whole thing looks like something out of a postcard. I'm tempted to sit and enjoy it for a minute, but I make myself get up and head into the bathroom to wash up. It's my first morning on the job, and I don't want to make a bad impression by showing up late. Not that I know what "late" is—we didn't discuss my work hours or Slava's schedule yesterday.

I'm clean from my nighttime shower, so my morning routine takes mere minutes. The shirt and underwear I hand-washed are still a little damp, but I throw them on anyway and make a mental note to talk to Pavel or someone about the laundry situation as soon as possible. Also, about my hours.

I need to understand what Nikolai's expectations are, so I can meet and exceed them.

My pulse begins to race at the thought of him, and I focus on gathering my hair into a bun to distract myself from the increasingly active butterflies in my stomach. I went to bed with my hair wet, so it's got all sorts of weird kinks in it, and in any case, it's more professional to keep my hair off my face.

Returning to the bedroom, I make the bed, pull on my sneakers, and square my shoulders.

I can do this.

I have to do this, no matter how my new boss makes me feel.

14

CHLOE

I don't see anyone in the dining or living room downstairs, so I walk around until I find the kitchen. Walking in, I see a curvy woman with bleached blond hair cut in a short, poufy bob. Dressed in a flowery pink-and-white dress, she's bent over a sink, washing a plate, so I clear my throat to warn her of my presence.

"Hi," I say with a smile when she turns around, drying her hands on a towel. "You must be Lyudmila."

She stares at me, then bobs her head. "Lyudmila, yes. You Slava teacher?" Her Russian accent is even thicker than her husband's, and her round, rosy-cheeked face reminds me of a painted matryoshka doll, one of those that have other dolls inside, like onion layers. I'm guessing she's in her mid-to-late thirties, though her skin is so smooth she could easily pass for ten years younger.

"Yes, hi. I'm Chloe." Approaching, I extend my hand. "It's nice to meet you."

She clasps my fingers cautiously and gives my hand a brief shake as I ask, "Do you know where Slava is, and if he's already had breakfast?"

She blinks uncomprehendingly, so I repeat the question, being careful to enunciate every word.

"Ah, yes, Slava." She points at the big window to my left, which turns out to look out over the front of the house, where I parked my car. Only the car isn't there. I frown, then realize Pavel must've re-parked it yesterday, when he brought up my suitcase.

I'll have to ask him where it is, along with my car keys. I don't think they ever gave them back to me.

Before I can pose the question to Lyudmila, I spot my young student. He's scampering up the driveway, with Pavel on his heels. The man-bear is carrying a huge fish on a hook, and the boy has an equally big smile on his face. The two of them must've done some early-morning fishing.

I steal a glance at the clock on the microwave and wince.

Nope, not early-morning. More like mid-morning.

It's nearly ten.

My stomach growls, as if on cue, and a smile splits Lyudmila's round face. "Eat?" she asks, and I nod, smiling back ruefully.

At least my stomach speaks a universal language.

"Is it okay if I take something?" I ask, gesturing at the refrigerator, but Lyudmila bustles over there herself and takes out a platter of what looks like stuffed crepes.

"This good?" she asks, and I nod gratefully. Picky eater I'm not, and if those crepes are anything like the delicious Russian food I had last night, I'm going to be in seventh heaven.

"Thank you," I say, walking over to take the plate from her, but she pops it into the microwave and gestures at the counter behind the sink.

"Go. Sit. I make for you."

I thank her again and sit down on one of the bar stools behind the counter. I don't want to be a burden, but with the language barrier, my polite protest might be misinterpreted as refusal or dislike.

"Tea? Coffee?" she asks.

"Coffee, please. With milk and sugar if you have it."

She gets busy making it, and I look around the kitchen. It's as modern as the rest of the house, with glossy white cabinets, gray quartz countertops, and black stainless-steel appliances. Part of the big kitchen island in the middle is occupied with a long row of potted herbs, and a wine rack with a variety of bottles hangs artfully above them.

The microwave pings after a minute, and Lyudmila brings the platter of crepes over to me, along with a clean plate, utensils, and a jar of honey.

"Wow, thank you," I say as she plates one of the crepes for me, drizzles honey onto it, and then mimes for me to cut and eat it. "That looks amazing."

I cut a piece of the crepe and examine its contents. It looks like ricotta cheese with raisins, and when I fork the bite into my mouth, I find it both sweet and savory —and even more delicious than I expected. My stomach growls again, louder, and Lyudmila grins at the sound.

"You like?"

"Oh, yes, thank you. This is so good," I mumble, my mouth already full with the second bite, and Lyudmila nods, satisfied.

"Good. You eat. So small." She moves her hands in the air, as if measuring the size of my waist, and tsk-tsks disapprovingly. "Too small."

I laugh uncomfortably and apply myself to the food as she goes back to doing the dishes. It's funny, her blunt criticism of my figure, but also true. I've always been slim, but after a month of sporadic meals, I've become downright skinny, the muscles on my body melting away along with what little fat I had. Even the booty I'd once deemed too prominent is barely there now; I'll probably have to do a million squats to get it back.

Which I will, once all of this is over.

If it's ever over.

No, not if. I refuse to think that way. I've come this far, eluding my pursuers against all odds, and now things are looking up. For the first time since this nightmare began, I've slept the whole night, I have a full belly, and I'm somewhere they can't ambush me. And in six days, I'll have my first paycheck, and with it, more options—including leaving here, if that's what I need to do to be safe.

If the darkness I sensed in Nikolai is anything more than a product of my imagination.

In this bright, sunlit kitchen, my fears about mafia feel overblown, irrational, as does my conclusion that he wants me. As Lyudmila pointed out, I hardly look my best, and I'm sure a man as rich and gorgeous as my employer is used to world-class beauties. The more I think about it, the more it seems my attraction to him might've led me to misinterpret the situation last night. The pet name, the probing questions, the low, seductive tone of his voice—it could've all been a case of cultural differences. I don't know much about Russian men, but it's possible they're always that way with women—just as it's possible that wealthy Russians are used to having guards due to high levels of corruption and crime in their country.

Yes, that's probably it. With all the stress of the past month, I've let my imagination run wild. Why would a mafia family settle here, in this remote wilderness? New York, sure; Boston, very likely. But Idaho? That makes no sense.

Shaking my head at my foolishness, I polish off the rest of the crepes and drink the coffee Lyudmila made. Then, feeling upbeat and hopeful for the first time in weeks, I get up, bring the dishes to the sink—where Lyudmila takes them despite my protests—and head out to find my student.

I can do this.

I really can.

In fact, I'm looking forward to it.

I'm rounding the corner to the living room, walking fast, when I run smack into a large, hard body. The impact knocks the air from my lungs and nearly sends me flying, but before I can fall, strong hands close around my upper arms, hauling me against said body.

Stunned, completely out of breath, I look up at my captor—and my heartbeat goes through the stratosphere as I meet Nikolai's tiger-bright gaze.

"Good morning, zaychik," he murmurs, his beautiful mouth curved in a mocking smile. "Where are you off to in such a rush?"

15

CHLOE

EVERY CELL IN MY BODY IGNITES WITH HEAT, MY PULSE jumping impossibly higher. My lower body is flush against his, my thighs pressed against the hard columns of his legs and my stomach molded against his groin. I can smell his cologne, something subtle and complex, with notes of cedar and bergamot, and underneath, the clean musk of warm male skin. And it *is* warm. Even with us both fully dressed, I can feel his animal heat— and, to my shock, the growing hardness pressing into my belly.

"Are you okay?" he murmurs, and I realize I'm staring up at him dazedly, like a rabbit caught in a trap. Which is pretty much how I feel. His long fingers completely encircle my upper arms, his grip unbreakable. And he's huge. Up until this moment, I hadn't realized just how tall and muscular he is. I'm of average height for a woman, but he dwarfs me in every way—and judging by the thickness of the bulge pressed against me, he's consistently big all over.

My skin heats another thousand degrees, and my insides contract on a sudden empty ache. "I'm... I'm fine." Only I sound anything but fine, my choked voice betraying my agitation. I can't think, can't process anything except the fact that his erection is pressing against me, and for whatever reason, he's not letting go of me.

He's holding me against him as if he might *never* let go, his gaze growing more intent by the second. Slowly, as if drawn by a magnet, his eyes move down to my lips and—

"Kolya." Alina's voice is tight. "Konstantin wants to talk to you."

Nikolai stiffens and raises his head, his fingers tightening on my arms to the point of pain. An involuntary gasp escapes my throat, and he loosens his grip—but still doesn't release me.

"Tell him I'll call him back," he tells his sister. His tone is cool and even, as if we were all sitting at a table instead of him holding me like we're about to tango. My face, on the other hand, is burning with embarrassment.

I can't even imagine what Alina's thinking right now.

"He wants to speak to you right away," she insists. "He's going into a meeting in a few minutes and will be busy afterward."

Nikolai mutters what sounds like a Russian curse

and finally releases me. Shaken, I stumble back on unsteady legs and turn to face Alina, who's watching her brother stalk off with a narrowed stare. Then her gaze swings to me, and her full red lips tighten.

"I ran into him," I blurt before she can accuse me of anything. "It was an accident. I would've fallen, but he—"

"My brother doesn't do accidents." Her eyes are like jade dipped in ice. "You'd do well to remember that, Chloe."

And with that, she walks off, leaving me more shaken than before.

After a few minutes, I've composed myself enough to resume my search for Slava—this time, at a much more sedate walking pace. When I get to his room, however, he's not there, so I go back downstairs to look for him.

I don't see him or Pavel in any of the common areas, so I return to the kitchen, hoping to find Lyudmila there. But she's also gone.

Maybe they're all outside?

Opening the front door, I step out into the bright sunlight. It's a gorgeous, cloudless day, the forest-scented breeze cool and refreshing on my face. Nobody's on the driveway, but I walk out there anyway, drawing lungfuls of fresh mountain air to further calm myself.

There's no reason to freak out.

Nothing happened.

Nikolai caught me when I would've fallen, that's all.

Except... something could've happened if Alina hadn't interrupted. I'm ninety percent sure Nikolai had been about to kiss me. And I definitely didn't imagine the hard bulge pressed against me.

He does want me.

There's no longer any doubt about that.

I take another deep breath, but my heart continues to pound, my palms sweating like crazy. Wiping them on my jeans, I walk around the side of the house, taking in mountain views in an effort to calm my racing thoughts.

It's fine. Everything's fine. Just because Nikolai is attracted to me doesn't mean anything is going to happen between us. I'm sure he realizes how inappropriate the whole thing is. No matter what Alina said, it *was* an accident, us bumping into each other. I don't know why she would imply otherwise. Maybe she thinks I was coming on to him? But no. It seemed almost as if she was warning me away from him, as if—

The sound of voices catches my attention, and as I round the corner, I see Pavel and Slava. They're standing by a tree stump some fifty feet away, with the big fish laid on top of it. As I approach, I see the man-bear slice it open halfway, then hand the sharp-looking knife to Slava.

What the hell? Is he expecting the child to finish the job?

He is. And Slava does. By the time I get there, the

boy is scooping out fish innards with his little hands and throwing them into a plastic bag Pavel is helpfully holding open for him.

Okay then. I guess they know what they're doing. I've cleaned fish a few times myself—my freshman-year roommate, a fishing-and-hunting enthusiast, taught me how—so I'm not grossed out, but it is unsettling to see a four-year-old doing it.

They're *really* not worried about him with knives.

Stopping in front of the stump, I put on my brightest smile. "Good morning. Mind if I join you?"

The boy grins up at me and rattles off something in Russian. Pavel, however, looks less than pleased to see me. "We're almost done," he growls in his thickly accented voice. "You can wait in the house if you want."

"Oh, no, I'm fine out here. Do you need any help with that?" I gesture toward the fish.

Pavel glowers at me. "You know how to remove scales?"

"I do." I'd actually rather not do it, lest I get my only clean clothes dirty, but I want to continue teaching Slava, and the best way to do that is to spend time with him, engaged in whatever activities he's doing.

In my experience, children learn best outside of a classroom—and so do most adults.

"Here then." Pavel thrusts a descaling knife at me. "Show the kid how to do it."

Judging by the smirk on his brick-like face, he thinks I'm bluffing—which is why it gives me great pleasure to take the knife from him and say sweetly, "Okay."

Taking care not to get any splatters on my shirt, I get to work, explaining to the boy the entire time what I'm doing and how. I tell him what every part of the fish is called and make him repeat the words, then let him try the descaling himself. He's as good at it as he was at the slicing, and I realize he's done it before.

When Pavel told me to show him, he was just testing me.

Hiding my annoyance, I let Slava finish the job and put the cleaned fish back into the bucket. Pavel carries it into the house, and Slava and I follow. The man-bear goes straight for the kitchen—probably to prepare the fish for lunch—and I tell him I'm taking Slava upstairs to get changed. Unlike me, the boy has fishy splatters all over his shirt.

Pavel grunts something affirmative before disappearing into the kitchen, and I shepherd Slava into the nearest bathroom. We both thoroughly wash our hands, and then I lead Slava up to his room.

To my surprise, Lyudmila is there when we walk in, presciently laying out a clean shirt and jeans for Slava on the bed.

"Thank you," I say with a smile. "He's in dire need of a change."

She smiles back and says something to Slava in Russian. He walks over to her, and she helps him out of the dirty clothes. I tactfully turn my back—the boy is old enough to be shy in front of strangers. When it seems like they're done, I turn around and find Lyudmila helping him with the buckle of his belt.

"All good," she announces after a moment, stepping back. "You teach now."

I grin at her. "Thank you, I will." Seeing her gather Slava's dirty clothes, I ask, "Is there a washing machine somewhere in the house? I need to do laundry."

She frowns, not understanding.

"Laundry." I point at the pile of clothes in her hands. "You know, to wash clothes?" I rub my fists together, mimicking someone doing laundry by hand.

Her face clears. "Ah, yes. Come."

"I'll be right back," I tell Slava and follow Lyudmila downstairs. She takes me past the kitchen and down a hallway to a windowless room about the size of my bedroom. There are two fancy washers and dryers—I guess to run multiple loads at once—along with an ironing board, a drying rack, laundry baskets, and other conveniences.

"This, yes?" She points at the machines, and I nod, thanking her. Returning to my room, I gather all my clothes and bring them down. Lyudmila is gone by then, so I begin loading the washers. In a half hour, I'll come down again to move the clothes over to the dryers, and by dinnertime, everything will be clean.

Things really are looking up, the situation with my boss notwithstanding.

My heart rate speeds up at the thought, the butterflies in my stomach roaring back to life. Slava and Pavel provided a much-needed distraction, but now that I'm away from them, I can't help thinking about what happened. My mind cycles through everything, over and over, until the butterflies turn into wasps.

I felt Nikolai's erection against me.

He looked like he was about to kiss me.

He didn't let go of me when his sister was there.

It's that last part that freaks me out the most, because it means I was wrong. He does intend to act on this attraction. If Alina hadn't insisted he take the call, he would've kissed me, and maybe more. Maybe at this very moment, we'd be in bed together, with his powerful body driving into me as—

I stop the fantasy before it can progress any further. Already, I feel overly warm, my breasts full and tight, my sex pulsing with a coiling ache. It must be some weird aftermath of my impromptu masturbation session last night; that's the only explanation for why I've suddenly acquired the libido of a teenage boy.

Taking slow, deep breaths to calm myself, I finish loading the laundry. The situation is undoubtedly tricky. An affair with my employer would be unwise on many levels, yet I'm less than certain of my ability to resist him. If I go up in flames merely thinking about him, what would it be like if he touched me? Kissed me?

Would my self-control evaporate like water on a frying pan?

There's only one solution I can see, only one thing I can do to prevent this disaster.

I have to avoid him—or at least, being alone with him—for the next six days.

Thus resolved, I set the washers to run, and turn around—only to freeze in place.

Standing in the doorway, golden eyes gleaming and mouth curved in a devastating smile, is the very devil who occupies my thoughts.

"There you are," he says softly, and as I watch, paralyzed in shock, he steps deeper into the room and shuts the door.

16

CHLOE

"I was looking for you," Nikolai continues, approaching with a panther-soft stride. "Pavel said you were upstairs with Slava."

I swallow hard as he stops in front of me. "Yes, I just came down here for a moment to throw in some laundry. I hope that's okay." Despite my best efforts, my voice wavers, and it's all I can do not to step back in an effort to put more space between us. Not that he's overly close—at least three feet separate us—but now that I know the smell of his cologne, I can pick up the subtle cedar and bergamot notes in the air, and my memory fills in the rest, from the heat coming off his skin to the hard contours of his body pressing against me. And that big, thick bulge... My knees wobble, and I almost sway toward him but catch myself at the last moment, stiffening my legs and spine.

A dark heat invades his gaze, and I know he's

noticed my reaction. My cheeks burn and my heart hammers faster, icy-hot prickles running over my skin.

Why is he here?

Why was he looking for me?

Why did he shut that door?

"Yes, of course, that's not a problem." His voice is soft and deep, that unsettling heat still in his eyes. "You're living here now, so think of this as your home."

"I will, thank you." Dammit, now I sound all husky and breathless. Pulling myself together with effort, I give him my best model-employee smile. "I was actually going to ask you something. Do I have a work schedule? That is, are there any specific times you'd like me to work with Slava? Ideally, I'd like to teach him throughout the day, as opposed to having formal lessons, but if you prefer otherwise, I'm flexible."

There, that's better. I actually managed to steady my voice and sound semi-professional. Hopefully, that'll remind him I'm here to teach his son, not melt at his smoldering stare like—well, probably like every straight woman he's ever met.

Another wickedly sensual smile touches his lips. "It's up to you, zaychik. Your pupil, your methods. All I'm after are the results. The only thing I ask is that you join our family for mealtimes, so Pavel and Lyudmila don't need to cook and clean extra."

"Yes, of course. What time are breakfast and lunch?" Now I feel bad that I made Lyudmila give me those crepes; as late as I woke up, I could've waited until the next scheduled meal.

"We usually eat breakfast at eight and lunch at twelve-thirty. Does that work for you?"

"Absolutely." If there's anything I've learned over the past month, it's that food, anytime, anywhere, of any variety, works for me.

A full stomach is something I'll never take for granted again.

"Good. Then I'll see you at lunch today." He turns to walk away, and I exhale a shaky breath, again relieved and perversely disappointed—only to have my heart miss a beat as he stops and faces me again.

"Almost forgot," he says, eyes gleaming. "Your new clothes are getting delivered this afternoon. Pavel will bring them up to your room, and I'd appreciate it if you wore one of the dresses for dinner."

"Oh, sure. Thank you. I will." One of the dresses? How many did he buy? And how is he getting them delivered so fast? I'm dying to ask, but I don't want to prolong this nerve-racking encounter.

I'm still cognizant of that closed door.

"Good. Let me know if something doesn't fit." His gaze travels over my body, and the icy-hot prickles return, my breathing turning shallow as my nipples tighten in my bra. *Another thin cotton bra that's doing little to hide my reaction.* My face burns with the heat of a thousand suns, and as his eyes meet mine again, I feel the shift in the atmosphere, sense the air taking on that dangerously electric charge.

Mouth dry, I take a half step back, though what I really want is to lean toward him. The pull is so strong it's like a physical force—and judging by the way his jaw flexes as he watches my retreat, I'm not alone in experiencing it.

Run, Chloe. Get out.

Mom's voice is quieter this time, less urgent, but it clears away some of the haze in my brain. Gathering the withering shreds of my willpower, I take another step back and say as evenly as I can manage, "Thank you. I will."

His nostrils flare, and I again have the sense of being in the presence of something dangerous... something dark and savage that lurks underneath Nikolai's urbane veneer.

"All right," he says softly. "Good luck with your laundry, zaychik. I'll see you soon."

And opening the door, he walks out.

17

NIKOLAI

I ABSTAIN FOR ALL OF FIFTEEN MINUTES AFTER I GET TO my office. I check my email, pay a few invoices, fire off a reply to one of my accountants. Then, cursing under my breath, I turn up the sound on my laptop and bring up the camera feed from my son's room.

As expected, Chloe is there, having finished her task in the laundry. Hungrily, I watch as she plays cars and trucks with Slava, speaking to him the entire time as if he can understand her. Every once in a while, she points at something like a wheel and makes Slava repeat the English word after her, but for the most part, she just talks—and Slava listens to her raptly, as fascinated by her facial expressions and gestures as I am.

At one point, he laughs at the way his truck overtakes her car, and she grins and ruffles his hair, her slender fingers casually sliding through his silky strands. My chest squeezes painfully, my lust for her mixing with intense jealousy. I don't even know which of them I envy more—Slava, for experiencing her touch, or Chloe, for winning my son's affections. All I know is I want to be there, basking in her sunny smile, hearing my son's laugh in person instead of through the camera.

Fuck.

This is pathetic.

What am I doing?

I move to close down the feed but stop at the last second, hovering the cursor over the X. She's opened a book and is reading to Slava now, her voice a soft, slightly husky croon that makes me want to burst into my son's room, snatch her up, and carry her off to bed. I want to hear that voice moan my name as I drive into her tight, wet heat, to hear her plead and beg as I take her to the brink over and over before finally granting her the sweet mercy of release.

I want to torment her nearly as much as I want to fuck her, to make her pay for making me feel this way.

Clenching my teeth so hard I risk a toothache, I close the screen and propel myself to my feet. Despite the largely sleepless night I had, I'm brimming with restless energy. I need another hard run, or maybe a sparring session with Pavel.

I cast a glance at the clock above my office door.

Less than an hour before lunch.

Pavel is likely busy preparing food, and if I go for the kind of long, hard run I need, I won't have a chance to shower and change before it's time to join everyone at the table.

Exhaling a frustrated breath, I sit and open my inbox again. It's too soon to expect anything from Konstantin—I only asked him to do a deep dive on Chloe's missing month this morning—but I still check for his email.

Nothing.

Fucking hell. I really need a distraction. My fingers are itching to open up the camera feed again and watch her interact with my son. But if I do, this restlessness will only grow worse, my hunger for her more intense. Having held her this morning, I know how she feels pressed against me, how sweet and clean she smells, like wildflowers on a crisp spring morning. It took all of my strength to turn her loose, even with Alina there, and when I found her alone in the laundry room, every dark, primal instinct insisted that I take her, that I strip her naked and bend her over a washer, claiming her on the spot.

And I would've done exactly that if she'd leaned toward me.

If she'd done anything but back away, I'd be balls deep inside her instead of sitting here, wrestling with myself like a fool.

No, fuck this.

I launch to my feet.

I need a hard, bloody fight, and since Pavel's unavailable, the guards will have to do.

Arkash and Burev are out patrolling the compound when I get to the guards' bunker, but Ivanko, Kirilov, and Gurenko are sitting around a campfire out front with a few of our American hires. Like the barbarians they are, they're roasting a whole deer on a spit and trading their usual insults.

Ivanko spots me first. "Boss." Snatching up his M16, he jumps to his feet. "Something wrong?"

Kirilov and Gurenko are already on their feet as well, weapons ready, just like in our Crimea days.

"Easy, boys." Smiling grimly, I strip off my shirt and drape it over a nearby tree branch. "Everything's just right." Or it will be soon.

Three against one is exactly the type of odds I was hoping for.

18

CHLOE

TO MY RELIEF, LUNCH WITH THE MOLOTOVS IS A MUCH more casual affair than dinner. Well, Alina is still dressed like she's at an upscale cocktail party, but Nikolai is wearing dark jeans with a white polo shirt, and nobody chides Slava for his shorts and T-shirt as we sit down at the table—which is again laden with all sorts of mouthwatering salads, cold cuts, and sides.

Do all Russians eat like czars, or just this family? If this is an every-meal thing, I have no idea how they're not fat. I'm still full, having had breakfast only a couple of hours ago, but there's no way I'm not going to gorge myself on this spread.

Everything looks so freaking good.

"How was your first night with us, Chloe?" Alina asks when we've all filled our plates. "Did you sleep well?"

I smile at her, relieved both by the innocuous question and the friendly tone. I was afraid she might still be mad at me after this morning's incident. "I slept very well, thank you." And it's true—the nightmare aside, it was the best sleep I've had in weeks.

"That's good," Alina says, cutting into what looks like a fancy deviled egg. "I thought I heard something from your room around three, but it must've been my brother returning from one of his middle-of-the-night runs." She shoots Nikolai a sidelong glance, and I busy myself with the food on my plate, grateful for the explanation.

I must've screamed out loud last night. That, or Alina heard me fall out of bed.

"I did go for a run," Nikolai says, "so that must've been it." When I look up, however, his gaze is trained on me, studying me with an unreadable expression.

Does he suspect something?

God, I hope *he* didn't hear me scream or fall.

Fighting the urge to squirm in my seat, I lower my gaze—and freeze, staring at his hands. He's holding a knife in one and a fork in the other, European style, but that's not what draws my attention.

It's his knuckles. They're red and swollen, as if he's been in a fistfight.

My pulse spikes as I look away, then sneak another look at his hands.

Yep. I didn't imagine it. Nikolai's knuckles are a mess. In general, his big, masculine hands look like they've seen a lot of action, with calluses on the edges of his thumbs and faded scars in a few places. Even his short, neatly groomed nails can't hide the truth.

These aren't the hands of a wealthy playboy. They belong to a man intimately acquainted with either hard manual labor or violence.

The suspicions I'd all but suppressed return, and this time, I can't pretend they're baseless. Something about the Molotovs unnerves me. Who are they? Why are they here? I can see a rich foreign family spending a couple of weeks in a place like this as a "nature detox," but to actually move here? Someone as glamorous as Alina belongs in Paris or Milan or New York, not a corner of Idaho where there are more bears than people. Same goes for Nikolai, with his smooth, cosmopolitan manners and insistence on *Downton Abbey* attire at dinner.

My new employers are the very epitome of the jet set—at least if one ignores Nikolai's street brawler hands.

I force myself to look away from those angry-looking knuckles and focus on the child next to me, who's again eating calmly and quietly. Disconcertingly so, I realize. What four- or five-year-old doesn't play at least a little with his food? Or demand adult attention on occasion? I know the boy can smile and laugh and play like any other child his age, so why does he turn into a kid-sized robot at mealtimes?

Feeling my gaze on him, Slava looks up, his big golden-green eyes strikingly solemn. I smile at him brightly, but he doesn't smile back. He just refocuses on his plate and resumes eating. I eat as well, but I continue watching him, my sense of wrongness intensifying by the second. There's something unnatural about my student's behavior, something deeply concerning. Maybe the boy is more traumatized by his mother's death than he seems on the surface, or maybe something else is going on... something far worse.

I steal another glance at Nikolai's knuckles, a horrible thought slithering into my mind.

To my infinite relief, the injuries look fresh, as if he's just pounded something or someone into the ground. Since Slava's been with me all morning, he couldn't have been that someone. Besides, only an impact of great force could've caused those types of contusions, and there's nothing about the way Nikolai's son is sitting or moving that would indicate he's been beaten so severely—or at all.

Whatever my employer is guilty of, it's not child abuse, thank God. I don't know what I'd do if that were the case. No, scratch that. I know. I'd call Child Protective Services and run, taking my chances with my mom's killers.

Which reminds me: I still don't have my car keys.

I'm about to ask Nikolai about them when Alina smiles at me and asks, "Have you always wanted to be a teacher, Chloe?"

I nod, setting down my fork. "Pretty much. I've always loved both children and teaching. Even as a child, I'd often play with kids younger than myself so I could cast myself in the role of their instructor." I grin, shaking my head. "I think I just liked having them look up to me. Stroked my ego and all that."

As I speak, I'm cognizant of Nikolai's eyes on me, intent and unwavering. A predator's stare, filled with both hunger and infinite patience. My skin burns under its weight, and it takes everything I have to keep my gaze on Alina and pick up my fork as if nothing is happening.

She asks about my choice of college next, and I tell her how I was lucky enough to get a full-ride scholarship there.

"I'd never even thought about applying to such an expensive school," I say between bites of delicious smoked fish and richly flavored beet salad. It helps if I concentrate on the food instead of the man staring at me. "My mom worked as a waitress, and money was tight for as long as I can recall. I was going to go to community college, then transfer to a state school, using a combination of scholarships, loans, and work-study to pay my way through. But just as I started my senior year of high school, I got an invitation to apply for this special scholarship program at Middlebury. It was for children of low-income single parents, and it covered one hundred percent of tuition, room, and board, in addition to providing an allowance for books and miscellaneous expenses. Naturally, I applied—and somehow got in."

"Why somehow?" Nikolai asks. "Weren't you a good student?"

I have no choice but to meet his penetrating stare. "I

was, but there were students in my circumstances who were far more qualified and didn't get it." Like my friend Tanisha, who'd gotten a perfect score on her SATs and graduated as our class valedictorian. I told her about the scholarship, and she applied to the program as well, only to be instantly rejected. To this day, I wonder why they chose me and not her; if it was a matter of surviving adversity, Tanisha had a "better" story, with her partially disabled mother raising not one but three children on her own, one of them— Tanisha's younger brother—with special needs.

"Maybe they saw something in you," Nikolai says, his eyes tracing over every inch of my face. "Something that intrigued them."

I shrug, trying to ignore the heat coursing under my skin. "Could be. More likely, though, it was just dumb luck." It had to have been, because a couple of months later, Tanisha got acceptance letters from every school she'd applied to, including Harvard, which she ended up attending thanks to a generous financial aid package. Not as generous as the scholarship I got—she graduated with seventy thousand dollars in student loans—but good enough that I stopped feeling guilty about taking the spot that should've been hers.

Being a nice person, she's never acted anything but happy for me, but I know how much the scholarship committee's rejection devastated her.

"I don't think it was dumb luck," Nikolai says softly. "I think you're underestimating your appeal."

Oh God. My heart rate jacks up, my face burning

impossibly hotter as Alina stiffens, her gaze bouncing between me and her brother. There's no mistaking his meaning, no waving it off as a casual compliment about my scholastic abilities, and she knows it as well as I do.

Still, I try. Pretending like it's all a joke, I grin widely. "That's very nice of you to say. What about you two? Where did you go to school?"

There. Change of topic. I'm proud of myself until I realize that if, for some reason, either of the siblings *didn't* go to college, my question could offend them.

Thankfully, Alina doesn't bat an eye. "I went to Columbia, and Kolya finished Princeton." She's composed again, her manner friendly and polite. "Our father wanted us to attend college in America; he thought it provided the best opportunities."

"Is that why you speak English so well?" I ask, and she nods.

"That, and we both attended boarding school here as well."

"Oh, that explains the lack of accent. I've been wondering how you both managed not to have it."

"We also had American tutors back in Russia," Nikolai says, a mocking half-smile playing on his lips. Clearly, he knows I'm trying to diffuse the tension, and he finds my efforts amusing. "Don't forget that, Alinchik."

His sister stiffens again for some reason, and I busy myself with clearing the rest of my plate. I have no idea what landmine I've stepped on, but I know better than to proceed with this topic. As I'm finishing up my food, I glance over at Slava and find him done as well.

"Would you like some more?" I ask, smiling as I gesture at his empty plate.

He blinks up at me, and Alina says something in Russian, presumably translating my question.

He shakes his head, and I smile at him again before looking over the other adults at the table. To my relief, they appear to have finished also, with Nikolai just sitting back, watching me, and Alina gracefully patting her lips with a napkin. Miraculously, her red lipstick leaves no traces on the white cloth—though I probably shouldn't be surprised, given that the bright color survived the entire meal without smearing or fading.

One of these days, I'm going to ask her to share her beauty secrets with me. I have a feeling Nikolai's sister knows more about makeup and clothes than ten YouTube influencers combined.

I'm about to excuse myself and Slava so we can resume our lessons when Pavel and Lyudmila walk in. He's carrying a tray with pretty little cups, a jar of honey, and a glass teapot filled with black tea. He sets it on the table while Lyudmila clears away the dishes.

"None for me, thank you," I say when he places a cup in front of me. "I don't drink tea."

He gives me a look suggesting I'm little better than a wild animal, then whisks my cup away and pours tea for everyone else, my student included. The delicate china looks ridiculous in his massive hands, but he handles the task deftly, making me wonder if he worked in some high-end restaurant prior to joining the Molotov household.

"Thank you for a wonderful meal. Everything was delicious," I tell him when he passes by me, but he just grunts in response, stacking the dishes that his wife didn't get to in a carefully arranged pyramid on top of the tray before carrying them all away. It's not until he's gone that I remember something important.

I turn to Nikolai, my face warming again as I meet his tiger gaze. "I keep forgetting to ask... Did Pavel repark my car somewhere? I didn't see it in front of the house. Also, I don't think I ever got my car keys back."

"Really? That's odd." Adding a spoonful of honey to his tea, Nikolai stirs the liquid. "I'll ask him about that." He hands the honey jar to Slava, who adds several spoonfuls into *his* cup—the boy must have a serious sweet tooth.

"That would be great, thank you," I say, picking up my glass of plain water—the only liquid besides coffee I like to drink. "What about the car? Is there a garage or something nearby?"

"At the back of the house, just underneath the terrace," Alina replies in her brother's stead. "Pavel must've moved it there."

"Okay, awesome." I grin, inexplicably relieved. "I was half-afraid you guys decided it's too much of an eyesore and pushed it into the ravine."

Alina laughs at my joke, but Nikolai just smiles and sips his honey-sweetened tea, watching me with an inscrutable expression.

19

CHLOE

THE REST OF THE AFTERNOON FLIES BY. AS SOON AS
lunch is over, I find the garage—the entrance to it is at
the back of the house, just past the laundry room—and
verify that my car is indeed there, looking even older
and rustier next to my employers' sleek SUVs and
convertibles. Then, since the weather is beautiful—low
seventies and sunny—I take Slava for a hike in the
forested portion of the estate rather than teaching him
in his room. We tromp through a wildflower-filled
meadow, climb down to a small lake we find about a
half mile to the west, and chase a dozen squirrels into
the trees. Well, Slava chases them, giggling maniacally;
I just observe him with a smile.

He's an entirely different boy out here than in the
dining room with his family.

As we make our way through the woods, he
chatters in Russian, and I reply in English whenever I
can guess what he's saying. I also make sure to give him

English words for everything we encounter, and I do my best to learn the Russian words he teaches me.

"*Belochka,*" he says, pointing at a squirrel, only to break into giggles when I mangle the word in my attempt to repeat it. He, on the other hand, pronounces English words perfectly almost from the first try; I suspect he's either been watching English-language cartoons or he has perfect pitch.

Musically inclined kids tend to master accents faster than their peers.

"Do you like music?" I ask as we're returning home. I hum a few notes to demonstrate. "Or singing?" I do my best rendition of "Baby Shark," which causes him to whoop in laughter.

In case there was any doubt, I'm *not* musically inclined.

As we approach the house, Pavel comes out to greet us, a fierce glower on his face. "Where were you? It's almost five, and he hasn't had his snack."

"Oh, we were—"

"And your clothes have been delivered. They're in your room." Eyeing Slava's dirty shoes with disapproval, he picks up the boy and carries him into the house, muttering something in Russian.

Chagrined, I take off my muddy sneakers and follow them in. I probably should've cleared our hike with Slava's caretakers, or at least kept better track of time. I did bring a couple of apples for Slava to munch on if he got hungry—I grabbed them from the kitchen before leaving—but I guess that's not as complete of a meal as the cheese-and-fruit tray Pavel brought up yesterday.

When I get to my room, I wash my hands and fix my bun; a bunch of fine strands have escaped the confinement and are framing my face in a messy halo. Then I head into my closet to check out the delivery.

Holy shit.

The walk-in closet—ninety-five-percent empty after I unpacked my suitcase—is now packed to the brim. And it's not just the fancy gowns my employers mandate for dinner. There are jeans and yoga pants, tank tops and T-shirts and sweaters, casual sundresses and sleek pencil skirts, socks and pajamas and hats. And underwear, all kinds, from thongs to comfy cotton panties to sports bras and lacy push-up bras, all improbably in my size. There's even outerwear—lots and lots of outwear, ranging from light rain jackets and sleek wool coats to puffy parkas that would withstand arctic weather.

It's a closet for all seasons and all occasions, and judging by the tags, everything's brand-new.

Stunned, I turn over a tag hanging from a soft-looking white sweater.

$395.

What the fuck?

I grab a tag from the nearest parka, a pretty blue one with a fur-lined hood.

€3.499. Made in Italy.

"You like?"

I give a start and spin around to face Alina, who's standing at the entrance of the closet.

"Sorry, didn't mean to scare you," she says, flicking her glossy black hair over her shoulder. She's already changed into another stunning gown, a red ankle-length piece with a thigh-high slit that shows a sliver of one long, toned leg. She's also refreshed her makeup, extending the eyeliner to emphasize the feline quality of her tip-tilted eyes.

"I knocked, but no one answered," she continues, "so I figured you were exploring your new things."

"I was—I am." I glance over my shoulder at the packed hangers and shelves. "Is that... all for me?"

"Of course. Who else would it be for? I don't need any more, that's for sure." Strolling over to stand next to me, she pulls out a long yellow dress and holds it up to my chest, then hangs it up and pulls out a pale pink one.

"But it's way too much," I say as she holds the pink dress against me, only to reject it as well. "I don't need all of this. A few dresses for dinner, sure, but the rest—"

"That's my brother for you. Nikolai doesn't do half measures." She flips through the rest of the gowns with practiced speed and pulls out a shimmery peach number. *Versace*, the label on it states, and there's no price tag in sight—probably because the amount would be scary. Holding it up against me, Alina gives a satisfied nod. "Try this on." She thrusts it into my arms.

"Right now?"

She arches her eyebrows. "I can turn away if you're shy." Matching action to words, she gives me her back.

Suppressing an exasperated sigh, I quickly scramble out of my clothes and into the dress—which somehow fits perfectly, the gold-speckled peach chiffon draping over my body with stunning elegance. The A-line skirt falls gracefully to my feet, and the square-cut bodice has a built-in bra that lifts my modest B cups, giving me a hint of cleavage. The wide straps conceal my shoulders, but my arms and the upper portion of my back are left bare, exposing the scabs from where the shards of glass pierced my skin.

Dammit. I was hoping to avoid showing those until they've healed.

"Ready?" Alina sounds impatient.

"Just one sec." I twist my arm behind my back, trying to get the zipper all the way up. "Actually, do you think you could...?"

"Of course." She zips me up and steps back to give me a once-over. Instantly, her gaze homes in on the scabs. "What happened here?" she asks, a tiny frown creasing her smooth brow.

"It's nothing." I grimace, as if embarrassed by my clumsiness. "I tripped and fell on some broken glass."

The explanation must satisfy her because she lets it go and resumes her perusal. "Very nice," she finally declares. "But that bun has to go."

"Oh, no, that's okay—"

"Come." Grabbing my hand, she drags me out of the closet and into the bathroom, where she makes me stand in front of the mirror. "See? You need to wear your hair down with this. Also, makeup is a must."

I stare at my reflection in the mirror, messy bun, dark circles, and all. She's right. A dress this glamorous deserves the works. Unfortunately, I only have a tube of lip gloss with me, having trashed the majority of the items in my makeup bag when I was clearing out my dorm room after graduation. I figured I'd go shopping with Mom when I got home. She loved that sort of thing, and we always—

I stop that line of thought and inhale to clear the painful constriction in my chest. "I can take my hair down, but I don't really have—"

"Yes, you do." She pulls open one of the drawers next the sink, revealing a selection of tubes and bottles that would make a professional makeup artist proud. "I made sure Nikolai got all the necessities," she explains.

"You helped him buy all this?"

"Who else?" She grins, revealing that perfectly imperfect little gap between her straight white teeth. "None of my brothers know mascara from lipliner."

My ears perk up. "Brothers?"

She nods, reaching into the drawer. "There are four of us. I'm the youngest and the only girl." She uncaps a foundation bottle and grabs my hand, turning it palm up. Smearing a streak of bronze color on my inner wrist, she eyes it critically, then opens a slightly more golden shade and tests that.

"Where are your other brothers?" I ask, watching her work in fascination. I did just think it might be nice to get a lesson from her one day, and here we are. I've always had trouble finding the right foundation; most drugstore brands offer shades that are either too light, too dark, or too ashy. But the second color Alina tries blends into my skin perfectly—she definitely knows what she's doing.

"They're both in Moscow," she replies, capping the bottle. "Well, at this moment, Konstantin is on a business trip in Berlin, but you know what I mean." She sets the bottle on the counter in front of me, along with mascara, eyeliner, and a bunch of other stuff, including an egg-shaped sponge that she wets under the faucet. Meeting my gaze in the mirror, she asks, "Do you mind if I do your face? Or would you rather do it yourself?"

"No, please, go ahead." I'm more than eager for her to continue. Beauty lesson aside, this is a chance for me to learn more about my mysterious employers without Nikolai's darkly magnetic presence scrambling my brains.

"All right then, wash your face and come along."

I do as she says while she sweeps all the makeup she laid out into a little silver case. After I pat my face dry and moisturize with a fancy-looking face cream I find in yet another drawer, she leads me back into the bedroom, where she stands me in front of the floor-to-ceiling window—natural light is best, she explains. Placing the makeup case on the nightstand nearby, she steps in front of me and, bending her head with a look of intense concentration, begins applying foundation with the damp sponge.

"You always want to pat, not rub," she explains, dabbing at my cheeks. "The color blends in best that way."

"Good to know, thank you." I wait until she's done with my chin before asking, "So what made you and Nikolai decide to come here? I imagine it must be a big change from Moscow."

She pauses, her eyes meeting mine. "Oh, it is. Moscow is... a whole other world." Her red lips tilt up without humor. "Not always a nice world."

"Oh?"

She resumes her careful dabbing. "It's quiet here. Calm. And the nature is beautiful. Nikolai wanted that for his son."

"So you're here for Slava?"

"My brother is." She frowns, studying my face, and uses the pointed end of the sponge to add a little foundation under my eyes. The dark circles must be bugging her. "Me, I just needed a break," she continues as she moves on to the bridge of my nose, "a little timeout, if you will."

"From life in Moscow?"

"Something like that. Close your eyes."

I obey, silently digesting what I've learned as she sweeps eyeshadow onto my lids and applies mascara to my lashes. It makes sense that they'd be here for the boy—the timing of their move to this compound lines up with Nikolai's learning of his son's existence. And I suppose if quiet, calm nature is what you're after, you can't do much better than this place.

Still, something doesn't smell right. I'm sure there are spots of wilderness untouched by civilization in Russia and other countries nearby. Why move halfway across the globe if pretty nature is all you're after? The time difference alone must make it difficult to stay in touch with family, or conduct any type of business— assuming there *is* a business.

I wait until Alina is done tracing my lips with a pencil before opening my eyes to ask, "What do your brothers do, work-wise?"

"Oh, this and that." She carefully applies lipstick, has me close my lips on a tissue to smudge off some of the color, and repeats the process two more times. Finally satisfied, she puts the lipstick away and picks up a little container of blush and a long-handled makeup brush. "Our family owns a bunch of companies in various sectors—energy, technology, real estate, pharmaceuticals," she says, swiping the brush across the apples of my cheeks with quick, expert strokes. "Nikolai oversees it all... or he did until recently. When we learned about Slava, he handed over most of the responsibilities to Valery and Konstantin, so he could move here and spend time with his son."

I stare at her in disbelief. Is she talking about the same Nikolai? The coolly distant father who barely interacts with his son? I can't picture him leaving a business meeting early to be with Slava, much less stepping down as head of some major conglomerate.

I must be missing something. That or Slava is a convenient excuse for something shady.

"What about you?" I ask when she steps away and surveys her work with a critical eye. "Are you involved with the family business as well?"

She laughs, a light, trilling sound. "Oh, that's not for me." Taking half a step forward, she smooths my left eyebrow with her thumb. "Not bad," she declares. "Now we just need to do your hair. Come." Clasping my hand, she drags me back into the bathroom, where she takes out an entire array of styling products from another drawer while I gape at my reflection in the mirror.

I have never, ever looked this way before, not even when Mom shelled out fifty bucks to have my makeup professionally done for my high school prom.

The girl in the mirror is beyond pretty, her skin smooth and glowing, her brown eyes large and mysterious above delicately contoured cheekbones and soft, plump lips the color of dusky rose.

I don't look like Alina, with her bright red lips and dramatic cat-eye makeup. In fact, I don't look like I'm wearing makeup at all. Instead, it's as if I've been Photoshopped, all my imperfections blurred and smoothed out.

"Wow." I lift my hand to touch my face. "This is…"

Alina slaps my hand away. "Don't touch, you'll mess it up. In general, the less you touch your face, the better. You have nice, clear skin, but it'll be even better if you keep your hands off it. The oil and dirt on our fingers clog the pores, causing them to look larger over time."

"Right, okay." Chastened, I keep my hands at my sides as she goes to work on my hair, first freeing it from the bun, then misting it with water and applying various styling products to tease out the wave in my otherwise-limp strands.

"There, all done," she says after a few minutes. "Now you need shoes, and we'll be all set."

Oh, crap. "I don't think I have any—" I begin, but she's already walking out of the bathroom.

I follow and see her beeline for my closet. A second later, she emerges with a shoebox. *Jimmy Choo*, the logo on the box proclaims. Setting it down on the floor, she takes out a pair of strappy gold heels and hands them to me. "Try these."

They bought me shoes as well? Stopping my brain from doing the math on the not-so-small fortune that must've been spent on my wardrobe, I put on the heels —like the dress, they fit perfectly—and walk over to the full-length mirror hanging next to the closet.

"How do they feel?" Alina asks, coming to stand next to me. To my surprise, she's now only a couple of inches taller than I; those high heels she always wears have fooled me into thinking she possesses a model's height.

I experimentally shift my weight from foot to foot. "Surprisingly comfortable." Not as comfortable as my sneakers, obviously, but I can stand and walk in them better than in any dressy shoes I've worn before. Likewise, the peach gown doesn't pinch or scratch anywhere; all the seams are smooth and soft against my skin, the silky inner lining pleasantly cool.

No wonder Alina is able to dress like a queen at all times. If all her clothes are of this quality, looking glamorous is nowhere near as big of an inconvenience as I imagined.

"You just need one more thing," she says, smiling at my reflection. "Stay here. I'll be right back." She hurries out of the room, and I stay in front of the mirror, marveling at the way the shimmery gown drapes over my too-skinny body, giving the illusion of healthy curves.

I'll never be as beautiful as Alina, but I'm definitely the best version of myself.

She returns a minute later with a small jewelry box in her hand. Setting it down on the nightstand, she opens it and takes out a pair of diamond studs and a heart-shaped pendant on a thin gold chain.

"Thank you, but I couldn't possibly," I say as she comes toward me, holding the jewelry. "That looks really expensive."

"Don't worry. It's just a little trinket." Ignoring my protests, she drapes the gold chain around my neck and locks it into place, then inserts the diamond studs into my ears. "There, now the outfit is complete."

She steps back, and I turn to face the mirror again.

She's right. The jewelry has added that final touch of polish, the heart-shaped diamond glittering an inch above the faint hint of cleavage created by the bodice of the dress. I look equal parts elegant and sexy, like a modern-day princess about to attend a ball.

If Mom saw me like this, she'd be so proud. She'd make me take a million pictures in dozens of different poses, and she'd set up the best ones as her screensaver and phone background, so she could show them off to her coworkers at the restaurant. She'd—

I blink the sting out of my eyes and turn back to face Alina. "Thank you," I say, my voice only slightly strained. "I appreciate this."

"It's my pleasure." Her green eyes gleam as she gives me a final once-over. "Let's go down to dinner. I can't wait for Nikolai to see you like this."

And before I can wonder what she means, she heads out of the room, leaving me no choice but to follow.

20

NIKOLAI

"WHAT THE FUCK DO YOU THINK YOU'RE DOING?" MY voice is low and pleasant, my expression neutral as I address my sister in Russian. Across from me, Chloe has her head bent toward Slava, talking to him about the food on his plate as if he can understand her, and all I can think about is how much I want to reach across the table and rip that pendant off her smooth, slender throat—right after I throttle the person who gave it to her.

"You asked me to help her get dressed." Alina's tone matches mine, even as chilly amusement glitters in her eyes. "Don't you like the results?"

"Where did you get it?" I drop my voice further as Slava glances at us curiously. Unlike his American teacher, he understands exactly what we're saying, if not the context of it all. "I thought it was lost."

"Mom's favorite necklace? Hardly." Alina's smile is as icy bright as the diamond glittering on Chloe's chest.

"She gave it to me for safekeeping. Right before... you know." She waits for my response. Getting none, she flaps her lashes with exaggerated innocence. "Don't you like it on her? I thought it was just perfect for this dress—and for your pretty new toy."

My molars squeeze together, but my outward demeanor remains calm. I now understand what game Alina is playing, and I don't intend to let her win. "You're right. It *is* perfect, and so is she. Thank you for being so helpful."

Not waiting for her reaction, I turn my attention to Chloe, ignoring the white-hot rage streaking through my veins each time the glimmering stone catches my eye. That pendant is all I've been able to see since Chloe came to the table, so now I take in her actual appearance—and as I do, the burning fury inside me transforms into scorching lust.

She's beautiful. No, more than that. She's breathtaking, a painting of a Grecian goddess come to life. Like in the picture I saw earlier, her hair tumbles down to her slender shoulders in a cascade of sun-streaked brown waves, and her smooth skin glows with a mysterious inner light. Whatever my sister has done has enhanced the radiance that's captured me from the beginning, emphasizing Chloe's bright, tender beauty.

The kind of beauty that all but begs for a despoiling touch.

My gaze trails from her face to her fragile collarbones, then, determinedly skipping over the pendant, to the hint of shadow between her breasts, temptingly pushed up by the tight bodice of her dress. With vivid clarity, I imagine how her erect nipples will feel when I palm those small, delicious globes, how they'll taste when I suck them. She'll moan, her head arching back and her slender arms rising to—

I stop, the fantasy evaporating as I stare at the dark red scabs on her left bicep.

What the fuck?

They look like puncture wounds, deep ones.

"She said she fell on some broken glass," Alina murmurs in Russian, as uncannily tuned in to me as always. "Interesting, isn't it?"

It is indeed. While it's theoretically possible to fall on broken glass and end up with puncture wounds, one is far more likely to get sliced up—and I don't see any marks of that kind on her arm.

"I wonder if she was stabbed or caught some shrapnel," Alina continues, again echoing my thoughts. "What do you think? My bet is on the latter."

I force myself to sound disinterested, bored by the topic. "I think she fell on some broken glass." I haven't told my sister about the additional report I commissioned from Konstantin's team, and I'm not planning to do so.

Chloe is my mystery to unravel, my puzzle to solve.

My pretty toy to play with.

Her eyes meet mine, and she quickly looks away, her hand tightening on her fork as her small chest rises and falls in a faster rhythm. I smile darkly, watching her. I unsettle her, make her nervous, and it's not just the sexual tension that heats the air between us. I caught the way she looked at my banged-up knuckles during lunch, saw the questions in her eyes.

My zaychik is smart enough to be wary of me.

She knows, deep down, what kind of man I am.

I study her throughout the meal, feasting my eyes on her while she feasts on the fruits of Pavel's kitchen labor. She's still discreet and subtle about it, but at least three heaping portions of *plov*, Pavel's Georgian rice pilaf specialty, disappear from her plate in short order, followed by a serving of every salad and side dish on the table, along with an entire plate of lamb kebab, tonight's main dish.

Her off-the-charts appetite both amuses and upsets me because it reveals something important.

It tells me she's known real, true hunger in the recent past.

The realization adds to my frustration, as do the marks on her arm. Konstantin still hasn't come through with the report, and it's driving me mad. I want to know what happened to her. I *need* to know it. It's fast becoming an obsession—and so is she. This afternoon, when she went hiking with Slava, I found myself climbing walls because I couldn't watch her through the cameras. I want to know what she's doing every moment of every day, and no matter how hard I try to distract myself, she's all I'm able to think about.

As the meal draws to a close, I contemplate getting her to stay for an digestif with me, but when I catch her covering a yawn, I decide against it. Alina's skill with makeup has hidden the outward signs of Chloe's exhaustion, but she's still fragile, still breakable... too much so for all the dark, dirty things I want to do to her. Besides, I can't be certain of my self-control tonight.

The desire searing my veins feels too powerful, too savage for a smooth seduction.

Soon, I promise myself as I watch her walk out of the dining room and disappear up the stairs.

Soon I'll get to the bottom of what makes Chloe Emmons tick, and appease this hunger.

It's nearly two a.m. when I admit defeat and get up to go for a run. After barely sleeping last night and working off much of my restless energy by sparring with the guards, I should've been dead to the world. Instead, I lay awake for hours, my body burning with unfulfilled desire and my mind filled with restless thoughts. Each time I'd come close to drifting off, I'd see the fucking pendant dangling above me, and rage would flood my veins, jerking me awake.

My sister knew what she was doing when she hung that bauble around Chloe's pretty neck.

The night sky is clear when I exit the house, the light from the half-moon illuminating my path as I begin jogging down the driveway. Not that I need it—I have excellent night vision. As the forest thickens around me, I speed up until I'm sprinting down the road leading to the gate. Halfway there, I take a sharp right and enter into the woods, my sneakers crunching on leaves and twigs as I weave through the trees. It's darker here, more dangerous, with the uneven ground and fallen branches, but the challenge is what I'm after. Running like this forces me to focus, to exert myself both mentally and physically. At the same time, something about the night forest soothes me. The quiet rustling of wild creatures in the bushes, the hooting of an owl above my head, the loamy scent of decomposing vegetation—it's all part of the experience, part of what attracts me to this place.

I run until my lungs burn and my muscles feel like lead, until sweat runs down my face in rivulets. When my legs threaten to give out, I turn back and run up the mountain, pushing myself past the point of exhaustion, past the limitations of my body and the memories encroaching on my mind. I run until I can't think about anything, much less picture the heart-shaped pendant on Chloe's chest.

Finally, I stop and walk the rest of the way, letting myself cool down. By the time I enter the dark, silent house, my breathing has calmed and my legs are starting to feel like they're attached to me. Toeing off my dirty shoes, I lock the front door and make my way up the stairs, the weight of sleep deprivation descending on me like a layer of bricks. I can't wait to fall into my bed and—

A choked cry stops me short.

I freeze on top of the stairs, all my senses on high

alert as I scan the dark hallway.

A moment later, I hear it again.

A muffled scream, coming from Chloe's room.

Adrenaline blasts through my body. I don't stop to think, I just act. Soundlessly, I pad down the hallway, every muscle in my body coiled for battle. If someone's broken in, if they're hurting her... The mere thought of it paints my vision red. Only a lifetime of training keeps me from kicking down the door and rushing in. Instead, I stop three feet from her bedroom and press my palm against the wall, feeling for a tiny ridge. When I find it, I push in, and with a quiet whoosh, a small square of the wall slides away, revealing one of the mini arsenals I've hidden throughout the house.

Moving silently, I reach into the niche and grab a loaded Glock 17, then approach Chloe's door.

All is quiet again, but I don't let it fool me.

Something isn't right. I know it. I feel it.

Clicking off the safety with my right thumb, I carefully twist the knob with my left hand and open the door a crack.

Another cry rings out, followed by a choked sob.

Fuck it.

I push the door wide open and charge inside, prepared to do battle.

Only no one attacks me.

There are no flying bullets, no movement of any sort.

The faint moonlight reveals no one in the dark bedroom besides me and a small bundle underneath the covers on the bed—a bundle that jerks suddenly, emitting another one of those muffled cries.

Of course.

I lower the gun, the worst of the tension draining from my muscles. This must be what Alina heard last night. No wonder Chloe looked so uncomfortable when my sister brought up the topic.

She has nightmares. Bad ones.

I should leave now that I know she's safe, but I remain rooted in place, staring at that bundle of covers as my heartbeat takes on a hard, thumping rhythm. *She's here, sleeping only a couple of meters away.* The adrenaline in my veins transforms into a sharp, hot need, a hunger so fierce and potent I shake from the effort of containing it. I want to feel her smooth, warm skin under my fingers, smell her crisp, sweet wildflower scent… sink deep into her tight, wet heat… My pulse roars in my ears, my body so hard it hurts, and my legs move against my will, carrying me forward.

No. Fuck, no.

I stop half a meter from the bed, jaw clenched.

Move the fuck back. Now.

By some miracle, my feet obey.

One step.

Another.

A third.

I'm halfway to the door when the bundle on the bed jerks again and begins thrashing wildly, filling the air with raw, heartrending cries.

21

CHLOE

"No!"

My feet slip in the blood as I lunge forward, dropping to my knees over Mom's body. Her beautiful, expressive face is slack, her soft brown eyes glazed and unseeing. Her pink robe, my Christmas gift from last year, gapes open at the top, revealing her left breast, and her right arm is flung out to the side, blood from the deep vertical gash in her forearm pooling on the clean white tiles, seeping into the immaculately maintained grout. Her left arm is pressed against her side, but there's blood there too. So much blood...

"Mom!" I press my icy fingers to her neck. I can't feel a pulse, or maybe I just don't know where to find it. *Because there's a pulse. There's got to be. She wouldn't do this. Not now. Not again.* I'm simultaneously frantic and numb, my thoughts hurtling along at lightning speed even as I kneel there, stiff and frozen. *Blood. So much blood on the kitchen floor.* My head jerks up on autopilot, my eyes searching for a roll of paper towels on the counter. Mom will be so upset about the stains on the grout. I need to clean this up, need to—

Call 911. That's what I need to do.

I scramble to my feet, frenziedly patting my pockets as my gaze bounces around the kitchen.

My phone. Where is my fucking phone?

Wait, my purse.

Did I leave it in the car?

I spin toward the front door, breathing in shallow gasps. *Keys.* The car needs keys. *Where did I put my fucking keys?* My gaze falls on a little table by the entrance, and I race toward it, heart hammering so fast it makes me sick.

Keys. Car. Purse. Phone.

I can do it.

Just one step at a time.

My fingers close around my furry keychain, and I'm about to grab the door handle when I hear it.

The low, deep rumble of male voices in Mom's bedroom.

I turn to stone, every muscle in my body locking tight.

Men. Here in the apartment. Where Mom is lying in a pool of blood.

"—was supposed to be here," one of them is saying, his voice growing louder by the second.

Without thinking, I leap into the wall niche in the hallway that serves as our coat closet. My left foot lands on a pile of boots, my ankle twisting agonizingly, but I bite back the cry and yank the winter coats around me like a shield.

"Check the phone again. Maybe there's traffic." The other man's voice sounds closer, as do his heavy footsteps.

Oh God, oh God, oh God.

I slap both hands over my mouth, the keys I'm clutching digging painfully into my chin as I hold still, not daring to breathe.

The footsteps stop next to my hideout, and through the bulky layers of coats, I see them.

Tall.

Powerfully built.

Black masks.

A gun in one gloved hand.

Prickles of terror race up and down my spine, my vision dappling with dark spots from lack of air.

Don't pass out, Chloe. Stay still and don't pass out.

As if hearing my thoughts, the man closest to me pivots to face my hideout and yanks off his mask, revealing a shark's head. Baring his knife-like teeth in a macabre grin, he points the gun at me.

"*No!*"

I jerk back violently, only to get tangled in the coats. They're all over me, smothering me, holding me captive. I flail with increasing desperation, hoarse pleas and panicked sobs tearing from my throat as the black-gloved finger tightens on the trigger and—

"Shhh, it's okay, zaychik. You're okay." The coats constrict around me, only this time their weight is comforting, like being enveloped in a hug. They smell good too, an intriguing mixture of cedar, bergamot, and earthy male sweat. I inhale deeply, my terror easing as the shark's head and the gun recede into a foggy mist and awareness of other sensations trickles in.

Warmth. Smooth, hard muscle under my palms. A deep, rough-silk voice murmuring soothing nothings into my ear as powerful arms hold me tight, protecting me, keeping me safe from the horrors hovering beyond the mist.

My sobs quiet down, my jerky breaths slowing as the nightmare releases its hold on me. And it *was* a nightmare. Now that my brain is beginning to function, I know there's no such thing as a shark's head on a human body. My sleeping mind conjured that up, embellishing the memory, just as it's now embellishing—

Wait, this doesn't feel like a dream.

I stiffen, a spike of adrenaline sweeping away the lingering haze and bringing the realization that a big, warm, bare-chested, *very real* man is rocking me on his lap. My face is buried in the crook of his neck, my hands gripping the hard muscles of his shoulders as his large, callused palms stroke soothingly over my back. He's murmuring words of comfort in a mixture of English and Russian, and his soft, deep voice is terribly familiar, as is his beguiling male scent.

It can't be.

It's not possible.

And yet...

"Nikolai?" I whisper, feeling like I'm imploding on the inside—and as I lift my head from his shoulder and open my eyes, the weak moonlight streaming through the window illuminates the starkly carved lines of his face, giving me the answer.

22

CHLOE

A BIG, WARM HAND SETTLES ON MY NAPE, MASSAGING away the tension permeating every muscle in my body. "Are you okay, zaychik?" he murmurs, the pale moonlight reflecting in his eyes as his other hand strokes up and down my arm. "Is the bad dream gone?"

I can't find the words to respond. The shock is like a million tiny needles stinging my skin, my inner thermostat flipping from hot to cold and back again.

Nikolai and I are in bed.

Together.

He's holding me on his lap.

The thermostat dials up all the way to scorching, spiking my pulse and sending a dizzying spear of heat straight to my core. We're all but naked—my pajama tank and shorts are beyond flimsy, and he must be wearing only shorts or briefs as well because I can feel his bare thighs against mine. His skin is rough with hair, his leg muscles so hard they feel like stone.

And that's not the only stone-like hardness I'm feeling.

The entire world seems to fade away, replaced by the stark awareness of our intimate position and the dark, magnetic force that's pulled us toward one another from the start. My heart thuds violently in my ribcage, each beat reverberating in my ears as my breath stutters through my parted lips. His face is mere inches from mine, his powerful arms encircling me, holding me in an embrace that's equal parts protective and restraining.

"Chloe, zaychik…" A strained note enters his deep voice. "Are you okay?"

Okay? I'm burning up, dying from the firestorm of need inside me. He's so close I can feel the warmth of his breath, smell a hint of minty toothpaste mixing with the sensual notes of his cologne and the salty undertones of clean, healthy male sweat. His eyes gleam with moonlight speckled with shadows, his black hair blending with the night, and I have the surreal thought that *he* is made of darkness… that like a creature of the underworld, he exists out of the reach of light.

Trepidation curls through me, mixing with the heat burning in my veins, intensifying it in some peculiar, unsettling way. My nipples harden, my inner muscles clenching on a growing empty ache, and my body acts on a long-simmering impulse, my fingers tightening on the hard muscles of his shoulders as my lips press against his.

For a brief moment, nothing happens, and I have the horrifying thought that I've misjudged the situation, that the attraction is one-sided after all. But then a low, rough sound rumbles in his throat, and he kisses me back with savage hunger, his arms tightening to form an iron cage around me. His lips devour mine, his tongue stabbing deep, tasting me, invading me in a blatant imitation of the sexual act, and my mind goes completely blank, all thoughts and fears evaporating under the brutal lash of desire.

I've never known a kiss so raw and carnal, have never felt arousal so intense it hurts. My skin burns, my heart beats like a fist against my ribcage, and my core pulses with a desperate, coiling need. He bears me down to the bed, pinning me under his heavy weight, and all I can do is moan helplessly into his mouth as my nails dig into his shoulders and my legs wrap around his hips, grinding my throbbing clit against the hard bulge of his erection.

A ragged groan escapes his throat, and he sweeps a hand down my body, his touch trailing fire in its wake. Roughly, he pulls up my tank top, and his callused palm closes over my left breast, kneading it with hungry pressure as his lips crush mine, his kiss consuming me, stealing every exhalation from my lungs. Breathless, dizzy, I strain against him, my hands sliding up to grip fistfuls of his silky hair. The feel of his hot palm on my nipple is equal parts relief and aggravation; it soothes the feverish craving for his touch while intensifying the rapid build of tension. Like a loaded spring, the pressure coils ever tighter in my core, each grinding movement of my hips bringing me closer to the edge, to the relief I'm so desperately seeking.

I'm going to come. The realization sweeps through me a heartbeat before the climax does. My back bows, my legs tighten around his muscled ass, and a choked cry bursts from my throat as heated pleasure rockets through my body. The release is so powerful it wipes away all thought, all reason, and it's only as I come down from the high and open my eyes that I realize he's stilled on top of me, his head turned toward the door and his powerful body all but vibrating from tension.

A split second later, I realize why.

"Chloe, is that you? Are you—" Alina freezes in the doorway, her negligée-clad figure outlined by the light streaming in from the hallway.

A light she must've turned on when she heard us.

Or more specifically, heard *me*.

A hot flush sears my face and neck as I realize exactly what she heard—and what she's seeing.

Me, in bed with her half-naked brother in the middle of the night, my pajama top hiked up to my armpits.

There's no spinning this as an accident, no mistaking it for anything other than what it is.

"Excuse me." Alina's tone turns chilly. "The door was open. I didn't mean to intrude."

She disappears into the hallway, and Nikolai mutters something that sounds like a Russian curse. Rolling off me with an explosive motion, he strides to the wide-open door and slams it shut, plunging us back into darkness.

I scramble to a sitting position, yanking down my tank top as I hear his returning footsteps. *Fuck. Fuck. Fuck. What am I doing?* My hand pats frantically along the nightstand in search of the bedside lamp switch, and the light flips on just as the mattress dips under his weight.

For a few beats, we just stare at each other, and I register all sorts of panty-melting details, like the way his straight black hair is mussed from my fingers and how his sensual lips are red and swollen, glistening from our rough kisses. Mine must look the same because I can feel them, damp and throbbing, aching for more of his addictive touch and taste. He's wearing only a pair of running shorts, and his chest and shoulders are all lean muscle, his abs sharply defined. Unlike the powerful trunks of his legs, which are sprinkled with crisp, dark hair, his torso is smooth, his lightly tanned skin marred only by a pale, puckered scar on his left shoulder.

My heart rate kicks up.

Bullet wound.

I've never seen one, but I'm certain I'm right. It's either that, or a drill bit went through his shoulder.

The lingering glow of orgasm dissipates as fear born of clearer thinking filters in. Who is he, this gorgeous man who appears to be so intimately acquainted with danger?

Why is he in my bedroom, on my bed?

Slowly, I scoot away, not taking my eyes off his. The bullet wound, the bruised knuckles, the wall around the compound, and the guards... There's a story here, and it's not a good one. Violence, in some shape or form, appears to be part of my new employer's life, and I want nothing to do with it, no matter how much my body longs for us to finish what we started.

What *I* started, by kissing him so thoughtlessly, so brazenly.

At my retreat, his tiger eyes narrow, and I feel his frustration, the simmering fury of a predator witnessing the inevitable escape of his prey. Except it's not inevitable in our case—with his superior size and strength, he can stop me at any point, and the fact that he remains still despite the tension evident in his powerful muscles is more than a little reassuring.

He must realize what I'm thinking because his expression smooths out, his posture taking on a relaxed, almost lazy vibe. "Don't worry, zaychik. I'm not going to pounce on you." His voice is soft, his tone gently mocking. "If you don't want this, just say so. I'm not in the habit of bedding the unwilling... or anyone pretending to be that."

My face feels like someone is burning coals under my skin. He's no doubt referring to my impromptu orgasm, something I haven't let myself think about yet. Because as shameless as my behavior tonight has been, nothing beats dry-humping him like a bitch in heat—and coming from it.

"I'm not—" I stop, realizing I was about to launch

into childish denials. "You're right," I say in a more level tone. "I apologize. I shouldn't have kissed you. That was completely inappropriate and—"

"And it's going to happen again." His eyes are like amber jewels in the warm light cast by the lamp. "You're going to kiss me, and we're going to fuck, and you're going to come again and again. You'll come on my fingers and my tongue, and with my cock buried deep inside your tight, wet pussy. You'll come as I fuck your throat and your ass. You'll come so fucking much you'll forget what it feels like not to come—and you'll still beg for more."

I stare at him, my throat dry and my underwear soaking wet. My clit pulses in tune with his softly spoken words, my heart hammering like a woodpecker even as my lungs struggle to draw a single breath. I've never had a man speak to me this way, never knew dirty talk could simultaneously turn me on and make me burn with shame.

"That's not... I'm not..." I drag in oxygen. "It's not happening."

"Oh, but it is, zaychik. You know why?"

I shake my head, not trusting myself to speak.

"Because this is inevitable. From the moment I saw you, I've known it's going to be like this... hot and wild and raw, completely uncontrollable. And you've known it too. That's why you can barely look at me at mealtimes, why being alone with me makes you so scared." He leans in, eyes gleaming. "You want me, Chloe... and believe me, I want you too."

I search for something to say, but nothing comes to mind. Where thoughts should be is a big, blank gap. At the same time, my body thrums with electric awareness, each nerve ending viscerally conscious of his nearness and the dark heat in those leonine, hypnotic eyes. This is so far beyond my realm of experience that I have no playbook for this, no clue how to react, much less act. He's my employer, the father of my student, and even if he weren't, there'd still be that aura of danger, of violence, that he wears like a lethal halo. The only sane solution is to shut this down, deny that I want him, but I can't bring myself to voice the obvious lie.

He waits for me to speak, and when I don't, his lips tilt up in a mocking half-smile. "Think about it, zaychik," he advises softly, the muscles in his powerful body rippling as he rises to his feet. "Think about how good it'll be when you come to me."

By the time I finally formulate a reply, he's gone, leaving a faint trace of bergamot and cedar on my sheets—and utter turmoil in my mind and body.

23

NIKOLAI

IT TAKES EVERY BIT OF THE SELF-CONTROL I'VE cultivated over the years to walk into my bedroom and close the door behind me. Lust, dark and potent, pulses through me, demanding I get back to Chloe and continue where we left off.

I head into my bathroom instead. Stripping off my sweat-soaked shorts, I turn on the shower and set the temperature all the way to cold. Then I step under the spray, letting the chill of the water cool the fire raging in my blood.

Too fucking soon.

I could've pushed her further, I know, but it would've been too soon. She's not ready for this, for me. The nightmare made her lower her guard, but my sister's untimely interruption reminded her of all the reasons she shouldn't want me, all the reasons she thinks this is wrong. Her body may want me, but her mind is fighting the attraction. It frightens her, the intensity of what simmers between us, and I can't blame her.

It almost frightens me.

There's something different about my desire for the girl, something both tender and violent... a possessiveness that goes beyond simple lust. When I thought she was in trouble, all I could think about was getting to her, protecting her, destroying anyone who'd hurt her. And when she started thrashing around in the throes of her nightmare, the need to comfort her had been too powerful to deny. I retained just enough presence of mind to lay the gun down in the hallway, and then I was there, holding her as she shook and sobbed, her obvious terror tearing at me, filling me with frustration and helpless fury.

She's been traumatized, hurt by someone or something, and I don't know who or what.

I don't know, and I need to know.

I need it, so I can protect her.

I need it because in my mind, she's already mine.

I still under the cold spray, a dark realization threading through me.

Alina is right to fear for Chloe.

I *am* a danger to her, though not for the reason my sister imagines. She thinks I want the girl as a disposable fuck toy, a casual plaything, but she's wrong. As much as I want to bury myself in Chloe's tight little body, I want to get inside her mind even more. I want to know every thought behind those brown eyes, to lay bare her every want and need... every scar and wound.

I want to dig deep into her psyche, and not just because of the secrets she's hiding.

I don't just want to unravel the mystery she represents.

I want to unravel *her*.

I want to take her apart and understand what makes her tick.

I want that so I can make her tick solely for me, so she can be mine alone.

I want her the way my father must've once wanted my mother... a lifetime ago, before their love turned to hate.

For one long, stomach-hollowing second, I contemplate doing the right thing. I consider walking away, or rather, letting Chloe do so. First thing tomorrow, I could give her two months' pay, free of strings, and send her on her way... watch her drive out of here in her rundown Toyota.

I consider it, and I dismiss it.

It may be too soon for Chloe to occupy my bed, but it's too late for me to do the right thing.

It was too late the moment I laid eyes on her... maybe even the moment I was born.

I meant what I said to her tonight.

This *is* inevitable. I feel the certainty of that deep in my bones.

She'll come to me, drawn by the same dark, primal need that writhes under my skin.

She'll give herself to me, and it'll seal her fate.

Shutting off the cold water, I step out and towel off,

then pad silently into my bedroom. The recessed lights in the headboard are lit, casting a soft glow on the white silk sheets, but the bed doesn't feel welcoming. Not the way *her* bed felt, with her small, warm body in it. Not the way *she* felt, writhing against me, not asking but taking her pleasure from me, her lips like honey and sin, her taste like innocence and darkness combined.

My cock hardens anew, a wave of burning lust chasing away the chill lingering from the shower. Sitting down on the bed, I pull open my nightstand drawer and look at a pair of keys on a furry pink keychain—the ones Pavel gave me last evening, right after he re-parked Chloe's car.

Carefully, reverently, I pick them up and bring them to my nose. The keys themselves smell like metal, but the pink fur holds a faint trace of wildflowers and spring, the fresh, delicate sweetness of her. I inhale deeply, absorbing every note, every nuance.

Then I drop the keys back in the drawer and slide it shut.

2 4

CHLOE

GROANING, I ROLL OVER ONTO MY BACK AND THROW AN arm over my eyes to shield them from the sunlight. It took me hours to fall asleep after Nikolai left, and I feel like a total wreck. All I want to do is shut out the stupid sunlight and—

Wait, sunlight?

I jerk upright, squinting at the bright light streaming through the window.

Dammit.

Am I late to breakfast?

I cast a frantic glance around the room, but there's no clock. There is, however, the TV hanging from the ceiling, and I spot a remote lying on top of my nightstand. I grab it and press the power button, hoping it's not one of those complicated home theater setups that requires a computer science degree to operate.

The TV comes on, conveniently tuned to a news

channel, and I exhale a relieved breath.

7:48 a.m.

If I hurry, I'll make it downstairs in time.

I dash to the bathroom and speed through my morning routine, then beeline for my closet. The TV is still on, the newscaster droning on about the upcoming elections as I grab one of my new pairs of jeans and a soft-looking long-sleeved shirt, another new purchase. According to the informative blue strip on the bottom of the TV screen, the temperature is in the high fifties this morning, significantly cooler than yesterday. Besides, it doesn't hurt to cover up those still-healing scabs on my arm—I saw Nikolai eyeing them last night.

I emerge from the closet fully dressed at 7:55 and, as a last-minute thought, grab the jewelry box with the pendant and earrings and slip it into my pocket, so I can return it to Alina. The news program is now showing a clip from last night's presidential primary debates, in which one of the frontrunners, a popular California senator, is decimating his opponents with a barrage of cleverly worded facts and figures. I don't really follow politics—my mom thought all politicians were the scum of the earth, and her opinions have rubbed off on me—but this guy, Tom Bransford, is prominent enough that I know who he is. At fifty-five years of age, he's one of the youngest candidates in the presidential race, and is so good-looking and charismatic he's been compared with John F. Kennedy. Not that he's got anything on my employer.

If Nikolai ran for president, the entire female

population of the United States would need a change of panties after each debate.

The time on the screen changes to 7:56, and I power off the TV. Maybe tonight I'll have a chance to watch something, preferably a light, funny comedy. Nothing romantic, though—I need to take my mind off Nikolai and the confusing situation between us, not be reminded of it.

I don't want another sleepless night where my body aches with arousal and my thoughts loop in an X-rated reel, replaying his dirty promises and the dark, heated images they conjure up.

———

To my surprise, Nikolai isn't at the table when I get down there at 7:59 on the dot. His sister is, though, and so is Slava. The child gives me a bright grin that contrasts with Alina's much cooler smile, and I smile back at them both, even though the thought of what Alina saw last night makes me want to slink away and never show my face in this house again.

"Good morning," I say, taking my usual seat next to Slava. It's tempting to avoid Alina's gaze, but I'm determined not to give in to my embarrassment.

So what if she caught me making out with her brother? It's not like I'm a governess in Victorian times who was seen canoodling with the lord of the manor.

"Good morning." Alina's tone is neutral, her

expression carefully controlled. "Nikolai is on a call, so he won't be joining us for breakfast."

"Oh, okay." I again experience that strange mixture of disappointment and relief, as if a hard test I've been studying for has been rescheduled. Though I've tried not to think about Nikolai this morning, I must've been subconsciously psyching myself up for seeing him here because I feel deflated despite the easing of the tension in my shoulders.

Slipping my hand into my pocket, I take out the little jewelry box and hand it to Alina. "Thank you for loaning me this last night."

Her long black lashes sweep down as she takes it from me. "No problem. Some *grechka?*" she asks, gesturing at a pot of dark-colored grain sitting next to her. Breakfast here appears to be a much simpler affair, with only a jar of honey and a few platters of berries, nuts, and cut fruit accompanying the main dish.

Nodding gratefully, I hand Alina my bowl. "I'd love some, thank you." I'm beyond happy she's acting normally. Hopefully, it'll continue.

When she hands the bowl back to me, I try a spoonful of the grain she called "grechka." It turns out to be surprisingly flavorful, with a rich, nutty taste. Mimicking what Alina is doing, I add fresh berries and walnuts into my bowl and drizzle the whole thing with honey.

"It's roasted buckwheat," she explains as I dig in. "Back home, it's usually eaten as a savory side, often mixed with some variation of pan-fried carrots, mushrooms, and onions. But I like it this way, more like oatmeal."

"I think it's tastier than oatmeal."

Alina nods, ladling Slava his portion of the grain. "That's why I like it for breakfast." She tops Slava's bowl with berries, nuts, and a generous drizzle of honey and places it in front of the boy, who immediately sticks his spoon in. Instead of eating, however, he starts chasing a blueberry around the bowl while making engine noises under his breath.

I grin, realizing I'm finally seeing him play with his food like a normal kid. Catching his gaze, I wink and start stacking my blueberries on top of each other, like I'm building a tower. I make it only to the second level before the berries roll off each other, landing in the portion of the grain made sticky by the honey.

I grimace, feigning dismay, and Slava giggles and starts building a berry tower of his own. It turns out much better than mine since he uses honey as glue and props up his blueberries with cut strawberries.

"Very good," I say with an impressed expression. "You really are a natural-born architect."

He beams at me and proudly scoops up a spoonful of the grechka along with a chunk of his berry creation. Stuffing it into his mouth, he chews triumphantly while I praise him for being so clever. Encouraged, he builds another tower, and I make him laugh again by having one of my blackberries chase a blueberry that keeps rolling away from my spoon.

"You really do like children, don't you?" Alina

murmurs when Slava and I tire of the game and resume eating. Her expression is decidedly warmer, her green gaze filled with a peculiar wistfulness as she glances at her nephew. "It's not just a job to you."

"Of course not." I smile at her. "Children are amazing. They can make us see the world as we once did... make us feel that sense of joy and wonder that the passing years steal from us. They're the closest thing we have to a time machine—or at least a window to the past."

Her lashes sweep down again, concealing the look in her eyes, but there's no missing the sudden tension bracketing her mouth. "A window to the past..." Her voice holds a strangely brittle note. "Yes, that's exactly what Slava is."

And before I can ask what she means, she changes the topic to today's cooler weather.

NIKOLAI

"WE HAVE A PROBLEM," KONSTANTIN SAYS IN LIEU OF A
greeting as his face—a leaner, more ascetic version of
mine, with black-rimmed glasses perched high on his
hawkish nose—fills my laptop screen.

I lean closer to the camera, my pulse speeding up
with anticipation. "What did you find out?"

Konstantin frowns. "Oh, about the girl? Nothing
yet. My team's still working on it." Oblivious to the
sharp sting of disappointment he's just delivered, he
continues. "It's my nuclear project. The Tajik
government has just pulled our permits."

I inhale and slowly let the air out. At times like this,
I want to strangle my older brother. "So what?" He has
to know I don't give two fucks about his pet projects,
especially ones that verge on science fiction.

Then again, maybe he doesn't. Despite his genius-
level IQ—or possibly because of it—Konstantin can be
remarkably unaware of what's going on around him,

especially if it involves people instead of zeroes and ones.

"So Valery thinks it's the Leonovs," he says, eyes gleaming behind the lenses of his glasses. "Atomprom is bidding against us, and Alexei was spotted having lunch with the head of the Energy Commission in Dushanbe."

Fuck. It's all I can do to hide the flare of rage searing through me.

I was wrong. My brother is very much aware of what he's doing by involving me in this. If it were anyone but the Leonovs, I *wouldn't* give two fucks— business is business—but there's no way I'm letting their interference slide.

Not after Slava.

"Did Valery—" I begin grimly, but Konstantin is already shaking his head.

"The Energy Commission refused to talk to him. Some bullshit about avoiding undue influence. Valery has a few ideas on how to proceed, but I figured I'd speak with you before we go down that path."

I take another steadying breath and force my tense shoulders to unclench. "You did the right thing." The persuasion tactics our younger brother likes to use might draw unnecessary attention, and after the stunt the Leonovs pulled two years ago, we're already on thin ice with the Tajik authorities.

A more delicate touch is required, which is why Konstantin has come to me with this.

"I'll call the Commission head and set up a meeting,"

I say. "We were in boarding school together. He'll see me."

Konstantin dips his head. "I'll meet you in Dushanbe. How soon can you be there?"

"Tomorrow. I'll fly out this morning." The sooner I get this bullshit over with, the sooner I get back here.

For the first time since I've left Moscow, this quiet retreat in the wilderness excites me more than any city in the world.

26

CHLOE

BY THE TIME WE'RE DONE WITH BREAKFAST AND I GET Slava to myself, gray clouds replace the bright sunshine that woke me up, and the temperature drops further as a light rain begins. According to Alina, we're supposed to get thunderstorms by noon, so I scrap the idea of taking my student on another hike.

Instead, I let Slava choose what he wants to do indoors, and I join him in that activity—which happens to be more LEGO tower assembly. That works well for me, since it lets us practice some of the words he's learned. When he gets bored with that, we build a fort out of pillows and blankets and play campers and bears, where I growl as I chase him all around the house, earning us vaguely disapproving stares from Lyudmila and Pavel, who are prepping for the next meal in the kitchen. Afterward, I read him his favorite comic books, and we play with cars and trucks, our chosen vehicles racing against each other while I commentate like a NASCAR sportscaster.

The boy really is bright and funny; it's a pleasure to teach him. Yet no matter how engaging our games are, I can't concentrate on them, or on him, fully. A part of my mind is elsewhere, on a different pair of golden eyes. After Nikolai left, I lay awake for hours, my skin flushed and my heart racing. Each time I closed my eyes, I heard his deep, soft voice making those carnal promises, and the throbbing ache between my legs returned, making me slick and swollen and so sensitive I could barely tolerate the touch of my pajama shorts. It wasn't until I gave in and used my fingers to reach another orgasm that I was able to drift off—and even then, my sleep was fitful, filled with hazy sex dreams interspersed with fragments of nightmares.

But not my usual nightmares.

In these, there was only one man in a mask, and he didn't want to kill me.

He wanted to capture me.

He wanted to make me his.

―――――

Slava and I are lounging on our stomachs on his bed, flipping through a book about the ABCs, when I become aware of a tingling sensation between my shoulder blades. I cast a curious glance over my shoulder—and heat suffuses my entire body as I meet Nikolai's gaze.

He's leaning against the doorframe, watching us, his expression carefully veiled. I have no idea how long he's been standing there, but I don't remember hearing the door open, so it must've been a while.

"Go ahead, finish what you're doing," he murmurs. "I don't want to interrupt the lesson."

Swallowing hard, I return my attention to Slava and the book. He's also spotted his father, but his reaction is much tamer. He's slightly subdued as we resume naming letters and the objects that start with them, but by the time we get to P and I make *oink-oink* noises to go with the illustration of the piggy, he's back to being his animated, giggling self.

Unable to help myself, I sneak another glance over my shoulder—and my heart stutters for a beat. Nikolai is not looking at me now but at his son, and there's something soft and pained in his eyes... a strange, despairing sort of yearning.

I blink, and just that fast, his attention shifts to me, the odd expression disappearing, replaced with the familiar scorching heat. Flushing, I look away and resume the lesson, my pulse pounding unevenly. I must've imagined that look, or misinterpreted it somehow. It doesn't make sense for Nikolai to yearn for a son who's right in front of him. If he wants to be closer with the boy, all he has to do is reach out to him, smile at him, talk to him... get to know him.

He can try to actually *be* a dad instead of this distant authority figure that Slava doesn't seem to know what to do with.

Then again, I've always found it easy to relate to children. That's why I chose this career path. If Nikolai's had minimal exposure to kids prior to learning of his son's existence, maybe he's just feeling lost and uncertain—as hard as it is to believe of a man this powerful and self-assured.

On impulse, I twist up to a sitting position facing him. "Would you like to join us? Maybe the two of us can finish going over the last few letters with Slava."

A peculiar stillness steals over him. "The two of us?"

"Or you can do it yourself if you'd rather." I'm beginning to feel foolish. It's highly likely I've misread the whole thing, ascribing thoughts and emotions to Nikolai that reflect my own wishful thinking. Just because I've secretly dreamed of meeting my father and growing close to him doesn't mean every parent-child relationship needs to adhere to a specific dynamic or—

"I'll join you." Nikolai pushes away from the doorframe and approaches the bed with those long, graceful strides that remind me of a jungle cat.

I scramble back as he sits down on the mattress next to me, but with Slava stretched out between me and the wall, I can't go far. Nikolai is so close to me we're almost touching, and my breath catches in my throat as his sensual cedar-and-bergamot scent envelops me, reminding me of last night. Vivid sexual images invade my mind, and more heat surges through me, dampening my underwear and sending my heart into overdrive. Uncomfortably aware of Slava's wide-eyed gaze on us, I try to tamp down on my arousal, but the heat doesn't dissipate, my pulse refusing to settle into a steadier rhythm.

This was a bad idea. A very bad idea. I should be keeping my distance from my employer, not issuing what amounts to an invitation to cuddle on a twin-sized bed. There's barely enough room for me and Slava. The only way for us all to fit is if—

"Lie down, zaychik," Nikolai says softly, a wicked half-smile curving his lips as he reaches around me to pick up the book. "So I can properly join you."

The blood flowing to my face feels like lava as I reluctantly obey, turning to lie on my stomach next to Slava—who seems fascinated by what's happening. Nikolai stretches out next to me, his big, hard body flush against mine, and it belatedly occurs to me that Slava should be in the middle, serving as a buffer. Before I can suggest it, Nikolai drapes a heavy arm over my shoulders, pinning me in place, and places the book in front of me.

"Go ahead," he murmurs in my ear, his warm breath sending goosebumps down my arm. "Let's see you work your teaching magic."

Magic? The only magic around here is that I'm somehow intact and not a puddle of goo on the sheets —which is what my body feels like as I lie in what amounts to his embrace. My pulse is pounding in my temples, my breath sawing through my lips as my underwear grows even slicker, and only the presence of the child next to us keeps me from repeating last night's mistake by giving in to the dangerous, hypnotic pull Nikolai exerts on me.

Instead, I attempt to concentrate on the task at hand. Clearing my throat, I read, "T is for train: *choo-choo*. Also for truck." My voice is a shade too husky, but I'm just glad my brain is functioning enough to make out the words on the page. Luckily, Slava doesn't seem to notice anything amiss as I continue, pointing at the picture of the truck with a slightly unsteady finger.

Casting curious looks at his father, he repeats the words after me, his voice quiet and subdued at first, then increasingly livelier, and by the time we get to Z, he's laughing at the stripes on the zebra and purposefully mispronouncing the word, having forgotten all about the large man in bed with us.

After his third incorrect attempt, I tsk-tsk with mock disappointment and glance at Nikolai. "Why don't you try saying it?" I suggest, ignoring the way my pulse spikes as I meet his gaze. "Maybe you'll have better luck."

Nikolai's expression doesn't change, but the arm draped over my shoulders stiffens slightly. "All right," he says in a measured tone, and looking down at the book, he says in a thick, exaggerated Russian accent, "Zye-bruh."

Slava's eyes round. He clearly wasn't expecting his father to have trouble with the English word. I tsk-tsk again, shaking my head as if disappointed by Nikolai's attempt, and after a brief, tension-filled moment, Slava bursts out laughing.

"Zebra," he corrects through the giggles, his pronunciation as perfect as mine. "Zebra, zebra."

"Oh, I see." Nikolai glances at me, a mischievous gleam in his eyes. "So... zee-bro?"

Slava is all but dying from laughter now, and I can't help grinning as well. This is a side of my employer I've never seen before, and judging by Slava's reaction, neither has he. Giggling, he corrects his father's pronunciation, and Nikolai bungles it again, sending the boy into fresh peals of laughter. Finally, Slava succeeds in "teaching" Nikolai how it's done, and we triumphantly close the book, having covered the entire alphabet.

Immediately, the tension between me and Nikolai returns, the air crackling with a sexual charge. I've been doing my best to ignore the feel of him pressed against my side, but without the distraction of the book, it's impossible. His big body is warm and hard next to me, his arm heavy over my shoulder blades, and though we're both fully clothed, the intimacy of lying together like this is undeniable.

To my relief, Nikolai removes his arm and sits up. I do the same, quickly scooting back to put some distance between us—a retreat he observes with dark amusement before saying something in Russian to his son.

The boy nods, still flushed from excitement, and Nikolai rises to his feet.

"Let's go to my office," he says to me. "There's something I'd like to discuss."

27

NIKOLAI

I sit at the small round table in my office, and Chloe sits across from me, regarding me with those pretty, wary brown eyes. Her hands twist together on the table as she waits for me to initiate the conversation, and I let the moment stretch on, enjoying her nervousness. Lying next to her on Slava's tiny bed had been torture; if not for my son, I wouldn't have been able to control myself. As is, I'm still hard from being next to her, feeling her warmth and breathing in her crisp, sweet scent. It takes everything I have not to reach over and grab her right here and now, spreading her out on this very table.

With effort, I rein myself in. It's too soon, especially since I'm leaving in a half hour and won't be back for several days. A quick fuck isn't what I'm after. It won't be anywhere near enough.

Once I get Chloe into my bed, I intend to keep her there for hours. Maybe even days or weeks.

Besides, that's not why I called her into my office.

Placing my forearms on the table, I lean forward. "About last night…"

She stiffens, the pulse in her neck visibly quickening.

"… was it about your mother?"

She blinks. "What?"

"Your nightmare. Was it about your mother's death?" The question has been tormenting me all morning, and since Konstantin hasn't come through with the report, there's only one way I can learn the answer.

At the word "death," her chin wobbles almost imperceptibly. "It's… yes, in a way, it's about her…" She swallows thickly. "Her death."

"I'm sorry." Whatever she's hiding, her pain is unfeigned, and it tugs at me like a dull fishing hook. "How did she die?"

I know what the police report said, but I want to hear Chloe's take on it. I've already dismissed the possibility that she might've killed her mother—the girl I've observed for the past two days is no more a killer than I'm a saint—but that doesn't mean something *didn't* go down. Something that made her drop off the grid and sent her on a cross-country trip in a car that should've been junked a decade ago.

Chloe's hands lace tighter together, her eyes glittering with painful brightness. "It was ruled a suicide."

"And was it?"

"I... don't know."

She's lying. It's clear as day that she doesn't believe a word of that police report, that there's something she's not telling me. I'm tempted to press her harder, force her to open up to me, but it's too soon for that as well. She has no reason to trust me yet; if I push too hard, it'll only backfire.

The last thing I want is to frighten her, make her want to run while I'm gone.

"That's tough," I say softly instead. "No wonder you have nightmares."

She nods. "It has been kind of tough." Cautiously, she asks, "What about your parents? Are they back in Russia?"

"They're dead." My tone is overly harsh, but my family is not a topic I care to delve into.

Chloe's eyes widen before filling with expected sympathy. "I'm really sorry—"

I hold up a hand to stop her. "You don't have a phone or a laptop or any kind of tablet, right?"

She looks taken aback. "Right. I didn't bring any with me on the trip."

I get up and walk over to my desk. Opening one of the drawers, I take out a brand-new laptop, still sealed in a box, and bring it back to the table.

"Here." I place it in front of her. "I'm leaving for Tajikistan in"—I consult my watch—"fifteen minutes. I don't know how long I'll be gone, but it'll be at least three to four days, and I want you to keep me posted on Slava's progress."

"Yes, of course." She stands as well, her brown eyes gazing up at me. "Would you like me to send you a daily email or…?"

"I'll videocall you. Ask Alina to set up an account for you on the secure platform we use. Also"—I pull out my business card and hand it to her—"here's my cell number in case of emergencies."

I plan to watch her through the cameras in Slava's room as well, but it's not going to be enough. I already know that. I need more contact with her, need to hear her talking to *me*, see her smiling at *me*, not just my son. The videocalls won't be enough either, but it's the best I can do short of bailing on the trip altogether, and I'm not that far gone yet.

No, this will have to do, and keeping up to date on Slava's progress makes as good of an excuse for these calls as anything.

My chest tightens again at the thought of my son, but this time, the ache is accompanied by an unsettling sort of warmth. Slava laughed with me, looked at me with something other than wariness this morning… and it was because of her, because she was there, lending me her sweetness, her radiant magic.

I want more of it.

I want to take all of her sunshine, use it to light every dark, hollow corner of my soul.

Slowly, taking care not to spook her, I step closer and gently curve my palm over her silky-smooth cheek. She stares up at me, unmoving, hardly breathing, those soft, pouty doll lips parted, and my guts clench on a violent surge of need, a hunger as intense as it is dark. As much as I want to fuck her, I want to possess her even more.

I want to own her inside and out, to chain her to me and never let her go.

Something of my intent must show because her breath hitches, her throat moving in a nervous swallow. "Nikolai, I…"

"Keep the laptop on in the evenings," I order softly, and dropping my hand, I step back before I can give in to the dangerous maelstrom inside me.

To the beast that no amount of refinement can hide.

28

CHLOE

HEART POUNDING, I WATCH THROUGH THE WINDOW IN Slava's room as Pavel loads a suitcase into the backseat of a sleek white SUV and gets behind the wheel. A minute later, Nikolai approaches the car. Dressed in a sharply tailored gray suit and pin-striped white shirt, with a laptop bag slung over one shoulder, he looks every inch the powerful businessman. Moving with his customary athletic grace, he climbs into the front passenger seat and shuts the door.

I let out a shaky breath, my pulse slowing as the car pulls away and disappears down the winding driveway. I have no idea how I feel about his departure or what happened in his office. Had he been about to kiss me? If I hadn't said his name, would he have—

"Chloe?" a small, high-pitched voice pipes up, and I turn with a smile, putting all thoughts of my employer on hold.

"Yes, darling?"

Slava holds up a box of LEGO pieces. "Castle?"

I grin. "Sure, let's do it." I love that he remembered the word, and that he feels comfortable enough to call me by my name. He really is one of the brightest kids I've ever met, and I have no doubt I'll have a lot to report to Nikolai when he calls me.

My heart rate speeds up again at the thought of talking to him on video, and I busy myself by taking the LEGO pieces out of the box. A part of me is glad that Nikolai is gone... that for the next few days, I won't have to contend with his dangerous, magnetic presence. But another, weaker part of me is already mourning his absence. The overcast sky outside feels darker, grayer, the house emptier and colder.

It's as if something vital has disappeared from my life, leaving behind a strangely hollow feeling.

I spend the rest of the morning with Slava, playing various educational games, and then we eat lunch in the dining room, just the two of us, with Lyudmila bringing out all the dishes.

"Headache," she informs me when I ask about Alina. "You eat yourself, okay?"

I nod, biting back a laugh at the unfortunate phrasing. Maybe Pavel's wife would be open to some English lessons while I'm here? I'll have to ask her at some point. For now, I concentrate on giving Slava a generous serving of everything on the table and then doing the same for myself while Lyudmila disappears into the kitchen. I don't see her again until dinner—which Alina also skips, leaving me to dine alone with my charge.

I don't mind it. In fact, it's a relief. Despite the fancy clothes Slava and I put on as per the "house rules," the dinner feels infinitely more casual with just the two of us, the atmosphere lacking all the strain and tension that the Molotov siblings bring with them. I play with my food, making Slava giggle like crazy, and I continue teaching him words for various food items, along with basic mealtime phrases. Before long, he's asking me in English to pass him a napkin, and by utilizing a lot of gestures and facial expressions, we succeed in discussing which foods he likes the most and which ones he dislikes.

It's not until Lyudmila takes Slava away to put him to bed and I go up to my room that I realize I need Alina. She's the one who's supposed to set up an account for me on the secure videoconference platform. I doubt Nikolai will call me tonight—he's most likely still in the air—but he could easily call me tomorrow morning. Or in the middle of the night, if that's when he lands.

Still, I don't want to bother her if she's not feeling well.

I decide to begin by setting up the computer itself. It's a sleek, high-end MacBook Pro, and as I unpack it from the box, I realize I've never had a laptop this expensive. It's hard to believe Nikolai just had it sitting in his desk drawer like a spare pen.

Then again, why am I surprised? This family clearly has money to burn.

I boot up the laptop and go through the new computer setup routine. But when I try to get on Wi-Fi, I can't—it's password protected. I need Alina for this too. I suppose I can ask Lyudmila, but she's putting Slava to bed right now, and there's no guarantee she'd know the password, given how paranoid the Molotovs are about security, digital and otherwise.

Blowing out a frustrated breath, I close the laptop. Without internet, it's pretty much useless.

I guess tonight I get to laze around and watch TV.

I change out of my evening gown and into a pair of butter-soft leggings and a long-sleeved cotton tee—both new acquisitions—and make myself comfortable on the bed. Turning on the TV, I locate a nature show and spend the next hour learning about the plains of the Serengeti. The David Attenborough narration is as magnificent as always, and I find myself completely absorbed by the story unfolding on the screen, my mind calm for the first time in weeks. It's only when I'm watching a lion stalk a gazelle that my thoughts turn to the killers hunting me, and my disquiet returns.

I still don't know who those men are or what they wanted with my mom—why they killed her and made it look like a suicide. The most logical possibility is that she walked in on them while they were burglarizing the apartment, but then why was she wearing her robe like she was relaxing at home? And why didn't the police notice signs of forced entry or things missing?

At least I assume they didn't notice it. If they did and ruled her death a suicide anyway... well, that raises all kinds of other questions.

The other possibility, a likelier and much more disturbing one, is that they came specifically to kill her.

Turning off the TV, I get up and walk over to the window to stare out at the rapidly darkening landscape. My chest is tight, my mind churning anew. I've racked my brain ever since it happened, trying to think of reasons why someone might want to kill my mom, and I can't come up with a single one. Mom wasn't perfect—she could be sharp-tongued when tired, and she was prone to bouts of depression—but I'd never seen her be deliberately mean or unkind to anyone. For as long as I can remember, she'd worked two or more jobs to support us, leaving her with little time and energy to socialize and make friends—or enemies. To the best of my knowledge, she didn't even date, though men hit on her all the time.

She was beautiful... and barely forty when she died.

My throat cinches tight, a stinging pressure building behind my eyes. Not only have I lost the only person in the world who loved me unconditionally, but her murderers are out there, free. The police didn't believe a single word I told them, the reporters I contacted didn't reply to my emails, and nobody is looking for my mom's killers. Nobody is hunting them like the rabid animals they are.

Instead, the killers are hunting me.

Fuck this shit.

Pivoting on my heel, I stride to the bed and grab the laptop. I can't sit around, watching TV like my world didn't crumble a month ago. Not when I'm finally safe and have a computer on which I can do research at my leisure. For weeks, I've lurched from one crisis to another, all my energy focused on survival, on escape, but things are different now. I have a full belly, a safe place to rest my head, and—if I can only get that Wi-Fi password—an internet-connected laptop. No more sneaking into a library in some small town to huddle over their slow, ancient desktops while looking over my shoulder every minute; no more dashing off hastily composed emails before running to my car.

Here, in the privacy of my room, I can take my time and look for evidence to back up my claims, for some kind of proof to take to the police.

I can try to solve the mystery of Mom's murder and turn the tables on her killers, make them be the ones who have to run.

29

CHLOE

I DON'T KNOW WHICH ROOM IS ALINA'S, BUT IT HAS TO be close to mine for her to have heard me both nights. Holding the laptop against my chest, I knock on the door closest to my bedroom, and when I don't get an answer, I move on to the next one.

Still no luck.

I try three more bedroom doors, plus Nikolai's office, with the same lack of results. The only room that's left is Slava's, and since all is quiet there, he must already be asleep.

Suppressing my frustration, I go downstairs. I'm pretty sure Lyudmila and Pavel's room is near the laundry; I heard their voices coming from there when I was taking my clothes out of the dryer yesterday. Hopefully, Lyudmila hasn't gone to bed yet, and can either provide the password or locate Alina for me.

Nobody answers that knock either—nor is Lyudmila in the kitchen or any of the other common areas downstairs. I'm about to give up and go back to my room when a distant peal of laughter reaches my ears.

It's coming from outside.

Finally.

Leaving the laptop on a coffee table in the living room, I hurry to the front door and step out into the cool, misty darkness. It's no longer raining, but the air still holds a damp chill, with thick clouds blocking all hint of moonlight. If not for the light spilling from the windows and the solar path lights lining each side of the driveway, it would be too dark to see. As is, it's still more than a little creepy, and I wrap my arms around myself to stop from shivering as I walk toward the back of the house, following the sound of voices.

I find Alina and Lyudmila sitting on a pair of boulders near the edge of the cliff, a small fire crackling merrily in front of them. They're laughing and talking in Russian—and, I realize as I get closer, sharing a joint.

The grassy smell of pot is unmistakable.

At my approach, they fall silent, Lyudmila regarding me with open dismay and Alina wearing her usual enigmatic expression. Taking a deep drag, Nikolai's sister slowly blows out the smoke and holds out the joint to me. "Want some?"

I hesitate before gingerly taking it from her. "Sure, thanks." I'm no stranger to pot, having smoked more than my fair share my freshman year of college, but it's been a while since I've had any.

It used to help me relax, though, and I could use that tonight.

I sit on a boulder next to Alina and inhale a lungful of smoke, enjoying the acrid, grassy taste, then pass the joint to wary-looking Lyudmila. Alina murmurs something to her in Russian, and the other woman visibly relaxes. Taking a drag, she passes the joint to Alina, who takes a drag and passes it to me, and we go like that in a circle, smoking in companionable silence until only a small, useless stub remains.

"I told her you won't rat us out to my brother." Alina drops the stub into the fire and watches the resulting explosion of sparks. "Or her husband."

"They don't like pot?" My voice is raspy and mellow, my mind pleasantly fuzzy. Even the prospect of upsetting my employer doesn't faze me right now, though I know it should. Besides, Alina is technically my employer too, and she offered me the joint, so I'm not at fault. Or am I? Maybe only Nikolai is my employer, after all?

It's hard to think straight.

"Nikolai can be... uptight about certain things. And Pavel doesn't keep secrets from him." Alina nudges a glowing ember with the tip of her shoe, and I hazily register the fact that she's wearing stilettos and a blue cocktail dress that would be perfect for an art gallery opening. Her only concession to the wilderness surrounding us is a white faux fur draped around her slender shoulders—presumably to keep out the chill. She's also wearing her usual lipstick and eyeliner.

"Lyudmila said you had a headache," I say before I can think better of it. "Do you dress up and put on makeup even when you're sick?"

Alina laughs softly and lights another joint. Taking a drag, she offers it to Lyudmila, who does the same and offers it to me. I start reaching for it but change my mind. I know from experience that I'm about as mellow as I'm going to get; anything more will just make me slow-witted. Not that I'm not already—that first joint was potent stuff, as strong as anything I've tried. Besides, there was a reason I came out here, and it wasn't to get stoned.

"I'm good, thanks," I say, pulling my hand back, and with a shrug, Lyudmila returns the joint to Alina.

I watch the flames crackle and dance while the two of them smoke and converse in Russian. I wish I spoke the language so I could understand them, but I don't and the smooth rhythm of their speech reminds me of a burbling mountain stream, the words flowing into one another, defying comprehension.

Is that what it's like for Slava when I speak? Or for Lyudmila?

Is that what it was like for my mom when she was first brought to America from Cambodia?

She'd never spoken much about her early years; all I know is that she was adopted by the missionary couple when she was around Slava's age. I'd never pressed her for details, not wanting to evoke any bad memories. I'd figured we'd have a lifetime to talk about whatever, and she'd tell me eventually, if there was anything to tell.

I was a short-sighted idiot.

I should've learned everything there was to know about my mom when I had the chance.

Alina's laughter catches my attention, and I shift my gaze from the dancing flames to her face, studying each striking feature. It would be easy to envy her, both for her extraordinary beauty and her wealth, but for some reason, I don't get the impression that Nikolai's sister is particularly happy. Even now, when she must be more than a little high, there's a brittle edge to her laughter... a peculiar fragility underneath her glossy façade. And maybe it's the glow of firelight softening the porcelain perfection of her skin, but tonight, she seems younger than the mid-to-late twenties I pegged her for.

Much younger.

"How old are you?" I blurt, suddenly worried I might've accepted pot from a teenager. A split second later, I recall that she finished Columbia, so she has to be at least my age, but it's too late to take back my overly personal question.

To my relief, Alina doesn't seem to think it inappropriate. "Twenty-four," she replies in a dreamy tone. "Twenty-five next week." Her eyes slightly out of focus, she reaches over and touches my hair, rubbing one strand between her fingers. "Anyone ever mention you look a bit like Zoë Kravitz?" Not waiting for a reply, she trails her fingertips over my jaw. "I can see why my brother wants you. So pretty... so sweet and fresh..."

Laughing awkwardly, I swat her hand away. "You

are so stoned." I can feel Lyudmila's gaze on us, curious and judging, and my face warms as I reflect on how much of Alina's words she's understood—and what she already knows. These two seem to be good friends, and I wouldn't be surprised if at least some of their earlier laughter was at my expense.

"Extremely stoned," Alina agrees, throwing the second stub into the fire. "But that doesn't change the facts." Propping her elbows on her knees, she leans in, firelight dancing in her eyes as she says quietly, "Don't fall for him, Chloe. He's not your white knight."

I draw back. "I'm not looking for a—"

"But you are." Her voice stays soft, even as her gaze sharpens to a knife's edge, all haziness disappearing. "You need a white knight, noble and kind and pure, a protector to cherish and love you. And my brother can't be that for you, or for anyone. Molotov men don't love, they possess—and Nikolai is no exception."

I stare at her, my stomach turning hollow as the pleasant state of chemically induced non-worry dissipates, my head clearing more by the second. I don't understand what she means, not fully, but I don't doubt that she's sincere, that her warning is meant to protect me.

Drawing back, Alina lights a third joint and extends it toward me. "More?"

"No, thanks. I, um…" I clear my throat to rid it of residual hoarseness. "I actually need the Wi-Fi password. That's why I came out here to look for you. Also, Nikolai wanted you to set me up on your videoconference platform—if you're feeling up to it, that is."

She takes a deep drag and slowly blows out the smoke at my face. "I suppose that can be arranged." Handing the joint to Lyudmila, she rises to her feet. "Let's go."

And with a gait that's only slightly unsteady, she leads me back to the house.

When we get to the living room, I hand her the laptop and watch, with no small degree of amazement, as she navigates to the settings and inputs the password, her elegant fingers flying over the keyboard. If not for the strong smell of pot clinging to her hair and clothes—and if I hadn't personally witnessed her smoking the majority of those two joints, plus however many she'd shared with Lyudmila prior to my arrival—I would've never known she's high.

She's just as unerring with her installation of the videoconference software and setup of the account, her red-tipped fingers moving at a speed that would do a hacker proud.

"You're really good at this," I say after she hands the laptop to me and explains the basics of the software. "Did you major in computer science or something along those lines?"

"God, no." She laughs. "Economics and PoliSci,

same as Nikolai. Konstantin's the geek in the family—the rest of us are proficient at best."

"Gotcha. Either way, thanks for this." I close the laptop and tuck it under my arm. "I'm going to head to bed. Are you...?" I wave in the general direction of the front door.

She nods, one corner of her mouth lifting in a half-smile. "Lyudmila's waiting for me. Goodnight, Chloe. Sweet dreams."

3 0

CHLOE

Back in my room, I take a shower to clear the remaining haziness from my mind and change into my pajamas. Then, brimming with anticipation, I get comfy on the bed, open the laptop, and bring up a browser.

I start by looking for news coverage of my mom's death. There isn't much, just an obituary and a short article in a local paper reporting that a woman had been found dead in her East Boston apartment. Neither goes into details, tactfully omitting any mention of suicide. I'd already read both the article and the obituary when I stopped at a library in Ohio a couple of weeks back, so I don't spend much time on them. Instead, I make a note of the reporter's name and look up her contact info, then log into my Gmail and send her a long, detailed email outlining exactly what happened on that June day.

Maybe I'll have better luck with her than with the

other journalists I've contacted so far. None of them have bothered to reply—probably dismissing me as a mental case, just as the police had. But those were reporters at major news outlets, and they undoubtedly get harassed by all sorts of crazies. In the movies, it's always the small-time reporter who gets intrigued enough to investigate, and maybe that will be the case here too.

One can always hope.

Next, I type Mom's name into Google and see what else I can pull up. Maybe somewhere out there is a mention of her leading some secret double life, something that would explain why someone would want to kill her.

And maybe pigs will hop on a spaceship and fly to the moon.

I find exactly what I expected: a big fat nothing. The only thing my search brings up is Mom's Facebook profile, and I spend the next half hour reading her posts while fighting back tears. Mom didn't love the idea of putting her life on display, so her friend count is in the low double digits and her posts are few and far between. A photo of the two of us dressed up to go clubbing for my twenty-first birthday, a snapshot of the bouquet of flowers her co-workers at the restaurant gifted her for her fortieth, a video of me feeding lettuce to a giraffe during our recent vacation in Miami—her profile barely touches on the highlights of our lives, much less reveals anything I didn't already know.

Still, I diligently review all of her Facebook friends' profiles on the off chance that one of them may be a drug dealer who's stupid enough to announce it on social media. Because that's the best theory I can come up with.

Mom witnessed something she shouldn't have, and that's why those men came after her—just as they're now coming after me because I saw them and know her death wasn't a suicide.

Admittedly, the evidence for this theory is nonexistent, but I can't think of a reasonable alternative. Well, I can—a burglary gone wrong—but there are way too many issues with that idea. I mean, guns with silencers? What burglars carry those?

The more I think about it, the more convinced I become that those men came to kill her.

The big question is: why?

Three hours later, I delete my browser's history and clear the cookies—just in case I have to give back the computer unexpectedly—and close the laptop. My eyes feel like they've been rubbed with sandpaper from all the reading on the screen, and the mellowing effects of pot have long since worn off, leaving me tired and dispirited. I've googled just about everything I could think of in connection with Mom's life and death, have scoured the local papers for reports of other crimes around the same time—in the unlikely case that Mom's murderers were two serial killers working together—and have stalked each of her Facebook friends and restaurant co-workers with the perseverance of the most dedicated online troll. I've even looked into the death of her adoptive parents, in case there was something more to their car accident than I'd been told, but it seems to have been a straightforward case of a drunk driver ramming into them on the highway.

There's nothing, absolutely nothing to take to the cops. No wonder they didn't believe me when I burst into the station that day, shaking and hysterical.

I should probably call it a night and think about everything with a fresh head tomorrow, but despite my tiredness, my mind is buzzing with all sorts of unsettling questions—only some of which have to do with Mom's death. Because there's another mystery I haven't let myself think about yet, one that may have just as much bearing on my safety.

Who exactly is Nikolai Molotov, and what did Alina mean by her strange warning?

I look at the pillow, then at the computer. It's late, and I should really go to sleep. But the odds of being able to drift off while I'm this wired are low, almost nonexistent.

Screw it. Who needs sleep?

Opening the laptop, I type "Nikolai Molotov" into the browser and dive in.

31

NIKOLAI

The first thing I do upon arrival at my hotel is power up my laptop, open the video feed from Slava's room, and check that my son is peacefully asleep.

He is. The car-shaped nightlight he likes us to leave on illuminates his sleeping features, revealing a tiny fist tucked underneath his sweetly rounded cheek. My heart thumps harder at the sight, a now-familiar ache spreading through my chest. I don't understand it any more than I understand my growing obsession with his tutor, but I can't deny it's there, as real and concrete as my hatred for the woman who gave birth to him.

For Ksenia, and the entire Leonov viper clan.

Rage kindles in my stomach, and I wrench my thoughts away from them. Tomorrow will be soon enough to deal with their latest sabotage; tonight, I have more pleasant things to think about.

Opening a new window, I bring up the feed from the webcam on Chloe's laptop, and a warm glow spreads through me as her pretty face fills the screen. Despite the late hour, she's awake, her smooth forehead creased in a frown as she peers intently at her computer. She must be doing something online because I can see her browser being active, and when I go into her search history, I'm pleased to find her researching me.

I was hoping she'd be thinking about me, just as I'm thinking about her.

She has no idea I can see this, of course. The laptop I gave her is from a special batch altered by one of Konstantin's shadier ventures. It looks like a regular brand-new Mac but comes pre-installed with undetectable spyware that allows us to keep an eye on all sorts of influential businesspeople and politicians.

Many a business deal was pushed through thanks to this handy software and the secrets it has revealed.

I watch her for a few minutes, amused by her attempts to read an article from a Russian newspaper using free web translation tools. She wrinkles her nose in the most adorable way when puzzled, and her eyes go from wide to narrow and back, her teeth frequently tugging at her lower lip. I want to bite that plump lip and soothe it with a kiss, then do the same all over her delicious little body.

My cock stirs at the thought, and I take a breath to distract myself from the heat building inside me. As enjoyable as it is to observe her, what I want even more is to talk to her, to hear her soft, husky voice and see her sunny smile. I miss that smile.

Fuck, I miss *her*.

It's ridiculous, I know—I just met her this week, and we've been apart less than a day—but that's the way it is, that's the inevitability of it all. Fate brought her to me, and now she's mine, even if she doesn't know it yet. If not for this trip, she'd already be in my arms, but the Leonovs stuck their dirty paws into our business and here we are.

Drawing in another settling breath, I open Konstantin's video software and place the call.

32

CHLOE

I'M IN THE MIDDLE OF PAINSTAKINGLY COMPARING THE Bing translation of the Russian article to the Google version in the hopes of making sense of three particularly confusing sentences when a soft chime sounds and a videocall request pops up, with Nikolai's picture in it.

My heart rate shoots up, my breathing quickening uncontrollably. It's like he's the proverbial devil, summoned by my thoughts—or my research. Is that possible? Does he somehow know I'm reading about him at this very moment?

Is that why he's calling so late? To fire me for snooping?

No, that's crazy. He probably just landed, saw on the videoconference app that I'm online, and decided to check in.

Pulling in a shaky breath, I smooth my hair with my palms and click "Accept."

His gorgeous face fills the screen, making my heart pound harder. "Hi, zaychik." His voice is soft and deep, his gaze mesmerizing even through the camera. In general, the quality of the video is insane; it's like a movie in HD. I can see everything, from the artful swoops in the abstract painting hanging on the wall a few feet behind his chair to the forest-green flecks in his amber eyes. He must've just arrived because he's still wearing the shirt and tie I saw him leave in, but instead of looking tired and rumpled, as a normal person would after a transatlantic flight, he's the very picture of effortless elegance, every glossy black hair in place.

Realizing I'm staring at him like a star-struck groupie, I force my vocal cords into action. "Hi." My throat is still a bit raw from smoke, but I'm hoping he ascribes the raspiness in my voice to the late hour. "How was your flight?"

His sensuous lips curl in a warm smile. "Uneventful. Why are you still awake? It's past midnight over there."

"Just… not sleepy." Especially now that I'm talking to him. Getting this call was like downing five shots of espresso; even my tiredness is gone, replaced by a jittery sort of excitement—one that's only partially related to what I was reading.

As I suspected, the Molotovs are filthy rich and a huge deal in Russia. "One of the most powerful oligarch families" is a Google-translated quote from one Russian article, and there are plenty of mentions of Nikolai and his brothers—and before that, of Vladimir, their father—in the Russian press. I even found a photo from last year in which Nikolai is sitting next to the Russian president at some black-tie event in Moscow, looking as cool and comfortable as at his family dinners.

What I didn't find, to my huge relief, is anything about the Molotovs being mafia or having criminal affiliations, though maybe I just didn't dig deep enough. Even with the help of web translation tools, it's hard to come up with the right search terms in Russian, and there's surprisingly little written about Nikolai's family in English—a passing mention on CNN of a pipeline in Syria laid by one of their oil companies, a paragraph on Bloomberg about a new cancer drug developed by one of their pharmaceutical companies, a line about Vladimir Molotov in a *New York Times* article discussing the enormous wealth in Russia. There are no Wikipedia entries on them, nothing in the tabloids. They don't even appear on any *Forbes* lists, though several Russian billionaires do, and the Molotovs sound even richer.

Of course it's possible I couldn't find anything because of all the Molotov cocktail references clogging up search results. I'll have to ask Nikolai or his sister if they're any relation to the Soviet foreign minister the homemade explosives are pejoratively named after.

At my reply, Nikolai frowns into the camera, looking concerned. "You didn't have another nightmare, did you?"

I shake my head with a smile. "I just haven't gone to sleep yet."

Maybe it's the lack of any alarming discoveries in my search, or the simple reality that he's not here to make my body hum with physical awareness, but I feel calmer talking to him tonight... safer. After all, it's possible that my experiences over the past month have shredded my nerves, leading me to see danger where none exists, and all the supposed red flags—his bullet wound scar and busted knuckles, the guards and all the security measures—have innocuous explanations. In fact...

"Were you ever in the military?" I ask impulsively, and more tension leaves my shoulders as Nikolai nods, a faint smile dancing on his lips as he leans back in his chair.

"My family has a long history of distinguished service to the country, and my father insisted my brothers and I follow the tradition. All three of us enlisted at eighteen and served for several years." He tilts his head, regarding me thoughtfully. "Were you wondering about this?" He touches his left shoulder.

"I was," I admit sheepishly. I'm beginning to feel like an idiot for letting my imagination run wild before. "What happened? Were you shot?"

He nods. "A sniper sent a bullet my way. Luckily, he missed."

"Missed?"

His white teeth flash in a grin. "I'm not dead, am I?"

"No, thank God." Still, my chest squeezes as I

picture that scar and the pain he must've experienced as the bullet tore through his flesh. "Did it take you long to recover?"

"A few weeks. I was only twenty at the time, which helped."

"Still, I can't imagine it was fun." Unable to resist the temptation, I ask, "Do you keep up with your training to this day? Like… fighting and stuff?"

I'm trying to be subtle, but he sees right through me anyway.

Grinning wickedly, he holds up his hands, turning them to show the bruised knuckles to the camera. "You're asking about these, I assume? That's from sparring with a few of my guards. They're from my former unit, and we go at it once in a while—at least when Pavel can't oblige me."

I grin back at him, so relieved I could cry. Of course his guards are his army buddies; that makes so much sense, and speaks volumes about his character. "Was Pavel in the army with you as well?" I can easily picture the man-bear in army fatigues, toting an M16 and maybe carrying a tank on his shoulders.

To my surprise, Nikolai shakes his head. "He actually served with my father. He enlisted at fourteen, and they let him, since he was already his current size and looked all of twenty-five."

"Oh, wow. So he's known your family since before you were born?"

"Long before," Nikolai confirms. "My father hired

him straight from the army, and he's been with our family ever since."

"Lyudmila too?"

"No, they've only been married for about ten years." He laughs. "Alina just about had a fit when he first introduced Lyudmila to us. I think my sister was under the impression that Pavel was her exclusive property."

My eyes widen. "She had a crush on him?"

"Not precisely, no. I think she thought of him more as a second father." His smile fades, and something bleak flickers in his eyes before his lips take on their usual darkly sensual curve—that cynical, seductive smile that, I'm now realizing, hides his true emotions. Leaning closer to the camera, he says softly, "Enough about them. Tell me about your day, zaychik. What did you and Slava do while I've been gone?"

Right, that's why he's calling: to get a report on his son. Concealing an irrational pang of disappointment, I put on my tutor hat and fill him in on our activities and the progress Slava's making. He listens attentively, interrupting occasionally to ask follow-up questions, and as our conversation continues, I realize I have to revise yet another negative opinion I had of him.

Nikolai does care about his son. A lot.

I caught a glimpse of it this morning, when Slava and I lay there on the bed, and I see it now in the way his face softens when I talk about the boy. I don't know why he refuses to protect his son from such obvious dangers as a sharp knife, but it's not because he doesn't love him. He does—though judging by the way he is around Slava, I wouldn't be surprised if he has trouble admitting it.

I think Nikolai wants to be closer to his son but doesn't know how.

I think... he may be a good man, after all.

Alina's warning intrudes on my mind again, but I push it away. She was high, and there's clearly tension between brother and sister, some kind of history I'm not privy to. Besides, I don't know what she thinks is happening between me and Nikolai, but love is nowhere on the table. Sex, maybe—I'm realistic enough to admit that my determination not to sleep with my boss is proving to be no match for the powerful attraction between us—but love is a whole other game. I'd be an idiot to fall in love with a man like Nikolai, who's undoubtedly used to the most beautiful women in the world throwing themselves at him. If we slept together, it wouldn't mean anything to him—and I can't let it mean anything to me.

Better yet, we shouldn't sleep together.

That way, nobody gets hurt.

We talk about Slava for another twenty minutes before the late hour catches up with me and a yawn overtakes me in the middle of a sentence. I stifle it right away, but Nikolai isn't fooled.

"You're exhausted, aren't you?" he murmurs, eyeing me with concern. "You should've said something, zaychik. I didn't mean to keep you up."

"No, no, it's fine. I'm just..." Another uncontrollable yawn interrupts my words, and I cover it with the back of my hand before giving him a rueful smile. "Okay, yes, it's sleepy time for me. How are you so awake? You must be jet-lagged on top of everything."

The green flecks in his eyes gleam brighter. "I don't need much sleep."

Of course he doesn't. I wouldn't be surprised if he was part superhuman—that would explain those extraordinary good looks he shares with his sister.

"Well, goodnight anyway," I say, fighting another yawn. "And good luck with whatever business you have there."

"Thank you, zaychik." His smile holds a tender note. "Sleep well. I'll call you tomorrow evening."

He hangs up, and as I put away the laptop, I'm cognizant of my heart beating in a new, uneven rhythm, my chest filled with a warmth I don't dare examine.

33

NIKOLAI

I CLOSE MY EYES AFTER WE DISCONNECT, TRYING TO hang on to the unaccustomed feeling of well-being talking to Chloe has generated, but it's fading fast. In its place is grim awareness of what I must do today, mixed with dark anticipation.

It's been six months since I've been in this world. Six months since I've let myself get involved in our business on any level beyond the most superficial. And while I'd like to say that I hate being back, I can't deny that a part of me revels in it all... that my blood is pumping faster through my veins.

Opening my eyes, I close the laptop and rise to my feet.

Time to get to work.

Pavel is already waiting in the hotel lobby, and we walk out together. Our destination is a small tavern a few blocks away, or more specifically, its basement.

The sight that greets us when we descend isn't pretty. A man is hanging by his wrists from a chain bolted into the ceiling, the toes of his booted feet just barely scraping the bare concrete floor. His pale face is bruised and swollen, the area under his off-center nose crusted with dark blood. Two of Valery's men stand next to him, their faces hard and eyes emotionless.

"Any luck?" I ask one of them, and he shakes his head.

"Claims he doesn't have the entrance code. It's a lie. We saw him use it."

"Hmm." I approach the captive and make a slow circle around him, noticing how his breathing picks up as I do. An acrid urine scent emanates from his crotch area, and there are dirt and blood stains on his beige Atomprom uniform.

The poor guy knows he's fucked.

"What's your name?" I ask, stopping in front of him.

He stares at me, mouth trembling, then bursts out, "I don't know the code. I don't!"

"I asked for your name. You know that, don't you?"

"Iv—" His voice cracks, as if he were a teenage boy instead of a twenty-something man. "Ivan."

"Okay, Ivan. Tell you what: I know you don't want to piss off your employer, but you don't really have a choice." I give him a sympathetic smile. "You see that, don't you?"

"I don't know the code!" Beads of sweat form on his forehead. "I swear—I swear on my mother's life."

"But she's dead, Ivan. She died in a factory fire when you were fifteen. That was tragic, I'm sorry."

His face goes linen white, and I continue in the same sympathetic tone. "Look, you're not a bad guy, Ivan. You've had a rough life, and you've done all you can to help out your family and take care of your younger sister. She's what, in tenth grade now?"

"Y-you…" He's shaking almost too hard to speak. "You fuckers!"

I tsk-tsk. "Insults will get you nowhere. Now listen to me, Ivan. I can let them"—I gesture at the emotionless guards—"beat the answer out of you. And if they fail, there's always my associate"—I glance at Pavel, who's quietly standing in a corner—"and his skill with knives. Not to mention all sorts of other, less savory tactics that my brother likes to use. But why go there when we can make a deal, you and I?"

His Adam's apple moves in a nervous swallow. "W-what kind of deal?"

I smile at him gently. "You're afraid of the Leonovs, aren't you? That's why you're being so brave. You couldn't care less about the plant you're guarding. What's it to you if we get the entrance code, right? But the Leonov family…" I make another slow circle around him. "… they can do things to you, to your loved ones. To your baby sister." I stop in front of him. "Nod if I'm on the right track."

He dips his chin in a barely perceptible nod, sweat running down his face.

"That's what I thought." I pull out a tissue from my pocket and dab at his forehead. "So how about this: You tell us the entrance code and share everything you know about the security protocol at the plant where you work, and we put you and your family on the nearest flight to a destination of your choice. It can be any place: Zimbabwe, Fiji, Thailand... the Cayman Islands. Name it, and we send you there with a new identity and a hundred grand in cash as a relocation bonus. How does that sound?"

Breathing raggedly, he stares at me, hope warring with fear in his eyes.

"I know what you're thinking, Ivan," I continue softly, letting the soiled tissue drop to the floor. "How can you trust me to hold up my side of the bargain? What's to stop us from killing you as soon as you tell us what we want to know, right?"

He swallows again. "R-right."

"The answer is nothing." I let a hint of cruelty seep into my smile. "Absolutely nothing. But that doesn't matter, because trusting me is the only option you have. If you don't, you'll tell us everything the hard way —and when the Leonovs learn of the breach at the plant, they'll look for the culprit. When they discover it's you, they *will* come after your family. Do you understand, Ivan? Do you understand what you have to do if you want your sister to live?"

His chin quivers as he stares at me, tears leaking

from the corners of his eyes. Finally, he bobs his head in defeat.

"Good. Now tell these gentlemen what they want to know."

Turning away, I nod at Valery's men, and they promptly step up, pulling out their phones to begin recording.

"You didn't have to do this personally, you know," Pavel says in a low voice as we walk out of the tavern. "They could've gotten the answers out of him. If not, I would've stepped in. Would've been cheaper that way."

"Maybe. But this way, we know he's not bullshitting us to make the pain stop." I glance at my lifelong bodyguard, whose gaze is restlessly sweeping our surroundings despite the fact that Valery's guards have already secured the perimeter. "Numerous studies have shown that information obtained under torture is unreliable."

"Not the information I obtain," he says darkly, and I chuckle.

"Afraid your knife's getting rusty?"

Pavel doesn't deny it. He misses being in the thick of things, just like I do—or did. Right now, I'd much rather be in Idaho with Chloe. I want to be there in case she has another nightmare. I want to hold her, soothe her, comfort her... and eventually, seduce her. Her resolve is already wavering, I can feel it—which is why I decided to reassure her about the bruises on my knuckles and the scar on my shoulder.

I don't intend to lie to her about the kind of man I am, but I don't want her to fear me.

I won't hurt her... not in that way, at least.

"Did you already set up a meeting with the head of the Energy Commission?" Pavel asks as we stop at an intersection, and I nod, pulling my thoughts away from Chloe.

"I'm meeting him for lunch on Monday," I say, stepping onto the street as the light in front of us turns green. It took three phone calls to get through to the guy, but I succeeded, as I knew I would. "That's another reason I went this route with Ivan," I continue. "There was no time to break him properly—we needed that code ASAP."

"Wouldn't have taken me long either," Pavel mutters, and I laugh—just as a motorcycle roars around the corner and barrels straight at me.

34

NIKOLAI

I REACT IN A SPLIT SECOND, BUT PAVEL IS EVEN FASTER. He shoves me just as I dive to the side, and we both hit the ground hard as the bike roars past us, so close I feel a whoosh of hot air on my face.

Adrenaline propels me to my feet straight away, but the biker is already halfway down the block, weaving through the traffic with race car speed. All I can tell from this distance is that it's a man wearing a black leather jacket and a helmet.

Pavel is already on his feet as well, jaw taut with fury. "Did you see his face?"

"No." I straighten my jacket and tie and brush the dirt and gravel off my scraped palms. My shoulder throbs from landing on it, and cold rage burns inside me, but my voice is calm. "His helmet had a mirrored visor. Maybe one of Valery's guys caught his license plate." I take in the gathering crowd of eyewitnesses, some of whom are pulling out their phones, presumably to call the police. "We better get out of here."

Pavel nods grimly, and we swiftly make our way to the hotel.

———

Levan Abkhazi, Valery's local security chief, meets us in my room an hour later. A burly Georgian about Pavel's age, he's completely bald but sports a thick black unibrow and a matching beard.

Pulling out a folder, he lays out a series of grainy photos on the desk. "This is all we were able to pull from the nearby store and traffic cameras," he reports in heavily accented Russian. "The team stationed on the rooftops didn't have a good angle on the license plate at any point, and there were too many civilians to risk taking a shot at him."

Pavel and I examine the photos. On one of them, it's possible to make out a portion of a digit, but the other pictures show a corner of the license plate at best. The biker is either the luckiest son of a bitch to ever walk the earth, or he knew where Valery's team was stationed.

I look at Pavel. "Thoughts?"

"A pro, definitely." His face is set in harsh lines. "He didn't slow down, didn't react in any way to almost running you over. And he knew how to handle that bike—and how to avoid the cameras."

Abkhazi's unibrow bunches in a frown. "You don't

think it could've been an accident? If the guy's a pro, he should know that running someone down in the street is not the most efficient way to carry out a hit."

"That depends on whether you want to make it look like an accident or not," Pavel says. "Besides, it wasn't a hit."

The Georgian gives him a confused look. "What was it then?"

"A message," I say, placing the photos back in the folder. "From our friends, the Leonovs. They wanted me to know that they know. The question is: know what?"

35

CHLOE

I WAKE UP SMILING, AND FOR A COUPLE OF MINUTES, I just lie there, eyes closed, floating in that blissful state between dreams and full wakefulness.

And what dreams they were.

My hand slips between my thighs, and I press on the sweet ache that lingers there, trying to remember the sensual scenes that played in my head all night. I only recall fragments of them now, but I know all of them featured Nikolai... his wicked smile... his deep, smooth voice... Best of all, they were the only dreams I had last night.

The nightmares that have plagued me since Mom's death stayed away.

Smile broadening, I open my eyes and sit up. It's bright and sunny, so I've probably overslept. I'm not too worried, though. Nikolai isn't here to enforce the mealtimes, and in any case, now that I know him better, I don't think he'll fire me for such a minor transgression.

Still, I don't want to take advantage, so I hop out of bed and turn on the news. They're again reporting on the primary debates, but all I care about is the time— 9:20 a.m. It also happens to be a Saturday, I realize, looking at the date. I wonder if that means I get a day off.

I should probably ask Nikolai about that the next time we talk.

A warm glow fills my chest at the thought of him calling me again and the two of us talking late into the night—almost like a dating couple. Because that's how that videocall last night felt: like the kind of thing you do with your boyfriend while he's away, a long-distance date of sorts. Though we spent most of the time talking about Slava, as befits our employer-tutor relationship, there'd been a definite softness in the way Nikolai looked at me and the way he spoke... an undercurrent of tenderness that makes my heart skip a beat each time I think about it.

It's almost as if he's starting to care for me, as if there's something more between us than animal attraction.

I try not to think about it as I go about my day because it's such a foolish notion. There's no way Nikolai is developing feelings for me. Not only is it way too soon, but I'd be an idiot to imagine that a man like that would be interested in me for any reason other than proximity. I *am* the only available woman here; he can't exactly hook up with Lyudmila or his sister. So what if he called me as soon as he landed yesterday? That doesn't mean he was thinking about me during the long flight.

He could've just been concerned about his son.

Still, that warm glow stays with me as I sneak into the kitchen to grab myself a late breakfast—the official breakfast being over—before taking Slava for a nice long hike. And it persists through lunch despite Alina's presence at the table reminding me of her strange warning.

"How's your headache?" I ask when we sit down to eat, and she waves away my concern, claiming that she's fully recovered. However, I can't help but notice that she's quiet and oddly distant, frequently staring off into space during the meal. It makes me wonder if she's high again, but I decide not to ask.

Last night, the campfire and the pot lowered everybody's inhibitions, creating a false sense of intimacy, but today, she feels like a stranger again. So does Lyudmila, who doesn't even smile at me as she brings out the food. Maybe she's embarrassed I saw her stoned? Either way, I hurry through the meal, and as soon as Slava is done eating, I take him to his room for our play lessons.

We build another castle and review the alphabet, and I teach him how to count to ten in English.

Afterward, we play hide-and-seek and read some books, including, at Slava's request, a story about a family of ducks. Before we begin, he proudly shows me a book in Russian that appears to be a translation of it, and I realize he's trying to apply his knowledge of the plot and characters to better understand the English words and phrases I read out loud to him.

"You're such a clever boy," I tell him, and he beams at me. Though I doubt he understands exactly what I'm saying, my tone of approval is unmistakable.

I sit on the floor, my back leaning against the bed, and Slava climbs into my lap as we start the story— which turns out to be surprisingly complex for a children's book. The duck family isn't all happy and go-lucky; they squabble and have conflicts, and at one point, the main hero, a young duckling, runs away from home. When he returns, he finds Mama Duck gone, and he cries, thinking that he caused her to leave.

I keep an eye on Slava during this part, worried that this might bring up memories of losing his mother, but the boy's expression remains curious and relaxed. However, when we get to the part where the young duckling has to stay with his grandfather, Slava stiffens and insists on skipping over the next three pages.

"You don't like Grandpa Duck?" I guess, and the child shrugs, avoiding my gaze.

"Okay. We don't have to read about him. Forget Grandpa Duck." Smiling, I ruffle his hair and move on to a less problematic section of the book.

Alina doesn't join us for dinner—another headache, Lyudmila tells me gruffly—so Slava and I have another relaxed meal before I go up to my room for the evening. Changing out of the formal dinner attire, I make myself comfortable on the bed and open the laptop—to do some more research, I tell myself. Not to wait for Nikolai's call like some lovesick girlfriend. So what if he promised he'd call? Maybe he will, or maybe he won't.

I shouldn't care either way.

Determined not to sit there biting my nails, I resume my research into Mom's death. The reporter I emailed last night hasn't replied, so I find the contact info of a few more Boston-area journalists and message them. I also research the owner of the restaurant where Mom worked, as well as the corporation behind the upscale hotel where the restaurant is located.

There has to be a reason those men killed my mom.

I find the same thing as yesterday: nothing. What I really need is a private investigator, but there's no way I can afford one right now. Although... it doesn't hurt to get some rate quotes. Come Tuesday, I'll have money, and if I'm staying here—which I don't see why I wouldn't—I might as well use that money to get some answers.

Yes, that's it.

That's exactly what I'll do.

Encouraged, I look up a few promising leads and email them for a quote. Then, feeling accomplished for the evening, I switch over to my other project: learning everything I can about Nikolai.

I've thought of a few more phrases I can translate into Russian, and my search turns up several tabloid photos. One is of Nikolai at a Warsaw charity gala with a tall blond beauty on his arm; another is of him at a Moscow fashion show, sitting next to a bored-looking Alina. A couple more show him vacationing at various exotic destinations, invariably with some leggy model at his side staring at him with adoration.

I was right. He's all but drowning in gorgeous women. For all I know, he might be in bed with some stunning model at this very moment, having picked her up at some VIP nightclub last night.

The thought is like a splash of boiling water on my chest. I have no right to feel this way, but I suddenly want to rip out every hair on the head of this imaginary woman—right before I do the same to Nikolai.

Setting the laptop aside, I jump off the bed and start to pace.

Why isn't he calling?

He said he would.

He promised.

He has to know it's getting later here by the minute.

Is it because he's busy with work—or with some woman? I picture her glossy red lips wrapped around his cock, her eyes peering up at him through skillfully applied fake lashes as she—

A soft chime sounds from the bed, and I lunge toward the open laptop, my pulse skyrocketing. Plopping down on my stomach, I pull the computer toward me and, with an unsteady finger, hit "Accept" on Nikolai's videocall request.

His face fills the screen, his hotel room visible behind him, and I exhale a shaky breath, my irrational jealousy fading as I see the tender look in his tiger eyes.

"Hi, zaychik," he murmurs, his deep voice so velvety I want to rub it against my cheek. "How was your day?"

"It was good. How was yours? I mean, your morning—or your day yesterday?" I sound out of breath, but I can't help it. My heart is pounding in a techno beat, and every cell in my body is vibrating with excitement. As pathetic as it is, I've been looking forward to this call all day. Even when I wasn't consciously thinking about it, it was lurking at the back of my mind.

He gives me a wry smile. "My morning was okay, and so was the rest of yesterday. Some meetings, some bullshit—business as usual."

"What kind of business?" Realizing how nosy that sounds, I open my mouth to take back the question, but he's already answering.

"Clean energy. Specifically, nuclear energy. One of our companies has developed a proprietary technology that allows for small, portable nuclear reactors that can be used to provide low-cost electricity in small villages and other remote settlements."

"Wow. And they're safe? Not like—what was that famous one in Ukraine?"

"Chernobyl? No, they're nothing like that. For one thing, each reactor is only about the size of a car, so even if there was an accident, the amount of radiation released would be much less. More importantly, our engineers have added so many redundancies that an accident is next to impossible. Our moto is *Safety First* —unlike our rivals.'" His voice hardens on the last part.

"There are other companies doing the same thing?" I ask, fascinated by this glimpse into a world I know nothing about.

His eyes glint darkly. "One. They're bidding against us for a huge contract with the Tajik government. Whoever wins it will dominate this nascent industry in Central Asia—which is why my brother asked me to get involved."

"Oh?"

"The head of the Tajikistan Energy Commission was a classmate of mine at boarding school, and my brother's hoping I'll have better luck making our case to him." A wry smile touches his lips. "As you've probably guessed, personal connections are very important in business."

I widen my eyes exaggeratedly. "No! Really?"

He laughs. "I know. Hard to imagine, right? I have a lunch meeting with him on Monday, and then I'll hopefully be able to fly back."

"So you'll be back by Tuesday?" I'm already counting down the days until my first paycheck, and now I'll have another reason to wish I could put the next fifty hours on fast-forward.

"I should be, yes." He pauses, then says softly, "I miss you, zaychik."

My breath stops, literally, even as my heart hammers faster and my skin tingles with a flush. Regardless of what I thought I saw in his eyes last night —what I hoped he might feel—I never dreamed that I'd hear him say that to me tonight so casually... so openly.

Like a boyfriend.

He's looking at me, patiently waiting for my response, so as soon as my breathing resumes, I force myself to speak. "I... I miss you too. And Slava. He misses you. We both miss you. He really does." I know I'm not making any sense, but I can't help it. I've never had trouble expressing my feelings with the guys I've dated, but I've never dated anyone like Nikolai before —not that we're dating. Or are we? Maybe he just misses me in the friend sense? Or son's tutor sense?

God, I have no idea what's happening.

The corners of his sensuous lips twitch with suppressed amusement, and I once again have the unnerving suspicion that he's looking straight into my brain and seeing the confusion there. "Tell me more, zaychik," he murmurs, leaning closer to the camera. "What has my son been up to today?"

Slava, that's it. I grab on to the topic like a drowning man latching on to a buoy, and launch into a detailed description of everything Slava and I have done and learned. Nikolai listens raptly, his gaze filled with that special softness he reserves for his son. However, when I get to the book Slava and I read last—the story about the ducklings—and I laughingly mention Slava's apparent dislike for Grandpa Duck, all traces of softness disappear from Nikolai's expression, his eyes taking on a hard, sharp gleam.

"Did he say anything?" he demands. "Explain it in any way?"

"No, I... I didn't ask." I draw back at the look on his face, an expression so dark and cold it sends a chill through my body. This is a side of Nikolai I've never seen, and suddenly, my earlier concerns about mafia don't seem quite as foolish.

I can picture this man ordering a hit—even pulling the trigger himself.

In the next moment, however, his features smooth out, the chilling look disappearing as he asks me to continue, and I'm again left wondering if my unruly imagination played a trick on me. Maybe I read too much into that brief change of expression... or maybe I just got a peek into some Molotov family drama. It could simply be that Nikolai doesn't get along with Slava's grandfather—assuming there is one on his mother's side.

There's still a lot I don't know about this family.

Deciding to remedy that, I finish my report on Slava's progress by going over what I taught him at dinner, and then I carefully—very carefully, lest I step on any landmines—ask Nikolai to tell me about his brothers.

Thankfully, my request doesn't upset him. "I'm the second oldest," he tells me. "Valery is four years my junior, and Konstantin—the genius of the family—is two years older than me. He runs all of our tech ventures, while Valery oversees the entire organization."

"Which you used to do, right?" I ask, recalling what Alina told me.

"That's right." He doesn't look surprised that I know. "But it's hard to do remotely, so I asked Valery to step in while I'm away."

"Why *are* you away?" I ask, unable to resist the question that's been on my mind for so long. "What brought you to this corner of the world?"

He smiles at my blatant curiosity. "I know. It's odd, right?"

"Extremely odd." So odd, in fact, that I've concocted a crazy mafia story in my head, but I'm keeping my mouth shut about that.

He leans back in his chair, the smile fading until only a trace of the sensual curve remains. "It's a long story, zaychik, and it's getting late. You should go to sleep."

"It's okay, I'm not tired." And even if I were, I'd deny it because I'm dying to hear this story, whatever length it may be. Sitting up straighter, I arrange the computer more comfortably on my lap and give him my best puppy eyes, fluttering lashes and all. "Please, Nikolai... tell me. Pretty, pretty please."

I meant it as a joke, a light flirtation at best, but his face goes taut, his gaze darkening as he leans toward the camera. "I like hearing my name on your lips." His voice is a low, honeyed purr. "And I really, really like it when you beg."

My mouth goes Sahara dry, my heartbeat uneven as fire streaks through my veins and centers low in my core. With him so far away and our video chats staying mostly on safe topics, I've somehow let myself forget about the sexual tension that smolders between us, ready to ignite into a conflagration at the slightest spark. I've convinced myself that I imagined that feeling of being hunted prey... that alarming, yet strangely exciting awareness that I'm at the mercy of this dangerously alluring man.

"Is that—" I swallow, uncertain if I should venture there. "Is that your thing? Women begging?"

The dark heat in his eyes intensifies. "My *thing*, zaychik, is you. I want you in every way possible... sweetly and roughly... on your knees, and on your back, and on top, riding me... I want to eat your pussy for dessert after each meal and pour my cum down your throat every morning. I want to fuck you so hard you scream, and then I want to cuddle you for hours. Most of all, I want to drown you in pleasure... so much pleasure you won't mind the occasional bite of pain... In fact, you'll beg for it."

Oh. My. God.

I stare at him, my breaths short and shallow, my clit throbbing and my nipples pebble hard. My body feels like one of his nuclear reactors in meltdown, the heat under my skin so scorching I might spontaneously combust. *Or come.* If I put any pressure on my clit right now, I could definitely come.

I wet my lips, trying to ignore the pulsing ache between my legs. "So... you *are* into stuff. Like, kinky stuff."

As soon as the words leave my mouth, I cringe at how juvenile and vanilla I sound. And I'm not vanilla. At least I don't think I am. My sexual fantasies have always had a darker tinge to them, and I've had a boyfriend tie me up once or twice—and another time, spank me. None of that turned me on, but then again, my boyfriend wasn't really into it. It felt awkward and forced with him... childish, somehow.

I have a feeling it'll be nothing of the sort with Nikolai.

The man doesn't know the meaning of childish and awkward.

Sure enough, his lips curve in another darkly sensual smile. In a voice like heated silk, he murmurs, "Chloe, zaychik... I'm into everything—as long as it's with you."

This time, it's my heart that goes into meltdown mode. Because it sounds a lot like... "Are you saying you don't want to see other women?" I blurt, and immediately want to kick myself for once again sounding like I'm in high school. He's just flirting, not making any kind of exclusivity commitment. We haven't even—

"I don't," he says softly, bringing my thoughts to a screeching halt. "I don't want anyone but you. I haven't since the moment we met."

"Oh." I stare at him, unable to come up with anything else to say.

This is big.

Huge, really.

There's no possible misunderstanding here, no chance that I'm being a foolish romantic.

Nikolai is telling me that he wants me and no one else... that essentially, we *are* exclusive.

"Does this scare you?" he asks, disconcertingly astute. "Is this too much for you?"

It is. Way too much. And yet... "No," I say, gathering my courage. "It's not. And I—I don't want to see anyone else either."

His nostrils flare. "Good. Once you're mine, I won't deal kindly with any man who tries to steal you."

A startled laugh escapes my throat, but Nikolai doesn't smile in response. His gaze remains fixed on me, his expression darkly intent, and to my shock, I realize that he means it, that it's not a joke at all.

I attempt to make it into one anyway. "Possessive much?"

"With you," he says, his gaze unwavering, "very much."

My heart stutters to a halt again. "Why me?" I ask when I recover my voice. "Is it because I'm the only woman here, within arm's reach? Is it a convenience thing or…" I trail off as amusement brightens the dark gold of his eyes, highlighting the flecks of forest green.

"If I were so inclined," he says gently, "I could have a different woman flown in every week—and I often did before you came. There's no lack of candidates willing to make the trip, believe me, zaychik."

Oh, I believe him. Even before I came across those tabloid photos, I knew he must have a stable of gorgeous women at his beck and call. How could he not, with his looks, wealth, and sex appeal?

The wonder is not that women are willing to fly in, it's that they're not camped out in the woods.

"Why then?" I ask unsteadily. "Why me?"

He cocks his head. "Do you believe in fate, zaychik?"

"Fate? Like God or destiny?"

"Or predestination. All of us being connected, like threads in a tapestry that was woven long before our births."

I stare at him, bemused. "I don't know. I've never given it much thought."

His lips curve in a faint smile. "I have. And I think at some point in the weaving of this tapestry, your thread was joined to mine. Our paths were bound to intersect, our meeting date set long before I saw you. Everything that had happened in our lives had brought us to that point, to that place and time… all the good things and the bad." His voice roughens. "Especially the bad."

Like my mom's death. If not for that, I would've never been on this road trip, never seen the job listing, never met him. Not that it means this is fated. But Nikolai seems to believe that, and I have to admit that we wouldn't be here today without the violent upheaval in my life. And, it sounds like, without some upheaval in his.

"What bad things happened to you?" I ask softly. "Or is that the long story you keep promising me?"

His smile takes on a rueful edge. "More or less. Unfortunately, zaychik, you need to go to sleep, and I have to go meet my brother. How about I call you tomorrow around the same time, and we'll talk some more?"

"Oh, sure. I didn't mean to hold you up."

"You didn't." That tender look is in his eyes again, making my heart pound in an erratic, joyous rhythm. "If I could, I'd talk to you all day."

"Me too," I admit with a shy smile.

His answering smile is dazzling. "Until tomorrow then. Sleep well, zaychik."

And as he disconnects the call, I push the computer off my lap and do a dance around the room, grinning so hard my cheeks hurt.

36

NIKOLAI

"You're in a good mood for someone who was almost killed yesterday," Konstantin says after we place our orders with the waiter, and I realize I've been smiling so much even my socially oblivious brother has noticed. And it's all because of her.

Chloe.

She's fast becoming my feel-good drug.

I love that she's beginning to trust me, to accept what's happening between us. I didn't want to come on too strongly on our call today, but it was time she knew my intentions—and now she does. More importantly, I got her to admit that she reciprocates my feelings.

Her sweetly murmured "me too" is still playing in my mind on a loop.

"Do you have the report?" I ask, ignoring Konstantin's comment. It's none of his business what kind of mood I'm in or why. Besides, there's nothing like almost dying to make one appreciate life and all of its wonderful possibilities—such as taking Chloe to bed as soon as I get back home.

"Not yet," Konstantin says, picking up his cup of chamomile tea. "Hopefully, either later today or tomorrow. But we have verified the info the security guard provided, and it all checks out. The operation is a go for tonight."

"What's taking so long? Your hackers usually come through within hours."

He blinks behind the lenses of his glasses. "You're still talking about the report on the girl?"

I grit my teeth. "What else?"

"My team's been busy, and it's not an easy task you've assigned them."

"How so? All I've asked is for you to look into her mother's death and her movements for the past month. How difficult is that? I know she's been off the grid, but there's got to be traffic cameras, gas station cam—"

"There seems to be some interference." He sips his tea. "A few of the security tapes my guys have pulled have been damaged or wiped clean."

I still. "Wiped clean?"

"A professional job, from the looks of it." He sets down his cup. "You said she's just a civilian, right? No affiliation?"

"None that I'm aware of," I say evenly.

Is it possible?

Could she have fooled me?

Is sweet little Chloe involved with the mob... or worse, the government?

"Why didn't you tell me this before?" I ask Konstantin, who, once again oblivious to the bombshell he's delivered, is calmly spreading sundried tomato pesto on a piece of freshly baked rye bread. "Don't you think it's important for me to know?"

He bites into the bread and chews leisurely. "I'm telling you now," he says after he swallows. "Besides, my guys only realized what's going on last night. A couple of damaged tapes could be just shit luck. But several—that's a pattern."

"So let me get this clear. You're telling me someone's erasing all the security tapes where she appears."

"Not all the tapes." He reaches for another piece of bread. "My team's been able to reconstruct her movements for the majority of the past month. Just certain tapes... ones I suspect may hold the answers you're after."

Fuck.

This is big.

I don't know what I thought Konstantin's hackers would uncover, but it wasn't this.

A thought slithers into my mind, a suspicion so awful my stomach turns over. "Do you think it's the—"

"Leonovs?" Konstantin sets down his bread. "I doubt it. My guys have come across their hackers' work before, and this doesn't feel like it."

"Feel like it?"

Light glints off the lenses of his glasses. "It's hard to explain to a non-techie, but yes. There's a certain sloppiness to the way this was done that doesn't fit the Leonovs."

"I thought you said it was professionals."

"There are different levels of professionalism. My guys are top notch, the Leonovs' team isn't far behind, and many are way, way worse. These guys are somewhere in the middle, which is why I think my team's going to come through for you. They just need more time."

I take a breath and let it out slowly. Just the possibility that Chloe could've been hired by my enemies is enough to spike my blood pressure. But Konstantin knows what he's talking about, and if he doesn't think it's them, I have to lay that suspicion to rest for now. Besides, if the Leonovs knew enough to plant Chloe in my compound, I doubt they would've sent a guy on a motorcycle as a warning.

There would've been no warning, just straight-up war.

"About the biker," I say. "Any luck tracking him down?"

"No. And that does have Leonov fingerprints all over it. If I had to guess, Alexei's pissed that you're here, interfering with his bid."

"You're probably right." I fall silent as the waiter brings out our food. Once he leaves, I continue. "He must've found out about my meeting with the Commission head."

"Valery's doubling your security until then, just in case. Now"—Konstantin drizzles dressing onto his

Greek salad—"let's discuss your talking points for tomorrow."

And as he goes over the technical specifications of our product, I do my best to focus on his words instead of the growing number of questions about Chloe and my increasing obsession with her.

37

CHLOE

I've never felt as giddy as I do this Sunday. All day long, I catch myself smiling uncontrollably and walking around like I'm floating on a cloud. It's embarrassing, really, but I can't stop. Each time I think about last night's call, my pulse races with excitement.

Nikolai wants me.

He misses me.

He wants us to be exclusive.

I feel like a teenager whose movie star crush just asked her out on a date. Which, in a way, is what's happening.

Nikolai wants us to date, or more precisely, to be in a relationship.

It should seem crazy, and on some level, it does. We've known each other less than a week, and for the past couple of days, he hasn't been here in person. It's way too soon to be talking about exclusivity, much less destiny and fate. But I can't deny the strength of the attraction that burns between us, of that powerful, magnetic force that's terrified me from the start. It wasn't the attraction itself I feared, though—it was getting hurt. I was afraid of falling for a man who, at best, thought of me as a few nights of entertainment. But that's not how it is for Nikolai. He made that clear last night, and though it may be naïve of me, I believe him.

I see no reason for him to lie to me.

There are other obstacles to our relationship, of course—like his status as my employer and the fact that I'm on the run from a pair of ruthless killers. At some point soon, I'll have to disclose that, and I have no idea how he'll react. But that's a worry for another day.

Right now, all I want to think about is seeing him on my computer screen tonight.

"Someone chasing you?" Alina inquires at dinner, and I freeze, my heart stopping for a second before I realize she's referring to the speed with which I'm devouring my food.

"Just hungry," I say after I swallow. "Sorry if I'm being rude."

She shrugs her graceful shoulders, which are left bare by her strapless evening dress. "I don't care. Just curious why you're in such a rush."

I'm in a rush because I'm dying to get up to my

room in case Nikolai calls early, but there's no way I'm telling her that. "No reason other than yummy food."

Slava giggles at my side. "Yummy. I like yummy in my tummy."

I beam at him. "Yes, you do." We've spent all day learning various words and phrases, including this little rhyme, and I'm beyond pleased he remembers it.

"At this rate, you're going to have him speaking English in a week," Alina says, cutting a piece of chicken and placing it on his plate.

I grin at her. "I hope so—but more realistically, in a couple of months."

She smiles back at me and resumes eating, and I do likewise, eager to be done and ensconced comfortably in my bed with the laptop. Like Alina, I'm wearing an evening gown, and I'm looking forward to changing into my pajamas. Although... maybe I shouldn't. Nikolai might enjoy seeing me like this, even through the camera.

In fact, I should probably refresh my makeup before he calls.

"Want to race?" I ask Slava, and make engine-revving noises to remind him of our racing game with toy cars. "See who can eat faster?"

He blinks, not understanding, so I pick up my fork and begin shoveling food into my mouth with exaggerated speed. Catching on, he does the same, and we clean our plates in record time. Alina, who's eating at a normal pace, watches our race with amusement, and by the time we're done, she pushes away her half-eaten chicken.

"I guess I'm done as well," she says dryly. Louder, she calls, "*Lyuda, Slava gotov!*"

Lyudmila appears from the kitchen, wiping her hands on her apron. I smile and thank her for the delicious meal—though, truth be told, it was nowhere near as good as what her husband makes. The chicken was on the dry side, the potatoes were too salty, and most of the appetizers and side dishes were leftovers. But I'm not about to quibble: Food is food, and I'm grateful to have it.

Smiling back at me, Lyudmila picks up Slava, and just like that, my evening is free.

As soon as I get to my room, I completely redo my makeup—all I had on at dinner was a light layer of foundation and a coat of mascara—and fix up my hair. I still don't look nearly as polished as when Alina did this for me, but hopefully, Nikolai won't mind.

I was barefaced and in my PJs on our last two calls, so this is a definite improvement.

Feeling giddy again, I grin at my reflection. I look much better than when I first got here. My cheeks are no longer painfully hollow and the dark circles under my eyes have faded, as has the look of desperation in them. Last night was another one with no nightmares, only sex dreams, and I have Nikolai to thank for that. I may have woken up wet and aching, with my hand pressed between my thighs, but at least I slept through the night.

God, I can't wait to talk to him.

Hurrying over to my bed, I sprawl on my stomach and grab the laptop, willing him to call at this very moment.

He doesn't. I guess my mental powers aren't up to snuff.

Sighing, I go into my inbox to check for any replies from the journalists. There's nothing, naturally— though there *is* a quote from one of the PI firms, detailing their hourly rates and retainer fees.

I skim it and wince. It's a lot, way more than I can hope to cover with my first week's paycheck, at least given the number of hours I anticipate they'll have to spend. I'll need at least a couple weeks' pay for the retainer alone. Maybe the other PIs will be cheaper, but they haven't responded yet, so I have to wait.

Like I'm waiting for Nikolai, *who's still not calling.*

Taking a breath, I remind myself to be patient. He said he'd call me around the same time as yesterday, and it's nowhere near that. For now, I need to distract myself with something, so I begin researching my mom's friends and co-workers again on the off chance I missed something the first time.

I'm scrolling through the pictures of her manager's daughter's quinceañera when the call request pops up, sending my pulse skyrocketing.

Beaming, I smooth my hair and click "Accept."

38

NIKOLAI

CHLOE'S SMILE IS SO RADIANT I FEEL LIKE I'VE STEPPED out of an underground bunker onto a sunlit beach. "Hi," she says, slightly breathless as she sits back against a stack of pillows and places the computer on her lap. "How's it going? How's your nuclear bidding thing?"

I smile back at her, pleasure spreading through me like molten honey. "It's good, zaychik, thank you."

And it is. Valery's operation has gone off without a hitch, and the Energy Commission is already swarming around the Atomprom plant, seeking to contain the fallout from the reactor that exploded overnight. The radiation leakage is minimal, as expected, but the damage to Atomprom's reputation is significant—which sets us up well for my lunch meeting with the Commission head today.

More importantly, for the past hour, I've been watching Chloe's online activities and examining her browser history from yesterday, and I've concluded that she's unlikely to be affiliated with any government or rival organization. If she were a plant, she'd know everything about me already and wouldn't need to translate Russian articles with the aid of free online tools. Nor would she be researching her mother's friends and co-workers using nothing more than their public social media—or looking into PI firms.

Something else is going on with Chloe, something I find both worrisome and intriguing.

My best bet is to get her to open up to me, to tell me the truth, but if I press her on it now, she might get spooked and try to run—and I don't want that. Not when I'm an ocean away. The next best option is to get Konstantin's team to hack her Gmail; the spyware allows me to see what sites she's on but not the content of them, like individual emails.

Either way, I'm going to get the answers. I just need to be patient a little longer.

"How was your day?" I ask, settling more comfortably into my chair. "What did you and Slava do?"

Her smile turns impossibly brighter, and she tells me all about my son's amazing progress, her small face so animated I can't take my eyes off it. She sounds as proud as any parent, and for the first time since I've learned of Slava's existence and Ksenia's death, my chest doesn't feel as painfully tight when I think of him and the future that awaits him because of the tainted blood running through his veins. Instead, I feel a sliver of hope as I picture Chloe with Slava, playing with him, cuddling him, loving him... giving him what his mother can't.

What *I* can't.

And that's part of it, I realize, part of why I want her so badly. I want her not just for myself but for my son. I want her sunshine to touch him, to warm him... to keep away the darkness of his heritage for as long as possible. I want her the way I've seen her through the cameras in Slava's room, gracing my son with her radiant smile, making him feel like he's the most important person in the world to her.

And I want him to be that.

I want her to love Slava even more than I want her to love me.

Hungrily, I listen to her talk about him, absorbing every word, drinking in every expression. She's wearing one of her new evening dresses, a pale-yellow number with thin straps that bares her delicate shoulders. Her brown eyes sparkle, and even through the camera, her bronzed skin glows in the golden light cast by her bedside lamp. She's breathtaking, this sweet mystery of a girl—and mine. All mine. I might not have claimed her physically yet, but it doesn't change the facts. She was made for me, her light the perfect foil to the dark void inside me, her warmth filling every cold, empty crevice in my heart. I don't care who she turns out to be or what secrets she's hiding.

Criminal or victim, she belongs to me, no matter what.

When she's done telling me about Slava, I ask her

about her favorite books and music, and we bond over our mutual love of eighties bands and Dean Koontz novels. I'm not surprised that we have things in common; that's how it often works when you find your other half, the puzzle piece that completes you. She's my opposite in so many ways, yet there are threads that connect us, that bound us together long before we met.

We talk for a solid hour, and I find out more about her childhood and teenage years, about her young mother and how hard she worked to raise Chloe by herself. She tells me about hanging out downtown with her friends and vacationing in Florida with her mother, about struggling with calculus in high school and working two jobs for three summers straight to buy her rickety Corolla on her own.

"It's almost as old as I am," she says fondly, "but it still runs. Even after all the miles I put on it driving across the country. Speaking of which, did you ever have a chance to ask Pavel about my car keys? I still don't have them."

I veil my expression, concealing the beast that stirs inside me at the thought of her getting into her rust bucket of a car and leaving. "He said he couldn't find them. We'll look for them when we get back."

It's a lie, but I can't tell her the truth. She wouldn't understand. I don't fully understand it myself. All I know is that I sleep better knowing the keys on that furry chain are in my possession, that my zaychik is safe and sound under my roof.

A tiny frown creases her forehead. "Oh, okay. But he'll find them, right?"

"I'm sure he will. If not, I'll buy you another car."

She laughs, clearly thinking it's a joke, but I'm completely serious. I *will* buy her a car, something better, safer than the Corolla. It's a miracle it hasn't broken down on some deserted road, leaving her stranded with no phone, at the mercy of any murderer or rapist who might be passing by.

Just the thought of her in that situation makes me break out in a cold sweat.

"I'll just call a locksmith," she says when she stops laughing. "There are locksmiths in Elkwood Creek, right?"

"I'm sure there's at least one." And I'm just as sure he's getting nowhere near Chloe's car. The more I think about her driving across the country all alone, the darker my mood turns. Anything could've happened to her, absolutely anything—and for all I know, it did.

Her nightmares could have nothing to do with what happened to her mother and everything to do with some lowlife assaulting her on the road.

Rage burns inside me as I picture her getting attacked, hurt and traumatized, and it's all I can do not to demand that she tell me the truth right now, so I can exterminate those responsible. Only the fear that she might pull back and try to leave keeps me silent. That and the recollection of those damaged tapes, the ones that indicate that something more is going on, that she's involved with someone or something with the resources to conceal her movements.

Oblivious to the storm inside me, she grins and says, "All right then. You can tell Pavel not to stress about it. I'm guessing he's upset he lost them?"

"I'll talk to him, don't worry." And I will. I need to explain the situation and ask him to apologize to Chloe. Right now, he has no clue that anything's amiss. "As to the—"

A soft chime interrupts me, and to my disappointment, I see it's time to head to my meeting. I set an alarm on my phone so I wouldn't be late.

"Do you have to go?" Chloe asks astutely, and I nod, buttoning my jacket.

"This is the meeting I'm here for. The good news is, if all goes as expected, I'm getting on a plane home right after."

Her eyes brighten. "Really? What time does your flight leave?"

"When I tell it to. It's my plane." Leaning into the camera, I murmur, "I can't wait to see you in person."

She gives me a sweet smile. "Same here. Good luck at your meeting and fly home safe."

"Thank you, zaychik." Voice roughening, I advise, "Sleep well tonight—you'll need it."

And as her lips part on a startled inhale, I hang up, eager to conclude the meeting so I can be in the air, on the way to her.

I'm already at the table when Yusup Bahori walks into Al Sham, one of the best Middle Eastern restaurants in Dushanbe and, according to Konstantin's research, a favorite spot of Yusup's. After the obligatory half hour of catching up on our favorite school memories and discussing our classmates and other mutual acquaintances, I shift the conversation toward our permits and the bidding for the contract with the Tajik government.

"Nikolai, you know I can't—" he starts, but I hold up my hand, stopping the bullshit in its tracks.

"Let's not play games. You and I both know our product is superior to Atomprom's. So why were our permits pulled?"

He blinks, not expecting me to be that direct. "Well, there were safety concerns and—"

"We've never had a meltdown or a leak. Our safety protocols go above and beyond any government requirements, and best of all, our reactors can provide cheap, clean energy to every settlement and village, no matter how inaccessible or remote."

He sighs, pushing away his half-finished kebab. "Look, I don't know the particulars, but if our inspectors—"

"Are these the same inspectors that greenlit Atomprom's bid? If so, for how much?"

He has the grace to flush. "We've just begun the investigation of last night's accident," he says stiffly. "If it turns out there was any improper conduct, we'll take appropriate measures. We don't tolerate corruption and bribery. The safety of our citizens and the environment is of utmost importance to us."

I nod, picking up my fork. "Which is why Atomprom was never the right company to partner with you. Their safety record is abysmal."

Calmly, I eat two bites of falafel, letting him mull it over, and I'm not the least bit surprised when he says abruptly, "Fine. I can look into the permits for you. Maybe some inspector did get overzealous."

"That would be much appreciated. And if it does turn out there's been a misunderstanding, we would be grateful if you reversed the decision and put in a good word for us during the bidding."

He licks his lips. "I understand."

Of course he does. Gratitude from the Molotov organization is a very lucrative thing. As is gratitude from the Leonovs—but he's already received it.

His new mansion in Khujand is proof of that.

It would be easy to point that out, to use the evidence of corruption Konstantin's hackers have uncovered to get him to do what we want, but unlike Valery, I believe in waving the carrot before grabbing the stick.

Things tend to go smoother that way.

Goal achieved, I return to neutral topics, and the rest of the meal passes in pleasant conversation. He doesn't bring up the specifics of our "gratitude," and neither do I. Let him have plausible deniability when our payment lands in his offshore account; it doesn't hurt us in the least.

When we're done, he heads out to his car, and I stop by the restroom before the long drive to the small airport where my jet is waiting. I'm washing my hands when the door opens and a tall, athletically built man about my age steps in.

A man I instantly recognize.

"Well, if it isn't the missing Molotov brother," Alexei Leonov drawls, leaning against the door and folding his tattooed arms across his chest. "Fancy running into you here."

39

NIKOLAI

I CASUALLY WIPE MY HANDS ON A PAPER TOWEL AND DROP it in the trash. In the process, I scan my enemy for any visible weapons. None are in sight, but that doesn't mean anything. He could have a gun strapped to his ankle or tucked into the back of his jeans. And there's definitely a knife or two in his biker boots.

Alexei Leonov is known for his appetite for violence.

"Coincidence is a funny thing," I say calmly, preparing to reach for the Glock strapped to my chest under my jacket. "What brings you to Dushanbe?"

He grins sharply. "Same thing as you, I imagine." Uncrossing his arms, he pushes away from the door and approaches me. Stopping in front of me, he asks, "How's life in... where is it you are these days? Thailand? The Philippines?" Even up close, his dark brown eyes look almost black, matching the hue of his hair.

"Life's great. How's your old man?" If he thinks I'm going to blurt out my location after all the trouble Konstantin's gone through to hide it, he's got another thing coming. "Still alive and kicking?"

His smile is all teeth. "You know how these old men are. Practically indestructible. You have to *really* try to get them to croak."

I don't take this bait either. "Say hello to him for me. And to your brother."

His eyes glint harshly. "Not my sister? Oh, yeah, she's fucking dead."

It takes everything I have to keep a poker face. "I've heard. I'm sorry." It's a lie—Ksenia deserves to rot with the worms—but anything more than the most neutral response may tip my hand, and he already seems to harbor some suspicions.

His savage grin returns. "Speaking of sisters… how's my intended?"

Now this I can't let slide. I hold his gaze, letting him see the ice in my eyes. "Alina's not yours. Never was, never will be."

"That's not what our betrothal contract says."

"That contract was voided by my father's death, and you know it."

"Do I?" He leans in until we're almost nose to nose. No hint of humor remains on his face, stamping his hard features with an unmistakable patina of cruelty. In a lethally soft tone, he says, "Tell Alina it's time. I'm done being patient."

And stepping back, he exits through the door.

Red-hot fury still burns in my chest when Konstantin's Tesla pulls up to the plane.

"Thanks for waiting," he says, climbing out. "I figured it'd be better to give this to you in person." He hands me a flash drive.

"Chloe?"

He nods. "It's a doozy. You were right to have me dig deeper. The girl isn't who she seems."

Fuck. "Mafia?"

"Maybe. Watch the video. My guys are doing their best to learn more."

Motherfucker. I want to demand all the answers, now, but the plane is ready to depart, and I need to fill him in on my encounter with Alexei. Swiftly, I do so, and when I get to the part about Alina, I see the same fury reflected on his face.

"I'll kill him if he so much as breathes her way," Konstantin says savagely. "If he thinks we're going to honor that fucking medieval contract, made when our sister was barely fifteen, he's—"

"I doubt he was serious. Most likely, he was trying to provoke me as payback for the explosion at their plant. Either way, he doesn't know for sure she's with me. He was shooting in the dark."

Konstantin takes a breath, visibly composing himself. Of the three of us, he's closest to Alina, having spent time babysitting her during school holidays and summer breaks. I never had that luxury; our father had decided early on that I was the son best suited to assume the mantle of leadership in our organization, and all of my childhood and teenage years were spent learning the family business.

"You're right," he says in a calmer tone. "He's pissed, and he wants to piss us off. Just in case, though, tell Alina to be on her guard."

"I don't think that's a good idea. She's been... having some trouble the last couple of days."

His eyebrows pull together. "The headaches are back?"

I nod grimly. "Lyudmila says she's been hitting the medications pretty hard while I've been gone. Pot, too."

Alina thinks I don't know about that last part, but I do—and I've asked Lyudmila to keep her company whenever she wants to smoke. I'm not a fan of mind-altering substances, but I know why my sister needs it, and weed is preferable to some of the prescriptions in her bedside drawer.

Konstantin's frown deepens. "She's spiraling again."

"Let's hope not." But if she is, that's another reason for me to hurry back. Though Alina and I barely get along, something about my presence keeps her on an even keel—maybe even the friction that exists between us. It gives her an external focus, a distraction from her inner turmoil.

With me, she has a clear and present target instead of the shadows lurking in her mind.

"Listen," I tell Konstantin, "I have to go. I'll let you know how she is when I see her in person. Just tell your team to keep doing what they're doing—Alexei can't find out where we are."

His jaw tightens. "Don't worry. He won't."

"Thanks."

With one last glance at my brother, I board the plane.

Pavel is waiting for me on the couch in the jet's main cabin, a laptop open on the coffee table in front of him. Wordlessly, I take a seat next to him and stick the flash drive into the computer.

There are two files on it, one titled "Updated report" and the other "Store camera, Boise, July 14."

My heart rate picks up as tension pervades my body.

That's the same day she applied to be Slava's tutor.

I click on the video.

The grainy recording shows a nondescript street with a few stores, a coffee shop, some parked cars, and occasional pedestrians. The time stamp in the corner tells me it's just after ten in the morning.

At first, it seems like nothing is going on, but after about thirty seconds, I catch sight of a familiar slender figure. Dressed in a T-shirt and a pair of jeans, Chloe is walking briskly down the street.

She's passing by a clothing boutique when it happens.

With a sharp *pop*, the display window to her left explodes.

Pavel emits a startled expletive, but I ignore him, all my attention on Chloe's small, frozen figure. Every muscle in my body is locked tight, fear and fury pulsing through me in sickening waves. Even on the blurry video, I can see the shock on her face as her wide eyes scan the street uncomprehendingly. Then screams about gunshots and 911 begin, and she lurches into a sprint—just as another *pop!* rings out and more glass around her goes flying.

Within seconds, she's gone from view, and the video cuts off.

"Motherfucker," Pavel mutters, but I'm already opening the other file.

The updated report.

40

CHLOE

I DON'T SLEEP WELL. AT ALL. WHO WOULD, WITH THAT kind of warning?

Sleep well tonight—you'll need it.

I can't think of anything Nikolai could've said that would've been *less* likely to make me get my zzzs. He might as well have told me that he intends to fuck me to exhaustion as soon as he returns home.

Actually, he did tell me that, more or less, before he left. His dirty promises have provided ample fodder for my wet dreams and shower masturbation sessions— including the lengthy one after our call last night.

I figured a couple of orgasms might relax me, but they actually made things worse. The entire time I played with myself, I kept thinking of what he'll do to me when he returns... how his hands and lips will feel on me... how his cock will feel inside me. My imagination went wild, painting all sorts of X-rated, non-PC scenarios, and they're still playing in my mind now, in the bright light of the morning, dampening my underwear and keeping my pulse racing.

It doesn't help that Alina is again nowhere to be seen. She doesn't come down for breakfast or lunch, and when I ask Lyudmila about that, she tells me Nikolai's sister has another headache.

"Does she get these a lot?" I ask at lunch, concerned, and Lyudmila nods, her face tight as she averts her eyes.

I wonder about that, but Lyudmila isn't exactly chatty around me, so I decide against questioning her further. Instead, I spend the afternoon teaching Slava and counting down the minutes until dinnertime, which is when Nikolai is expected to arrive.

My student is equally impatient. Lyudmila must've told him that his father is coming back today because he keeps jumping up and running over to the window as we're reviewing the alphabet.

"Do you want to surprise your daddy?" I ask when he returns from his expedition for the fifth time. "Make him happy?"

Slava's brows furrow. "Happy?"

"Yes, happy." I draw a smiling face with a yellow crayon. "Do you want your daddy to be happy?"

He nods, plopping down on the floor next to me.

"Then repeat after me: 'Hi, Daddy.'"

Slava is silent. He knows both of those words from the books we've been reading, and he's been repeating phrases after me when I request it, so I know it's not a comprehension issue.

Gently, I try again. "Hi, Daddy."

He stares at his sneakers. "Hi, Daddy." His voice is barely above a whisper, but the words are clear, as is the wariness in his large golden eyes when he lifts his gaze.

He's hesitant, and I can't blame him. Despite the small bit of progress we made with our joint reading session the other day, father and son are still virtual strangers.

I reach over to take his hands in mine. "I'm very proud of you. You're being brave and strong, like Superman."

His small face brightens. "Superman?"

"Superman," I confirm, squeezing his hands gently before releasing them. "Brave and strong."

"Brave and strong," he whispers, trying out the words. He points at his chest. "Brave and strong?"

I beam at him. "Yes, you are brave and strong, just like Superman. And you'll make your daddy very happy."

He gives me a big grin. "Happy, yes." He points at the smiley face drawing and puffs out his thin chest. "Very happy."

He's so adorable that I can't resist giving him a hug, and my heart melts when his short arms go around my neck, squeezing tightly. This, here, is why I love children so much. All they want is love and affection, and once they have it, they return it in spades.

Nikolai doesn't understand that about his son yet, but he will.

It's just a matter of time and a little effort on my part.

An hour before dinner, I leave Slava with Lyudmila and go to my room to change and get ready. I'm so excited and nervous I can barely keep my hands from shaking as I apply my makeup and smooth my hair into a semblance of the polished waves Alina was able to create for me. If she were feeling well, I'd ask her to repeat her magic, but since I haven't seen her at any point this afternoon, I have to assume she's still down with the headache.

Poor girl. I hope she feels better soon.

Once my hair and makeup are done, I flip through my ridiculously large collection of evening dresses to find the absolute best one. Without Nikolai here, I've been grabbing whichever one seems most comfortable and easiest to put on, but tonight, I want to put in extra effort.

I want to see his breath catch and his eyes kindle with that dark, savage heat that both excites and alarms me.

I settle on a delicate ivory gown that has subtle threads of gold woven in. Made of some diaphanous material, it's strapless, with a heart-shaped, corseted bodice that pushes up my breasts and defines my waist. The form-fitting skirt skims over my hips in the most flattering manner imaginable, and when I walk, a thigh-high slit on the left side reveals flashes of my leg. I pair the dress with the gold Jimmy Choos I wore on my first formal evening here, and I'm ready.

Ready to see Nikolai and take our relationship further.

The car pulls up as I'm coming down the stairs. I catch a glimpse of it in one of the large windows, and my heart beats faster. Lyudmila and Slava are already standing in the living room, with the boy dressed in his evening best. As I approach, he smiles up at me shyly, and I give him an encouraging shoulder squeeze.

"Remember, brave and strong, like Superman," I whisper, trying to control my own nervousness, and he giggles—only to fall silent at the sound of the front door opening, followed by footsteps heading in our direction.

Pavel appears first, but his house-sized frame barely registers in my vision. All my attention is on the tall, darkly beautiful man behind him, whose tiger-bright gaze homes in on me with an intensity that scorches my flesh and stills my lungs.

In the span of the past couple of days, I've forgotten what it's like to be near him, to experience the devastating impact of his presence. I don't just see him, I *feel* him with every inch of my skin, every cell of my being. Helplessly, my eyes trace over his features, taking in the uncompromising angles of his jaw and the sensuous shape of his lips, the startling thickness of his jet-black lashes and the way his raven's wing hair is brushed back from his forehead, revealing those high, wide cheekbones. He's dressed more casually than when he left, with a blue button-up shirt tucked into tailored slacks, and he looks so mouthwateringly hot that it's all I can do to remain standing. My heart races, my entire body buzzing as if a network of live wires resides under my skin, and I'm only peripherally aware of Lyudmila stepping up to embrace her husband while chattering excitedly in Russian.

Nikolai must be caught in the same potent spell because for a long moment, he stands still, eyes glittering as he takes in my appearance.

Then he comes toward me.

Breathless, I stare up at him as he stops in front of me. He's so much more up close than on a computer screen. Bigger, taller... more dangerously, primitively male. With his seductive charm and fine clothes, it's possible to forget that raw, animal quality he possesses, the sense that something feral lurks underneath his beautiful façade... something that draws me to him even as it makes the fine hair on the back of my neck stand up in warning.

At a distance, it was easy to dismiss my imaginings about him being dangerous.

Up close, it's infinitely harder.

"Hi, Daddy."

The sound of that small, high-pitched voice jolts me out of my trance—and it has an even stronger effect on

Nikolai. Every muscle on his face tightens as his gaze jumps to the boy standing bravely at my side.

For a moment, father and son just stare at each other. Then Nikolai slowly goes down on one knee.

"Hi," he says hoarsely as a medley of emotions plays across his face. "Hi, Slavochka."

My heart clenches with a surge of warmth. That version of the boy's name is an endearment; I've heard enough Russian over the past few days to know that.

Slava smiles uncertainly at his father before looking up at me.

"You did good," I say huskily, smoothing my palm over his silky hair. "Just like Superman." Smiling, I catch Nikolai's gaze. "Tell him he did well."

His face twists, something dark and agonizing flashing in his eyes before he regains control. "You did well," he says to the boy tonelessly, and rising to his feet, he steps back, his expression shuttered once more.

Confused, I start to speak, but he beats me to it.

"I need to talk to you," he tells me in a hard voice, and taking my hand in an inescapable grip, he leads me to his office.

41

CHLOE

My stomach churns and my pulse is sickeningly fast as he takes a seat across from me at the round table, his eyes filled with a darkness I can no longer convince myself stems solely from my imagination. No trace remains of the tender, seductive man I spoke to for so many hours over video, a man who was so open about his feelings for me. In his place is a beautiful, terrifying stranger, his face taut with fury.

The worst part is I have no idea what I've done, what happened to upset him so. Was it what Slava said? Or my clumsy suggestion that he praise the boy for—

"You lied to me, zaychik," he says in a lethally soft tone, and my heart plummets to my feet.

I was wrong.

This has nothing to do with Slava.

It's infinitely worse.

I gulp in a breath. "Nikolai, I—"

He holds up a hand, then opens a laptop that I just

now notice is on the table. "Watch this," he orders, turning the screen toward me.

I watch—and what I see turns my blood to icy slush.

It's me, that day in Boise.

The day they openly shot at me.

There's nothing more damning that Nikolai could've come across, no incident that speaks more clearly of the danger I pose to his family—a danger I haven't let myself think about in any real way, focusing instead on *my* situation, *my* survival. It's only now, with that grainy video in front of me, that I comprehend just how thoughtless, how selfish I have been.

I have two violent killers after me, and here I am, playing dress-up in the clothes he bought for me, pretending I'm safe in a compound he built for his son, a bright, sweet child I've already grown to adore.

A child who's in danger every second I'm here.

I'd blocked that out of my mind somehow, along with the crushing terror of that day, but I can do so no longer. Trembling, sick inside, I rise to my feet. "Nikolai, I'm so, so sorry. I'll leave. I'll go right now—"

"Sit." His voice is even softer, a frightening contrast to the savage ferocity in his eyes. "You're not going anywhere."

"But—"

"Sit."

My knees buckle underneath me, obeying his command.

He leans in, his gaze pinning me in place. "I want the truth. The full truth. Understand?"

I nod, even though I'm crumbling on the inside, all my hopes and dreams crashing around me.

I will tell him.

I will tell him everything.

After all the lies, he deserves the truth.

42

CHLOE

"It all started when I drove home after my college graduation," I say, trying—and failing—to keep my voice steady. "I was supposed to arrive in time for dinner, but the traffic was unusually heavy and I was almost an hour late. As soon as I found a parking spot in front of our building, I ran to the apartment, leaving my suitcase in the car. I figured I'd come back for it after we ate.

"I had my keys, so I came in and went directly to the kitchen, where I thought Mom was warming up some of the food. But when I got there—" I stop to swallow the lump threatening to overtake my throat.

"She was dead," Nikolai guesses grimly, and I nod, hot tears stinging the back of my eyes.

"She was lying in a pool of blood on the kitchen floor, her wrists slit. I couldn't feel a pulse, so I ran to get my phone—I was in such a rush I forgot my purse with the phone in the car. But before I could exit the apartment, I heard voices, male voices, coming from Mom's bedroom."

His eyes narrow dangerously. "They were there? In the apartment with you?"

"Yes. I jumped into the little closet niche by the door and hid behind the coats there. I saw them then. Two big men in ski masks. They exited the apartment, then immediately came back in. I heard them go back into the bedroom, and since I was right by the door, I ran. I ran down all five flights of stairs, and then I kept running until I got to my car." I drag in a shuddering breath, shoving down the recollection of that mind-numbing panic, of hyperventilating and sobbing as I fought to jam my keys into the ignition.

Nikolai gives me a moment to compose myself. "What happened next?"

"I called 911 and drove to the nearest police station. I told them what happened, and they dispatched a unit to my apartment. But the killers were gone by then, and the police, they ruled it—" My voice breaks. "They ruled it a suicide."

His eyebrows snap together. "I don't understand. You told them about the two men? As in, filed an official police report?"

"I did. I told them about the masks and the guns with silencers and—"

"Guns with silencers?"

I nod, wrapping my arms around myself. I'm so cold my teeth are beginning to chatter. "I saw them, through the coats in the hallway. Well, technically, I spotted just one gun, but later, when I saw them again, there were two, so I assume—"

"Later?" His jaw flexes. "You saw them up close again?"

"Not up close, no. They were about a block away. It was after this." I jerk my chin toward the laptop. "They ran after me, and I saw them. They each had a gun."

"Ski masks too?"

"Yes." I strain to recall the two figures, but other than their general size and the guns in their hands, they're blurry in my mind. "At least I'm pretty sure."

Nikolai's gaze sharpens. "But not certain?"

"I… no." Which is stupid of me. I should've been paying attention, should've memorized every tiny detail so I could—

"Was that the only other time you saw them? The only time they came after you?"

"No." A shiver racks my body. "Not even close."

His face is a mask of barely restrained fury. "Tell me everything."

So I do. I tell him about the black pickup truck with tinted windows that nearly ran me down as I was coming out of the police station, and how it happened again in a Walmart parking lot barely an hour after I reported the first attempt. I tell him about the fire at the local motel where I booked a room to avoid sleeping in the apartment, and about a van that nearly ran me off the road once I was already on the run. I tell him about my narrow miss at an Airbnb in Omaha, where I stopped for some much-needed rest a couple of weeks ago, only to end up escaping through the window in the middle of the night when I heard scratching noises at the door.

"The lock. They were picking it." Nikolai's jaw is clenched tight. "If you hadn't woken up—"

"Yes. And there were other instances where I thought they might've been close, like the time I spotted a black pickup with tinted windows pulling up to a gas station just as I was pulling out. I was so paranoid by then, though, that it could've been my imagination. Or maybe not. Maybe it was them. I don't know. All I know is they kept coming after me, and the only thing I could do was keep moving. That is, until I ran out of money."

"Which is when you came across my ad."

"Yes." I swallow thickly. "I'm sorry, Nikolai. I really am. I wasn't thinking straight when I applied for the position. I was down to a few dollars, and I was terrified because they'd just found me again, and they were getting bolder, shooting at me in broad daylight. I'll leave, I swear I will. You don't even need to pay me for the week. I'll find another job and—"

"What the fuck are you talking about?" Jerking up to his feet, he props his fists on the table and leans in. His voice is harsh. "I told you, you're not going anywhere."

I scramble to my feet and back away. "Nikolai, please. I really *am* sorry. I didn't mean to endanger your family. I'll go today. Right now. Before they figure out I'm here and…" My heart climbs into my throat as he advances on me, eyes like fire and brimstone. "Please. I swear I—"

His hands close around my upper arms in an iron grip. "You're not leaving," he growls, and yanking me toward him, he crushes his lips to mine.

43

NIKOLAI

I DEVOUR HER MOUTH WITH ALL THE FURY AND FEAR inside me, all the hunger I've been holding back. So much makes sense now: her starved appearance and her lumberjack appetite, the puncture wounds on her arm and the nightmares that assault her every night. For weeks, they've hunted her, seeking to exterminate her, snuff her out of existence, and on that day in Boise, they nearly succeeded.

A couple of inches to the right, and the bullet would've torn through her skull.

The entire flight home, I shook with rage, and that was before I knew the rest of it. Before I knew how many times she came close to dying. If she hadn't woken up to hear the locks getting picked, or jumped out of the way of that pickup truck... Fuck, if she'd just so much as breathed louder in that coat closet, she wouldn't be here today.

I wouldn't be holding her, tasting her.

I wouldn't know what it's like to have found the other half of my soul.

Her head falls back under the brutal pressure of my lips, her hands clutching desperately at my arms, and I know I should slow down, be gentle, but I can't. Whatever restraint I'd possessed is gone, burned to ash in the fires of my fury, decimated by my fear for her.

There was so little of what she told me in Konstantin's report, so many suspicious blanks in the police files he'd pulled for me. No mention of the two masked men in her mother's apartment, nothing about the attempted hit-and-runs. Even her emails to the journalists, the ones Konstantin's hackers found in her sent folder, don't appear to have reached their destination, as if someone has had her messages blocked or marked as spam. And then there are all the erased and damaged tapes, likely those that would've served as proof of the other attempts on her life.

Someone went to enormous trouble to kill her mother and cover their tracks, someone with massive resources, and the fact that I don't know who it is eats at me like acid.

Breathing hard, I wrench my mouth away from hers and meet her dazed gaze. "You're not leaving."

I wasn't going to let her go before, but now that I know she's in mortal danger, I will do whatever it takes to keep her here. I will literally chain her to me if I have to.

She blinks up at me, her kiss-swollen lips parting. "But—"

"But nothing. I don't want to hear it again. You're mine now, understand?" My voice is harsh, guttural. I'm frightening her, I can see it, but I can't stop myself, can't place the beast back on its leash.

She opens her mouth to respond, but I don't let her. Roughly, I slide my hand into her hair and grip a fistful, holding her still as I swoop in for another deep, marauding kiss. There's something dark and twisted in the way I need her, in this compulsion I feel to claim her. My hunger for her emanates from the deepest, most savage part of me, one that I've done my best to hide from her and from the world at large... one that my sister saw that awful winter night, much to her detriment.

Chloe is right to be wary of me.

I'm not a normal, gentle man.

Civilization is just another suit I wear.

She stiffens under my assault at first, but after a moment, her body softens against mine, her arms wrapping around my neck as she gives in to the heated need consuming us. She embraces me as I fuck her with my tongue and eat at her soft, lush lips, holds on to me as I bear her down to the table, my hands roaming greedily over her hips, her ribcage, the small, plump mounds of her breasts.

Her dress is in the way, so I tear it open at the bodice, too impatient to figure out all the hooks and zippers. She's braless underneath, and her breasts spill into my hands, round and perfect, tipped by gorgeous brown nipples. My mouth waters at the sight, and I bend my head, sucking one into my mouth. It tastes like salt and berries, like everything I've never known I craved, and as she arches into me with a gasping cry, her small hands fisting in my hair, I know I'll never get enough of her.

It's utterly impossible.

My cock is so hard it hurts, my balls tight against my body as I switch my focus to the other nipple, sucking it in deep before biting down with calculated force. She cries out again, her nails digging into my skull, and I soothe the sting with gentle strokes of my tongue before delivering another bite of pain.

She's panting now, writhing underneath me, and I know I was right about her, about our compatibility in this regard. The beast in me calls to its mirror image in her, heightening the dark chemistry between us. Pain and pleasure, violence and lust—they've coexisted since the dawn of time, feeding on one another, forming a sensual symphony like no other.

A symphony that I intend to play with her.

Releasing her nipple, I move down her body, ripping her dress in half along the way. It was a fine, pretty dress, but I'll buy her another. I'll buy her everything, take care of her every need. She'll never go hungry, will never know want again. Because she's mine now, her body and her mind, her secrets and her fears and her desires.

I want it all from her.

Gripping her hands, I pin them at her sides as I trail burning kisses over her heaving ribcage, her flat belly, the vulnerable V under her navel. She's wearing a white thong, and I rip it off as well, then pin her hands again as I continue my oral exploration of her body. It's beautiful, all slim and toned, her bronze skin like warm silk under my lips. The hair on her pussy is delicate and fine, as if it's just growing out after a waxing, and jealousy sears me like hellbroth as I imagine her grooming herself for an ex-boyfriend... for some man who isn't me.

Never again.

No one else will ever touch her.

I will eviscerate any man who tries.

Her breaths speed up as my lips approach her sex, the muscles in her thighs tightening even as her legs part and her hips rise off the table. She wants this, badly, and though I'm dying to taste her fully, I prolong her torment by nuzzling just the outside of her tender folds, breathing in her scent and letting the anticipation build.

"Nikolai, please..." Her voice quivers, her hands flexing in my grasp as I kiss and lick at the seam of her slit, giving her just a fraction more. "Oh God, please, just—" She gasps as my tongue finally delves between her folds, and I lap at the creamy evidence of her desire, tasting her sweet, rich essence. She's everything I've imagined, everything I've ever wanted, and my cock throbs violently with the need to be inside her, to slide deep into her tight, wet heat. Instead, I find her clit and greedily attack it, alternately sucking and licking, and as she comes with a choked cry, I push two fingers into her spasming flesh, intensifying her orgasm and preparing her for what's to come.

Because I won't be gentle when I take her.

I can't be.

Not this time.

44

CHLOE

Aftershocks are still rippling through my body when I open my eyes to find Nikolai leaning over me, one hand propped on the table next to me and the other possessively cupping my sex, two long, thick fingers buried inside me. His eyes are narrowed fiercely, his jaw taut. "I'm going to fuck you now." His voice is hard and guttural, dangerously savage. "Do you understand?"

I do. It's a warning as much as a statement of fact.

This is happening, and there's no going back.

The sane part of me wants to run, to shrink back from the dark intensity in his stare, even as something twisted in me revels in his loss of control, in the raw, unvarnished hunger on his face. His smooth black hair is disheveled from my fingers, his lips glistening with my wetness, and the top buttons on his shirt are missing, as if he's ripped them off.

This is not the elegant, sophisticated man who mandates rigid meal times.

It's the feral being I've sensed lurking underneath.

"I..." I wet my lips, my body clenching on his fingers. "I understand."

His jaw flexes violently, and then he's on me, his lips and tongue consuming me as his fingers thrust deeper, finding a spot that makes sparks dance at the edges of my vision. He tastes like the forest, primal and wild, his cedar-and-bergamot scent mixing with the musky undertone of my arousal. Gasping into his mouth, I arch against him, clutching at his sides as he starts to fuck me with those fingers, driving them into me with a hard, relentless rhythm that makes tension skyrocket in my core. I can feel the orgasm barreling at me with the speed of a runaway locomotive, and then it's crashing over me, blasting me with white-hot, dizzying pleasure.

Panting, I sprawl bonelessly on the hard surface of the table, but Nikolai's not done with me. Before I can recover, he pulls out his fingers and pushes away from me. Forcing open my heavy eyelids, I watch as he pulls down his zipper and rolls a condom onto his erection.

A very large erection.

I was right about his size. He's bigger than any guy I've known.

A frisson of purely feminine alarm snakes through me, but he's already over me, gripping my wrists to pin them above my head as he claims my lips in another scorching kiss. The broad, thick head of his cock prods at my entrance, and finding it, presses in.

I'm wet and soft from the two orgasms, but the stretch still burns, my body struggling to accommodate his size as he slides deeper. A sound of distress escapes my throat, and he stills, lifting his head.

Breathing heavily, we stare at each other, and unbidden, his words come to me. Crazy words, about predestination and threads of fate… about the inevitability of us. I still don't know if I believe it, but I can't deny the powerful connection that thrums between us, can't refute that this feels more like bonding than mere sex.

He must feel it too, because the savage fire in his eyes intensifies and his grip on my wrists tightens. "Yes, zaychik…" His voice is a deep, dark rasp. "You're mine now."

And with a heavy push, he thrusts in all the way.

The shock of the invasion is still reverberating through my body as he begins to move, his eyes locked on mine. His strokes are ruthless, so hard and deep they hurt, but the pain is soon edged out by a darker kind of pleasure, one that's only partially related to the fresh tension coiling in my core. Each merciless thrust slams his pelvis against mine, pressing on my clit, but it's the look in his eyes that drives my arousal higher and sends another orgasm blasting through me.

It's a look of possessiveness, complete and total, mixed with something dangerously tender and intense.

He comes a few moments after I do, still holding my

gaze, and my heart pounds wildly as I watch his gorgeous face contort with the pleasure-pain of his release as he grinds into me, emptying himself deep inside my body.

It's the most intimate thing I've ever experienced, and the most beautiful.

Our bodies are still joined, my wrists held captive in his grasp, when he lowers his head and presses the softest, sweetest kiss to my lips, then lays his cheek against mine, his warm breath washing over my bare shoulder. I want my hands free so I can hold him, but this feels right too, comforting in some strange way. The table is cold and hard under my back, my inner flesh throbbing from his rough possession, but I feel utterly at peace, my rapid breathing slowing as every remnant of tension drains from my body.

I could lie like that for hours, days, weeks, but after a few long moments, he stirs, raising his head to look at me with a tender smile. Releasing my wrists, he carefully withdraws from me and pushes up to stand. "You okay, zaychik?" he murmurs, running a warm, callused palm over my arm, and I nod, blushing as I sit up.

"More than okay," I admit, pulling together the edges of my torn dress as he disposes of the condom in a trashcan by the desk.

"Good," he says softly, zipping up his pants. "Because we're far from done."

And scooping me up against his chest, he carries me out of the office.

45

CHLOE

I HALF EXPECT TO RUN INTO ALINA OR LYUDMILA, BUT we make it to Nikolai's bedroom without encountering anyone. It's a huge relief, given the state of my dress—and, I realize as I catch a glimpse of us in a mirror, my face and hair.

With my lips swollen from his kisses and my hair wild, I don't just look freshly fucked.

I look ravished.

And that's pretty much how I feel as he lays me down on his king-sized bed and begins to strip, volcanic heat kindling anew in his golden eyes. I don't know if I'm up for more so soon, especially with the questions raised by the video hanging over us, but when he's fully naked, his magnificent body bared to my gaze, I can't find the will to protest as he climbs over me and takes my lips in a deep, tenderly erotic kiss.

It's a lovemaking this time, not a fucking. He

worships every inch of my body, bringing me to another orgasm with his lips and tongue before carefully sheathing himself in my sore flesh. Somehow, I manage to come again alongside him, and then, exhausted, I lie in his arms like a ragdoll before drifting off to sleep.

———

I wake up to the feel of being submerged in warm water. Blinking my eyes open, I realize we're both half-lying in a bubble bath, with Nikolai spooning me from underneath so I don't slip in and drown.

"Relax, zaychik," he murmurs in my ear, running a soapy sponge over my breasts and stomach. "Close your eyes, let me take care of you."

He doesn't need to ask twice. After the sleepless night I've had and with my body jellified by all those orgasms, I'm already drifting off to dreamland. Vaguely, I'm aware of him washing me all over, then lifting me out of the tub and wrapping a big, fluffy towel around me. At that point, I wake up enough to ask for privacy to use the bathroom, and then I stumble off to bed, where he's waiting for me with a tray of food.

Sleepily, I let him feed me grapes, cheese, and various spreads on crackers—since we missed dinner in favor of sex and all—and then I pass out in his embrace, feeling safe, secure, and cared for.

Feeling like I've found my new home.

46

CHLOE

WE MAKE LOVE TWICE MORE THROUGHOUT THE NIGHT, with Nikolai giving me two orgasms each time, and by morning, I'm so sore I can't move, yet so satisfied it's worth it. Of course it's possible I can't move because his heavy arm is slung across my ribcage, securing me to him as he sleeps—almost like a child with a teddy bear.

Grinning at the incongruous thought, I carefully wriggle out of his embrace and tiptoe into the adjoining bathroom, where I find a brand-new toothbrush considerately laid out for me. Trying to be as quiet as possible, I brush my teeth and take care of business, then put on a huge, soft robe I find hanging on the door. It's obviously his, but hopefully, he won't mind if I wear it long enough to get back to my room.

He did destroy my dress, after all.

The thought is both disturbing and exhilarating, my

pulse speeding up when I think about how he reacted when I proposed leaving. I don't know what I'd thought his reaction would be when he learned of my predicament, but it wasn't that.

Nothing is resolved between us, but there's one thing I now know for sure, and it fills me with immense gratitude and hope.

Despite the danger I've brought with me, Nikolai doesn't want me gone.

I'm not surprised to find him still asleep when I return to the bedroom. Between the jet lag and the long flight—plus all that sex—he must be exhausted. Holding up the sides of the robe to prevent it from dragging on the floor, I pad quietly toward the door, but as I'm passing by the bed, I can't resist the urge to stop and stare at my new lover.

Because that's what my gorgeous, mysterious Russian employer is now.

My lover.

Covered by a blanket up to his waist, he's lying half on his side, half on his back, face turned partially toward me and one muscled arm folded above his head. Some men look younger in repose, softer, but not Nikolai. Sleep only enhances that dangerous, animalistic quality I've sensed in him—even as it heightens his striking male beauty. With those intense eyes closed, I can see just how long and thick his jet-black lashes are, how sharply carved his cheekbones. His lips are slightly parted, but even in this relaxed state, there's something cynical in their curve, a wicked sensuality in the way their softness contrasts with the hint of stubble darkening the hard, molded lines of his jaw.

I could stand and stare at him for a solid hour, but that would be creepy, and in any case, I need to get back to my room and get dressed before the rest of the household wakes up. I don't know what time it is, but judging by the soft light seeping through the blinds, it's not long after sunrise—which makes sense, given how early I fell asleep last night.

With one last look at sleeping Nikolai, I tiptoe out of the room. As I hoped, nobody's around, the house completely silent as I make my way to my bedroom. I'm not particularly embarrassed by what happened—sooner or later, everyone will know we're dating—but Nikolai and I need to talk about it first, along with everything else.

I still feel terrible about endangering him and his family, and it's only the knowledge that they have all those guards and security measures that's preventing me from jumping into my car and fleeing anyway. Well, that and the fact that I still don't have my car keys.

I'm going to seriously insist they get a locksmith here ASAP.

Stepping into my room, I close the door behind me and am about to take off the robe when I spot the figure on my bed.

My heart leaps into my throat, even as I recognize who it is.

"Did you and Kolya have a nice fuck?" Alina asks,

rising to her feet—and as she comes unsteadily toward me, barefoot and wearing only a sheer peignoir, I see the overly bright glitter of her eyes and realize she's on something.

Something way stronger than pot.

47

CHLOE

"WHAT ARE YOU DOING HERE?" I DEMAND, MY HEART rate kicking higher as she stops in front of me, swaying. If I had any doubts about her state, they dissolve as I take in her huge black pupils and smell the sickly sweet odor of her breath. For the first time since I've known Nikolai's sister, she's not wearing makeup, and her beautiful face is pale and puffy, her green eyes red-rimmed and underlined by shadows.

"I was waiting for you." Her pretty lips are bloodless as they stretch into an uneven smile. "My brother wanted you to get paid for the first week by noon yesterday, but I didn't feel well enough to get out of bed until later in the evening, so that's when I came by to drop that off." She waves a careless hand at the thick envelope sitting on the nightstand.

"You've been here *all night?*"

She laughs, a too-bright peal of a sound. "Don't be silly. I dropped off the envelope and left. But I couldn't sleep, so I swung by to check on you again this morning—and you still weren't here. So..." Her gaze falls to my robe. "Did you have a nice time fucking my brother? Rumor has it, he's got mad skills."

Heat invades my face. "I think you better leave."

"I will. Just tell me, Chloe... Have you already fallen for him? Did that handsome face of his fool you into thinking he's your knight in shining armor, after all?"

I take a deep breath. "Alina, listen... I don't know what beef you have with your brother, but I think it's best if we talk when you're feeling better. Nikolai and I *have* started dating, but that doesn't mean—"

She sways toward me. "Poor child. He did fool you, didn't he?"

"Uh-huh." I grip her shoulders, steadying her; then I turn her around and march her toward the door. "We'll talk more about this later."

She twists out of my hold. "You don't understand. I'm trying to help you." Her glassy eyes are wide, imploring. "You need to listen to me. He's just like *him*."

I shouldn't listen to anything she says in this state, but I can't help myself. "Him?"

"Our father. Kolya is his carbon copy, in *all* ways." She grips the lapels of my robe. "Do you understand? He's a monster, a killer. He—" She stops, her face turning even paler as she realizes what she's said.

Releasing my robe, she backs away as I stare at her, my stomach churning as every suspicion I've ever entertained about the Molotovs surfaces like a poisoned cork in a well. Alina is clearly out of her mind, but to call her brother a killer?

That's not an accusation one throws around for no reason, even when drunk or high.

She's already reaching for the door handle when I shake off my shock-induced paralysis and dash after her. "What are you talking about?" Grabbing her arm, I spin her around to face me. "What the fuck are you talking about?"

She's shaking her head, tears leaking out of the corners of her eyes. "Nothing. It's nothing. Forget it. I just... didn't want you to end up like her."

"Her?"

"Just leave, Chloe. Go before it's too late."

I grit my teeth. "I can't. Pavel lost my car keys. But even if I had them, there's no way I'd just—"

"I found them. In Kolya's nightstand drawer."

I step back, reeling. "What? When?"

"Yesterday morning, when I went into Kolya's room to get the cash for you." Her jade-green eyes look haunted. "That's when I knew."

A chill wraps around my spine. "Knew what?"

Ignoring my question, she steps around me and unsteadily makes her way to the bed, where she starts digging through the folds of the blanket. "Here." She holds up a pair of keys on a pink, furry keychain. "That's another reason I came here—to give this to you."

The sick churning in my stomach intensifies. She's lying. She must be lying. She could've found the keys anywhere, wherever it was that Pavel had lost them. Because if she's not lying, if they were in Nikolai's nightstand yesterday morning, then they were never lost. That or Nikolai found them before leaving for his trip—before our video chat in which he claimed Pavel couldn't locate them.

As if reading my mind, Alina says unevenly, "Pavel doesn't lose things, by the way. I've known him all my life, and he's never misplaced so much as a holey sock —at least not by accident. He's like my brother in that regard. Whatever he does is planned."

My heart pounds at my ribcage like a mallet. "Give me the keys." Stepping toward her, I snatch them from her hand and stuff them into the robe's pocket. My mind is racing, my thoughts tumbling over each other like pieces of colored glass in a kaleidoscope. I don't know what to think, what to believe.

Why would Nikolai lie about my keys?

Why would Alina?

"What did you mean when you called your brother a killer?" I ask, staring into her drug-clouded eyes. "Who is this *her*?"

Her face crumples. "You don't want this. Believe me, you don't."

"I do. Tell me."

She shakes her head, more tears leaking from her eyes.

"Alina, please... I have to know. I have to know because—because you're right. I—" I suck in a breath, my chest tightening as the truth sinks its fangs into me. "I *am* falling for him, and fast."

Her shoulders shake with silent sobs as she sinks to the floor, her back against the bed and her long hair falling forward to hide her face as she hugs her knees.

Desperate, I kneel in front of her. "Please, Alina. I have to know. How's he like your father? How's he a monster? What happened? Who is he supposed to have killed?"

For several long moments, there's no response. Finally, she lifts her head, and through the black veil of her hair, I see the screaming agony in her eyes. "Our father." The words come out in a broken, ragged whisper. "He killed her. And then Kolya killed him. Sliced him open, right there—" Her voice cracks. "Right in front of me."

And as I stare at her, mute with horror, she buries her face against her knees and cries.

48

CHLOE

My stomach is a pit of ice and churning acid, my fingers numb and clumsy as I stuff my old clothes into my suitcase. Alina is on my bed, passed out, the drugs and the sleepless night having finally taken their toll.

I don't know where I'm going or what I'm doing; I just know I have to leave. Right now. Before Nikolai wakes up. Truth or lies, reality or madness, I stand no chance of sorting it all out while I'm here, under his roof and at his mercy, with that overpowering chemistry simmering between us, dragging me deeper under his lethal spell.

I'm not sure what I'd thought I'd hear from Alina. An admission that they're mafia, after all? And maybe they are. At this point, nothing would surprise me. From the beginning, my instincts have been warning me about Nikolai, and I should've heeded them.

I should've listened to that voice inside my head.

You're not leaving.

Yesterday, his fervently uttered statement seemed romantic, if somewhat autocratic, his possessiveness a turn-on rather than reason for alarm. But now, with Alina's revelations ringing in my ears and my no-longer-lost keys jabbing my leg through the pocket of my jeans, I can't help but view his words in a different, infinitely more sinister light.

Was he never going to return the keys to me?

Have I been a de facto prisoner all along?

Frantically, I throw in the last of my clothes and zip the suitcase, then slip on my old sneakers and grab the envelope with the cash from the nightstand, stuffing it into my pocket. My heart is pounding so hard I'm sick from it, or maybe I'm just plain heartsick.

I just... didn't want you to end up like her.

I still have no idea to whom Alina was referring; after the slicing-open bit, she became incoherent, sobbing until she passed out from exhaustion—and no wonder. It sounds as if she's witnessed Nikolai murdering their father, and maybe this mysterious "her" as well. An ex-girlfriend of his? Or worse, their mother? Or was the "he killed her" part referring to their father, who's allegedly also a monster?

I strain my memory to recall any mention of how Nikolai and Alina's parents died, but there was nothing in the Russian articles I came across. Nikolai did react strongly when I asked about his parents that one time, but I attributed it to grief. But what if there's more to it? What if there's guilt and anger, the self-loathing of a man who's done the unforgivable, committed the most heinous of crimes?

I don't know if I believe it of Nikolai. I don't want to believe it. Despite the darkness I've sensed in him, despite his savage hunger for me, I felt safe in his embrace last night. His roughness had been tempered with tenderness, his strength carefully leashed. And the way he cared for me afterward, washing me, feeding me, holding me so tenderly …

Is a monster capable of caring?

Can a psychopath fake emotion so well?

Maybe nothing Alina said is true. Maybe it's a ploy to make me leave, to break up a relationship she's disapproved of from the beginning. Maybe if I talk to Nikolai, he'll explain everything, prove to me that Alina is simply ill, out of her mind with all those drugs.

It's a tempting thought, so tempting that as I'm stepping out of my room, I stop and glance longingly down the hallway, where the door to Nikolai's bedroom is still firmly shut. I want to trust him so badly, and under different circumstances, I would. If we were a regular couple hooking up in an apartment in a city, I would march down that hallway and demand an explanation, hear his side of the story before deciding what to do. But I can't take that risk, not when I'm so completely in his power on this remote, highly secure estate.

Nobody knows I'm here.

Nobody will know or care if I disappear for good.

The only reasonable thing to do is to go now, to

leave and assess the situation from a distance. Once I'm in a motel somewhere, I can reach out to Nikolai, let him know what happened and why I left. We can talk it out over email or on the phone, and I can do some more online digging, see if I can find out anything about his parents' deaths.

This doesn't have to be forever, just for now.

Just until I know the truth.

Still, my heart feels agonizingly heavy as I carry my suitcase down the stairs and to the garage entrance in the back. Not only will I miss Slava, but the mere possibility that I might never see Nikolai again fills me with cold, hollow dread. So does the knowledge that I'm going out there, where my mom's killers are still hunting me. But I've evaded them before, and I have to believe that I'll be able to do so again—especially with all that cash on hand. When I fled Boston, all I had were a couple of twenties in my wallet, plus the five hundred I withdrew from an ATM before ditching my debit card along with everything else that could be tracked.

It's going to be fine.

I'll make it.

I have to believe that.

Swallowing the growing knot in my throat, I approach my car and throw my suitcase into the trunk. Then I press the button to open the garage door and watch it lift silently. No slow, noisy mechanisms here, thank God. As quietly as I can, I start the car and back out of the garage, then steer around the house to the driveway.

It takes everything I have to drive down the mountain calmly, sedately, like I'm in no rush. If the guards are watching the road, I can't have them getting suspicious. As is, icy sweat trickles down my back, and my knuckles whiten on the steering wheel as I pull up to the tall metal gate.

What if Nikolai gave them instructions not to let me out?

What if I'm a prisoner here for real?

But the gate slides apart at my approach, and nobody stops me as I drive through. Shaking with relief, I maintain my slow, steady speed for another thirty seconds or so, until I'm out of view, and then I floor the gas, speeding away from the safe haven that just might be the devil's lair.

From the man I yearn for with every fiber of my heart.

49

NIKOLAI

I WAKE UP WITH MY BODY HUMMING WITH CONTENTMENT and my mind filled with greater peace than I've ever known. Last night was everything I thought it would be, and more. I can still feel her, smell her, taste her on my lips. Smiling, I roll over, patting the sheets for her small, warm body, and when my hand encounters nothing but a bunched-up blanket, I open my eyes and survey the room.

Chloe is not here, which is disappointing but not surprising, given the bright sunlight. She's probably already had breakfast and is teaching Slava; maybe they're even out on a hike. Normally, I would've heard her get up—I'm a light sleeper—but I was coming off thirty-plus hours with no sleep and the jet lag kicked my ass hard.

My mood darkens a fraction, my adrenaline levels rising as I think of the video that dominated my thoughts on the flight over, keeping me from getting any shut-eye, and of everything else Chloe told me. The idea that someone out there wants to hurt her, kill her, fills me with incandescent rage, one tempered only by the knowledge that they can't get to her in my compound.

The precautions that keep my family safe from our enemies will keep Chloe safe from hers while I work to figure out who they are.

Eager to get started on that, I get up and fire off an email to Konstantin, detailing everything I learned last night. Then I hop into the shower for a swift rinse, get dressed, and go in search of Chloe.

I start with my son's room. Nobody's there, so I go downstairs. The dining room is empty, but I hear voices from the kitchen, and when I walk in, I'm surprised to find Lyudmila feeding breakfast to Slava all by herself.

He smiles at me shyly, and my chest fills with uncharacteristic warmth as I recall how he greeted me last evening. Even as laser-focused as I'd been on getting answers from Chloe, I couldn't help reacting to that small, sweet voice calling me *Daddy*.

I didn't know how badly I'd yearned to hear it until it happened.

Until *she* made it happen.

"Good morning, Slavochka," I murmur, going down on my haunches in front of his chair. Switching to Russian, I ask, "Did you have a good night?"

He nods, eyes big and wary, and my ribcage tightens with a familiar squeezing pain. I want to step away, end the conversation so I can be rid of the discomfort, but instead, I lean into it, letting myself feel it as I smile gently at my son.

He's so much—too much—like me, but maybe with Chloe in his life, he won't follow in my footsteps.

Maybe he won't grow up hating me the way I hated my old man.

"Where is Chloe?" I ask, and my smile broadens as his eyes brighten at the mention of her name.

"I don't know," he says shyly and glances up at Lyudmila, who's putting berries into his bowl of cream of wheat.

"I haven't seen her this morning," she says. "Maybe she's still sleeping?"

My smile fades, an unpleasant feeling stirring low in my gut. I haven't checked in Chloe's room, but I assumed she left my bed to start her day, not sleep in hers. Rising to my feet, I tell Slava, "I'm going to go find your teacher. You're eager for your English lessons, right?"

He nods vigorously, and I grin at him. On impulse, I ruffle his hair the way I've seen Chloe do it, and ignoring the surprised look on Lyudmila's face, I go back upstairs.

The door to Chloe's room is shut, so I knock and wait a few seconds. When no response comes, I open it and walk in.

The blinds are still closed, blocking most of the daylight, but I can see a small mound on the bed under the covers.

She *is* sleeping, after all.

A tender smile tugs at my lips as I approach the bed and sit down on the edge. She's lying turned away from me, the blanket covering her up to her neck, leaving only her hair spread out on the pillow. For some reason, it looks much darker in this light, the golden streaks missing.

Leaning over her, I lift my hand to gently brush the hair off her face—only to jerk my fingers back as my heart launches into a furious gallop.

"What the fuck are you doing here?" I growl at my sister as she rolls over onto her back and blinks open her eyes. "Where is Chloe?"

She blinks a few more times, then slowly sits up. "What?" she says hoarsely, pushing her hair off her face with an unsteady hand. She smells like a drug cocktail, I realize, my fury growing as she asks dazedly, "What are you doing in my room?"

I jackknife to my feet. "*Your* fucking room?"

She stares up at me. "I don't..." Her eyes sweep the bedroom, and the confusion on her face slowly morphs into horrified comprehension. "Oh, shit. Chloe."

My stomach tightens with an awful premonition, and it takes every shred of restraint I possess not to grab and shake her. "Where the fuck is she? What did you do?"

My sister's spine straightens, her eyes narrowing on my face. "Me? What are *you* doing in her bedroom?"

"Alina," I warn through clenched teeth, and whatever she sees on my face convinces her that she can't fuck with me right now.

"Look, I may have..." She dampens her lips. "I may have told her some things."

"What things?"

"About you and... and our father."

Fuck. "What exactly did you tell her?"

"Probably more than I should've," Alina admits, even as her chin lifts defiantly. "But she deserves to know what she's getting herself into, don't you think?"

My hands flex at my sides, rage pulsing through every cell in my body. If it were anyone but my sister, they'd already be bleeding out. "So you told her... what? That I killed him? Gutted him like a fucking fish?"

She whitens but doesn't look away. "I don't remember, exactly."

Of course she doesn't. She was fucking high—still is, probably.

Leaning over the bed, I yank the blanket off her. This is my fault for babying her, letting her wallow in her weakness. "Get up and get dressed," I bite out as she scrambles back, eyes wide. "We're going to search this place top to bottom, and when we find her, you'll tell her that you made it all up. Every last word, understand?"

"Kolya…" There's a strange note in her voice. "Have you looked in the garage?"

My blood ices over. "What?"

"I found the keys in your bedside drawer," she says defiantly. "And I gave them back to her. She's a person, not a thing, and if she wants to leave, you have no right—"

"You fucking idiot," I whisper, so overcome by rage and terror I can hardly speak. "She's got assassins after her. If she left here and they get to her…"

And as my sister blanches, I pivot on my heel and sprint to the garage.

Sure enough, the Toyota is gone, the garage door raised.

Cursing violently, I run back into the house—only to nearly mow down Lyudmila, who's stepped out of the kitchen to see what the ruckus is about.

"Tell Pavel I need him. Now," I bark into her startled face and race upstairs to my office.

Grabbing my computer, I pull up the footage from the gate cameras and rewind the recording until I see Chloe's car pulling up to the gate. The time stamp reads 7:05 a.m.—well over two hours ago.

By now, she could be anywhere.

She could be dead.

The thought is so unbearable, so paralyzing, that I cease breathing for a moment. Then logic kicks in.

Unless Chloe's enemies were camped out right outside my compound, there's no way they've found her so quickly. And with our infrared drones patrolling the area, my guards would've known it if they were there.

The most likely scenario is that Chloe is fine, albeit freaked out by Alina's revelations. I still have time to find her and get her back here, where she'll be safe.

A fraction calmer, I videocall Konstantin.

"I need you to scan the footage from every camera in a two-hundred-mile radius of my compound for any sighting of Chloe's car in the last two hours," I say as soon as my brother's face fills my screen. "Start with the gas stations—Pavel mentioned the car was low on fuel."

To Konstantin's credit, he doesn't ask any questions. "I'll get my guys right on it."

"Call my phone when you have it. I'll be in the car."

He nods and disconnects.

I call my guards next. "Get Kirilov and come up to the house," I order when Arkash picks up. "Full gear. We're going on a road trip."

I don't expect to run into trouble retrieving Chloe, but only an idiot doesn't prepare for the worst.

"Be there in ten," Arkash replies.

As I hang up, a knock sounds at my door and Pavel comes in.

"The girl?" he asks tersely, and I nod, already striding toward the wall in the back.

I press my palm to a hidden panel, and a section of

the wall slides away, revealing a small room full of weapons and battle gear—the main armory in the house.

"Gear up," I tell him, stripping off my shirt. "We're going to get her back."

I put on a bulletproof vest and button my shirt over it to avoid looking conspicuous. Pavel does the same, and we each strap on several weapons.

If we do run into trouble, we'll be ready.

Kirilov and Arkash are already pulling up to the house in an armored SUV when we step outside. Pavel and I jump into the backseat, and we tear down the driveway, gravel flying. I don't have a concrete destination in mind, but there's only one road leading down the mountain, and wherever Chloe is by the time Konstantin calls me, we'll be closer to her than if we stay here and wait. Besides, we can start with the nearby gas stations as well, see if someone might've spotted Chloe at one of them.

"What happened?" Pavel asks quietly as we clear the gate. "Why did she leave?"

My upper lip curls. "Alina."

"Ah." He falls silent then, staring out the window, and I do the same, trying to ignore the heavy thudding in my chest—and the growing pain of betrayal spreading through it.

My zaychik ran.

She left me.

Just like that, without so much as a goodbye.

It's unreasonable to feel this way, I know. I *am* the

kind of man she should fear and despise. Whatever my sister told her in her drugged-out state must've painted me in the worst possible light, but that doesn't mean Alina's story is untrue.

I did kill our father in front of her.

Still, Chloe's desertion hurts. She gave herself to me. She came willingly into my arms. Last night was so much more than sex, our connection so deep I feel it in my bones. But she must not. Because if she did, she would've known I'd never harm her; she would've trusted me to protect her. The fact that she'd rather be out there, facing mortal danger, speaks volumes about her opinion of me.

She's afraid of me.

She thinks I'm a monster.

My jaw hardens, a dark resolve settling in as the car picks up speed. I should've kept those keys in a safe, not my nightstand—and I definitely should've warned the guards not to open the gate for her car. It didn't occur to me that she'd run after last night, but it should've—and I won't make that mistake again.

When I get her back, she's not leaving.

I won't let her.

I'll do whatever it takes to keep her safe.

The first gas station we stop at is manned by a pale, pimply twenty-something with a hint of a beer belly.

"Nope, haven't seen her," he says after peering at

Chloe's picture. "Cute chick, though. What's her deal? She part-Asian? Latina?"

"What about a blue Toyota Corolla circa late nineties?" I ask softly, and whatever the guy sees on my face causes him to lose what little color he possesses. "Any car like that stop by?"

"No, sorry, man." He gulps. "I would've seen it. I've only had two other customers today."

I glance at Pavel, and he jerks his chin toward the exit.

Like me, he doesn't think the guy is lying.

The next closest gas station is the one by the town. A white-haired cashier looks up from a newspaper as Pavel and I walk in, her rheumy gaze sharpening as she takes in our appearance.

I approach the counter and pull out Chloe's photo. "Have you seen this girl? Or a blue Corolla circa late nineties?"

The old woman puts on a pair of glasses and carefully examines the photo before looking up at me. "You two cops or something?" she asks in a croaky voice.

I rein in my impatience with effort. "Or something. Have you seen her this morning or not?"

"Not this morning, no." She squints up at me through her glasses. "Would you look at that pretty face… just like one of them magazines. And so nicely dressed, too. You her boyfriend, dearie?"

My hand tightens on the edge of the counter. "When did you see her?"

"Oh, about a week ago. She stopped by to get gas, asked about a job listing in the paper. I haven't seen her since, and I told them that."

Ice fills my chest. "Them?"

"Two fellas, about your height. Came by yesterday, late in the day. Showed me her picture and all. I told them I only saw her that one time, and I have no idea where she went—"

"What did they look like, exactly?" Pavel cuts in as I stand frozen, my mind racing a mile a second.

They're here.

They know she was here.

Worse yet, they know she was looking at my job listing.

"The two fellas? Well, tall, like I said. One's got dark hair, a little lighter than his"—she waves at me—"the other's more like you. You know, salt and pepper, except kind of balding."

Pavel's jaw tightens. "Age? Race? Body build?"

"Caucasian. Thirties—forties for the older one, maybe. Kind of big and muscular." She looks me up and down. "Not as pretty as him, that's for sure."

"Anything else?" Pavel demands. "Tattoos, scars? What were they wearing?"

"Jeans, I think. Or khakis? I don't remember for sure. Black or gray shirts, maybe navy blue. Something dark. No scars, I don't think. Oh, but"—she brightens—"the older one had a tattoo on the inside of his wrist. I saw the edge of it under his sleeve."

"Did they ask about the job listing?" I ask, keeping

my voice even despite the rage and fear pounding through me.

I have to know how bad the situation is, how close they are to finding her.

The woman nods. "Sure did. Wanted to know all about it, who and what and where. I told them I don't know for sure, but it was probably that old Jamieson property up in the mountains, the one that was bought out by that rich Russian. Say"—she squints up at Pavel —"where's that accent of yours from? You boys wouldn't happen to be from—"

"Thank you," I say tersely and pull out my phone to call Konstantin as we hurry back to the car.

As soon as my brother picks up, I rattle off the description we've gotten and demand an update on the search.

It's infinitely more urgent that we find Chloe now, before the assassins do.

"Nothing yet," Konstantin says. "In fact— Wait a minute. Let me call you back. I think we just got a hit."

I was about to jump into the SUV, but now I pace in front of it, my adrenaline levels climbing with each passing second.

We may already be too late.

They know about my compound and Chloe's interest in it.

Maybe they weren't camped out by the gate when she drove out, but they couldn't have been far.

Spinning around, I rap on the window next to

Pavel. "Get a medical team over to the compound," I tell him tersely. "We might need it."

My phone vibrates in my pocket, and I snatch it up. "Yeah?"

"No sightings, but we got a partially erased tape," Konstantin reports. "Same digital signature as the others. Two hours wiped out—and it looks like it was done about a half hour ago. If I had to guess, I'd say they've caught her scent and don't want anyone to know that."

I'm already halfway inside the car. "Where's the tape from?"

"A gas station some forty miles west of you. I'll send you the coordinates."

I hang up and order Kirilov to hit the gas.

50

CHLOE

THE ROAD BLURS IN FRONT OF MY EYES FOR THE umpteenth time, and I jerkily wipe at the wetness on my cheeks. I don't know why I can't stop the tears from coming, why my chest aches like I've just lost Mom all over again. The banana I picked up at a gas station is lying on the passenger seat, half-eaten, and though it's the only food I've had today, the thought of taking another bite makes me want to vomit.

I'm driving blindly again, heading nowhere. I must've been in shock for the first couple of hours because I can barely recall how I got here. I know I filled up the car somewhere, because the fuel gauge shows the tank is full, but I have only a vague recollection of walking into a dingy store and paying. The banana came from there, I'm sure—I grabbed it on autopilot—but I don't remember eating it, though I must have.

I'm pretty sure they don't sell half-eaten fruit, even at the dingiest of gas stations.

The road ahead of me slopes up and curves sharply, and I force myself to concentrate. The last thing I need is to drive off a cliff. As is, I feel like that's more or less what I'm doing with every mile of distance I'm putting between myself and Nikolai.

I did the right thing, the smart thing.

I keep telling myself that, but it doesn't help, doesn't lessen the feeling that I've made a terrible mistake. It's only been a few hours since I left, yet I miss him so acutely it's as if we've been apart for months. When he was away on the business trip, I knew I'd see him again, knew we'd speak each evening, but there's no such certainty now.

He may refuse to talk to me when I call him.

He may be so angry that I left he won't want me to return.

Now that I'm out here, away from the compound, Alina's revelations seem even more like the ramblings of an ill, drugged-out mind, and though I can't dismiss them entirely, I shudder at the thought of confronting Nikolai and asking whether he did, in fact, kill his father.

What innocent man wouldn't be insulted by that query?

What boyfriend wouldn't be furious that his girlfriend believed such monstrous lies?

I should've stayed. Fuck, I should've stayed. Even if it felt risky at the time, I should've given Nikolai a fair hearing. The keys prove nothing. Alina could've had them all along; she could've even stolen them from Pavel. If Nikolai wanted to deprive me of my freedom, there are all kinds of other actions he could've taken—like telling the guards not to let me out.

And that's the thing, I realize with a start. That's why what seemed so rational when I was packing feels like such an awful error now. It's because the moment I drove through the gate, I got proof that I *could* leave, that Nikolai didn't plan to keep me there with some sinister intentions. I'd been too panicky to realize it at first, but the farther I drove, the deeper that knowledge settled, the consequences of my impulsive actions weighing on me more with every passing mile.

I should've turned back hours ago.

In fact, I should've done it the moment I cleared the gate.

I cast a frantic glance around me. Trees and cliffs everywhere. I'm deep in the mountains again, the road in front of me so narrow it's barely two lanes. I can't do a U-turn here; it would be suicide to try.

Clutching the wheel tighter, I keep driving—and finally, I see it.

A little extra space to the left of where the road curves.

I look in the mirror, then straight ahead and back.

Nothing. No cars. I'm all alone.

Braking hard, I make an illegal U-turn and head back.

I'm twenty minutes into my return trip and desperately trying to remember if I need to turn right or left at the upcoming intersection when a black pickup truck turns onto the road, coming toward me.

A chill ripples down my spine, the fine hair on the back of my neck rising.

It could be my paranoia working overtime again, but those tinted windows look familiar.

There's no time to second-guess myself; in another thirty seconds, we'll be passing next to each other. With a sharp tug on the wheel, I swing the car onto a small dirt road leading up the mountain to my right, and slam on the gas, ignoring the complaining whine from the Corolla's ancient motor.

If it's not them, they won't follow me.

I'll feel like an idiot, but better that than dead.

My heart thumps violently against my ribcage, each second marked by half a dozen beats as my gaze flits between the rearview mirror and the steep, pothole-filled road ahead. *Please don't let it be them. Please don't let it—*

The pickup truck appears in the mirror, its dark shape gaining on me swiftly.

I push the gas pedal to the floor, my breath coming in jagged gasps as my car bounces over a series of potholes. Adrenaline sloshes in my veins, ratcheting up my pulse until all I can hear is its roar in my ears.

Pop!

My right side mirror explodes, and my terror doubles as I catch sight of a man leaning out the truck's passenger-side window, gun in hand. Instinctively, I jerk the wheel left, and the next bullet shatters the back window and punches a hole in the windshield, barely a foot from my head.

The third bullet whines past my shoulder, and I taste death. I feel its icy, scaly fingers. It's everything left undone, unsaid, all the things that won't come to pass. It's Nikolai whispering into my ear how much he wants me, loves me, and Slava giggling as he hugs me tight. It's the bitter knowledge that these men will get away with this, like they did with Mom's murder, and regret that no one will ever know how I died.

A fourth bullet pierces the seat an inch from my right side, and I jerk on the wheel again, desperate to avoid the inevitable, to live at least a second longer. The pickup is right behind me now, looming over my Corolla like a black mountain, and as I try to swerve out of the next bullet's path, its bumper rams into mine, hard, making my head whip forward.

Pop!

Fire punches through my upper arm, the sensation so sharp and sudden it doesn't hurt at first. Instead, I feel something hot and wet slide down my arm as the truck slams into my car again, making it shudder from the massive jolt. The pain hits me then, a nauseating wave of it, and with the desperation of a dying animal, I jerk off my seat belt and push open my door.

Pop!

What remains of the windshield shatters as I hit the dirt so hard air whooshes out of my lungs. Stunned, I roll twice before landing on my back and watching in dazed horror as the truck rams one last time into my Corolla, forcing it off the road and squashing it against a thick tree. With an earsplitting screech of metal crushing metal, the old car crumples, and then, just like in the movies, catches fire. The truck immediately backs up, and some remnant of strength propels me to my feet.

Run, Chloe.

Dragging in a wheezing breath, I lurch toward the trees on legs that feel like broken matches, my knees threatening to buckle with each step I take. My foot catches on a root, and pain shoots through my left ankle—the same ankle I twisted hiding in Mom's closet —but I just clench my teeth and force my strides to lengthen, ignoring the hot blood dripping down my arm and the dizziness washing over me in waves. I can't give up, not if I want to live, so I keep going, keep limping forward at a zombie-like half-jog, half-run.

A male voice yells something behind me, and I force myself to pick up speed, ragged sobs sawing between my lips as another bullet whizzes past my ear, splintering a branch in front of me.

"Fucking bitch!"

Some sixth sense makes me duck, and a bullet slams into a tree instead of me as I lurch sideways.

Run, Chloe.

Mom's voice is clearer than ever, and with a surge

of strength I didn't know I possessed, I launch into a full-scale run. My ankle screams each time my foot strikes the ground, my vision blurring from nausea and waves of pain, but I run with everything I've got.

Only it's not enough.

Not nearly enough.

A truck-like force rams into me, knocking me off my feet, and a massive weight crushes me into the leaf-strewn dirt. I can't even wheeze as my ribcage flattens out—and then, miraculously, the weight is gone and I'm flipped over onto my back.

When my vision clears, I see a huge dark-haired man straddling me, gun pointed at my face and mouth twisted in a triumphant snarl.

"Gotcha, little bitch," he says, panting. "And since you made us work for it, you owe us some fun."

51

CHLOE

AIR RUSHES INTO MY OXYGEN-STARVED LUNGS, AND I swing my fist blindly, aiming at that smug face. He intercepts it with ease, brutal fingers catching my wrist and pinning it to the ground as he jams the barrel of the gun under my chin.

"Move again, and I blow your fucking head off," he growls, and I believe him.

I see my death in his flat, dark eyes.

"What the fuck, Arnold?" a second voice exclaims, and another man appears above us. Also armed with a gun, he looks to be some dozen years older than my captor, with receding salt-and-pepper hair and ruddy skin flushed from the exertion of the run. Breathing heavily, he orders, "Put a bullet in her and be done."

"Not yet," Arnold mutters, eyes glued to my mouth. "She's pretty. You ever notice that?"

The other man's voice turns gruff. "That's not the way we do things."

"Who gives a fuck? She's dead meat anyway. Who cares if we enjoy a bite before we bury it?"

My stomach heaves with a fresh surge of nausea, and only the cold barrel jammed under my chin keeps me from clawing the asshole's eyes out as he lets go of my wrist and presses a thick, dirty thumb to my tightly clamped lips.

"Just finish the fucking job already."

The older man's tone is sharper, more impatient, and for a moment, I'm half-afraid, half-hopeful that Arnold will obey. But he just leans in and drags a wet, jerky-scented tongue over my cheek, like a dog—and as an involuntary cry of disgust escapes my throat, he jams his thumb into my mouth, pushing it so far in I gag.

"That's nice, bitch," he whispers, eyes gleaming with lust and feral excitement. "That's real—"

A sharp *crack* shatters the silence, and he yanks his hand back. A millisecond later, he's on his feet above me, gun coming up as he spins around lightning fast— yet still not fast enough.

The second bullet slams him into the tree behind me, and as I scramble backward on my hands and ass, I see the older man already on the ground, mouth slack and skull blown open, brains spilling out like moldy cottage cheese.

52

NIKOLAI

I'M MOVING BEFORE THE SOUND OF MY LAST SHOT FADES, leaping out from behind the cover of the trees to close the distance between me and Chloe. Her gaze jerks up from the dead man at her side, her face streaked with dirt and blood, her brown eyes uncomprehending as she backs away, mouth opening in a silent scream at my approach.

"Shh, it's okay. It's me." Dropping to my knees, I gather her against me, feeling the convulsive trembling of her body—and of mine. I'm shaking with relief and rage and the aftermath of bone-chilling terror, the awful fear that we were too late.

We were almost at the gas station when Konstantin called me again with the news that his team had accomplished the nearly impossible feat of hacking into an NSA satellite, and that he was able to pinpoint the exact location of Chloe's car—and the black pickup truck that was less than a half hour behind her.

To say that we broke every speed limit in existence would be an understatement. Arkash is still recovering from the half-dozen times we nearly flew off a cliff. And we almost didn't make it anyway. The terror that assaulted me when I saw her car in a crumpled, burning heap... If it hadn't been for the empty pickup next to it and the sound of gunfire nearby, I would've lost my fucking mind.

Actually, I did lose it when I saw her on the ground with the dark-haired assassin straddling her, twisted lust painted on his face.

The motherfucker was going to rape her before killing her.

It was the only reason she wasn't already dead.

My arms tighten around her reflexively, and she makes a faint sound of distress.

I immediately pull back. "Are you hurt, zaychik? Injured in any way?"

She doesn't reply, just stares at me with huge, blank eyes, her pupils blown so wide her irises look black. She's in shock, and no wonder. Even a trained soldier would be traumatized.

Gently, I lay her down and begin inspecting her for injuries, starting with her ribs and stomach. I'm relieved to find only scrapes and bruises on her torso, but as my hand brushes over her right arm, she jerks with a pained cry, her face turning gray. I snatch my hand back, my pulse doubling at the sight of the red smear on my fingers as she squeezes her eyes shut, her breathing painfully shallow.

Fuck. She *is* hurt.

Steadying my hands, I rip open her sleeve.

"Gunshot?" Pavel asks in Russian, appearing at my side, and I nod grimly, ripping off a piece of my shirt to fashion a makeshift bandage.

"Looks like it went clean through, but she's losing a good amount of blood."

"So is he," Pavel says, and I tear my gaze from Chloe to glance at her assailant. He's sitting slumped against a tree trunk a few feet away, with Kirilov putting pressure on his chest wound and Arkash standing guard over them.

"I don't think he'll last long enough to get him back to the compound," Pavel says as I swiftly finish tying the bandage and resume my inspection of Chloe. Her color is a little better, but her eyes are still closed and her breaths are too shallow for my liking. "If you want to interrogate him, it has to be now."

Fuck. I deliberately tried to only wound the motherfucker so we'd be able to question him. If he dies, so does our chance to get answers.

I quickly finish patting down Chloe and leap to my feet. As much as I want to get my zaychik to a doctor right away, her injuries aren't life-threatening—but not knowing who her enemies are could be.

These men are pros, which means someone hired them, someone powerful, and I need to know who it is.

"Watch over her," I tell Pavel and step over to our captive.

He's breathing in jerky gasps, his face starkly pale and the entire front of his body soaked with blood.

Pavel's right. He doesn't have much longer. I meant to shoot him in the shoulder, but he spun around too fast, alerted to my presence by the bullet I had to put through his colleague's skull. With Pavel and the rest of the team unable to keep up with my terror-fueled sprint, I had no choice but to take out both assassins quickly, before they could do anything to Chloe.

In hindsight, I should've wounded them both.

As I crouch in front of the dying man, his lids lift, revealing baleful dark eyes.

"Who the fuck are you people?" he rasps, only to close his eyes, exhausted by the effort.

"Don't worry about that." Despite the volcanic rage boiling in my veins, my voice is lethally calm, controlled. "Who hired you? Why are you after her?"

His upper lip twists in a snarl. "Fuck you."

"You're dying, you know. I can let you fade away in peace or"—I take out my switchblade and flip it open—"I can mince you into pieces and make you feel every last slice."

His eyes open heavily. "Fuck off."

I throw a glance over my shoulder. Chloe is lying perfectly still, her eyes closed. Hopefully, she's passed out, or at least is so deeply in shock she won't register this next part.

Either way, there's no choice.

I need to get answers, fast.

I catch Arkash's gaze. "Do it."

The guard pulls out a syringe and stabs the dying assassin in the neck, injecting him with our pharmaceutical division's patented drug—the one the Russian military pays millions for.

The man barely reacts at first, only swatting at the site of the injection with a feeble hand. A moment later, however, his eyes go wide and he sits upright, his breathing speeding up as color rushes into his pallid cheeks.

"Epinephrine mixed with a few other fun substances," I tell him cruelly. "It'll keep you wide awake until the moment you croak. Which will be either a few neutral or a few terrible minutes from now. Your choice."

He's panting now, sweat running down his face. "Who the fuck *are* you?"

"If you don't start talking, the man who makes your last moments hell." I nod at Arkash and Kirilov, and they seize the man's arms, easily lifting them above his head despite his struggles.

"Last chance," I prompt, but the motherfucker just glares at me.

I smile darkly. I was hoping he'd prove difficult. As much as I prefer to play nice, this is the one time I'm looking forward to applying the skills Pavel taught me.

With the speed of a striking rattler, I stab my knife into the man's kidney and twist the blade.

The scream that rips from his throat is barely

human. The drug not only keeps him conscious, it enhances all sensations, magnifying pain a thousandfold.

Before he can recover, I yank out the blade and slice at his stomach twice, slashing through skin, fat, and muscle in a big X.

His eyes bulge, another inhuman scream tearing through his throat as I peel back the triangular flaps of flesh, revealing his insides.

"Have you ever wondered what it feels like to have your intestines cut out without anesthesia?" I ask conversationally. "No? Because you're about to find out. Actually, wait—I think that might kill you too quickly. We'll start lower." With another swift motion, I slash through the groin of his jeans, exposing his limp cock and balls.

"Wait!" His eyes are wild as my blade descends again. "I'll—I'll tell you."

I stop an inch from his shriveled dick. "Go ahead."

"I don't know why, okay? He never told us." He coughs, spitting up blood. "Just said we had to take them out."

"Them?"

"The woman and… the girl."

Fuck. "You were supposed to kill them both that day?"

"Yeah." His face is paler with each moment. "Only the girl was late. And then somehow she saw us and…" He coughs again, weakly, and I know the drug is losing the battle against his dying body.

"Who was it?" I demand urgently as his lids drift down. "Who hired you?" I press the sharp point of the knife against his balls. "Give me a fucking name!"

His eyes open blearily, and he croaks out three syllables—a name that nearly makes me drop my knife. My stunned gaze meets Arkash's and Kirilov's; written on their faces is the same slack-jawed look of disbelief.

"Did you just say—" I begin, returning my attention to the assassin, only to fall silent in frustration.

His eyes are vacant, his chest unmoving as his head lolls bonelessly to one side.

It's over. The motherfucker's gone.

I leap to my feet, my mind furiously sifting through what I know.

The man he named would definitely have the resources to do this, but what's the motivation? The connection? How would his and Chloe's paths have even crossed?

Unless... they didn't.

Chloe wasn't the only person on his hit list; her mother was on it too.

And then, like an avalanche, it hits me.

California. Young mother, still underage at the time of Chloe's birth. A father she never knew. A full-ride scholarship that came out of nowhere.

A different man, one with a normal, loving family, would never leap to a conclusion so twisted, so dark. But I'm a Molotov, and I know shared blood doesn't buy loyalty or safety.

I know love can be more violent than hate.

Heart thudding heavily, I turn to look at Chloe.

If I'm right, her very existence is a career-ending scandal—and another so-called father deserves my knife.

53

CHLOE

I'M IN HELL. EITHER THAT OR TRAPPED IN A NIGHTMARE. My arm is on fire, my insides are roiling, and each time the dark haze in my mind clears and I crack open my eyelids, I see Nikolai doing something ever more terrible as his deep, smooth voice utters threats that make bile churn in my throat. And the screaming that follows… My stomach lurches, and it's all I can do not to roll over and vomit.

This isn't real.

It can't be.

The dark haze threatens to swamp me again, and I focus on taking small, shallow breaths and keeping my eyes closed. It has to be a dream, a horrible, graphic dream, or a hallucination brought on by extreme terror. How else would Nikolai be here? How would he have found me?

Then again, how did my mom's killers?

My consciousness must cut out again, because

when I open my eyes next, I'm in the backseat of a moving SUV, comfortably ensconced on a man's lap. Nikolai's lap—I'd recognize that cedar-and-bergamot scent anywhere. His powerful arms are around me, holding me tight, and my pulse leaps with joyous relief as I realize this isn't a dream.

Nikolai is here.

He came for me.

I must make some kind of noise because he pulls back, eyes fiercely golden in his taut face. "Almost there," he promises, voice rougher than I've ever heard it. "The doctor is already waiting."

As he speaks, I become aware of a throbbing pain in my right arm and the general feeling of lightheadedness and extreme weakness, along with the sensation that I've been beaten all over with a club. The latter must be from jumping out of the car—and also from being tackled to the ground by the younger killer. My heart rate triples as I recall his face above me, the twisted hunger in those flat, dark eyes.

How did I go from there to here?

How is it that Nikolai—

Abruptly, my mind clears and the memories rush in, each more nauseating than the next. The older man with his skull blown off... Nikolai leaping toward me, gun held like an extension of his hand... His interrogation of the man who planned to rape me; the threats Nikolai made and the brutal, skilled way he wielded that switchblade... And the screams, those raw, blood-curdling screams...

I begin to shake as my gaze sweeps the car, taking in Pavel's stone-faced presence next to us and the two dangerous-looking men up front. I've never seen them before, but they must be guards from the compound. My eyes snap back to Nikolai's face, that perfectly sculpted face that can look alternately savage and tender, and I notice a reddish-brown streak over one high cheekbone.

Blood. Dried blood.

My shaking intensifies. Misinterpreting the cause, Nikolai strokes my jaw, his fierce expression softening. "It's okay, zaychik, you're safe. They can't hurt you."

But *he* can. I'm painfully, acutely aware that I'm at the mercy of this beautiful, terrifying man. Being held on his lap only highlights the size and strength differences between us; his large, powerful body surrounds me completely, the muscular band of his arm at my back as inescapable as any iron chain. Not that I'd be able to escape in any case—not with his men here, not while the SUV is driving at full speed.

I'm better off not knowing, but I can't hold back the question. "It was you, wasn't it?" My voice emerges as a strained whisper. "You shot him in the head."

It's as if a veil drops over Nikolai's face, all hint of expression disappearing. "I had no choice. If I'd only injured him, he could've killed you while I dealt with his partner. With the two of them there, I had to eliminate one, fast."

"And the other man…" I swallow down a surge of nausea at the recollection of the screams. "Is he…?"

"Dead from his injuries, yes." There's no remorse in Nikolai's voice, no sign of guilt in his level gaze, and shards of ice form in my veins as I realize he's done this before.

He's killed and tortured others.

Including, most likely, his own father.

"Stop the car!" The words fly out of my mouth before I can consider their wisdom. Ignoring the dizzying flare of pain in my arm, I wedge my hands between us and push against his chest—which, for some reason, feels like it's plated with steel. Desperate, I resort to begging. "Please, Nikolai, let me out. I need… I just need a minute."

He doesn't budge, and neither do any of his men as he says quietly, "We're almost home, zaychik. Just a few minutes longer."

Home? My panicked gaze jumps to the window, and fear squeezes my chest as I recognize the road leading up to the compound, the steep curves of which I navigated just this morning as I fled from the man holding me… the man I didn't truly believe was a killer.

"Don't worry. I had the doctor and his team come out here," Nikolai says, addressing a question that's just started forming in my mind. "They brought everything they need to treat you."

I take in his implacable expression, my fear growing with each passing second. "I would prefer a hospital. Please, Nikolai… just take me to a hospital."

"I can't." His chiseled features might as well be made of granite. "It's not safe."

"Safe? But—"

"Those two were just hired guns. There's plenty more where they came from."

My throat goes dry. In my panic, I almost forgot about the mystery of the killers' motivations. "Is that what he told you? The man you… questioned?" Is my theory right, after all? Did my mom witness something she shouldn't have?

"Yes, and Chloe…" He frames my cheek with his large, warm palm, the tender gesture belying the hard set of his features. "They were there to kill you both."

"What?" I jerk back. "No, that's not poss—"

"That's what the assassin said. If you hadn't been late coming home…" He drops his hand, a muscle flexing violently in his jaw.

"But that doesn't—" I stop short as fragments of the conversation I overheard that day surface in my mind.

Supposed to be here… Maybe there's traffic…

I heard the killers say that, but for some reason, I didn't put two and two together, didn't realize they were talking about *me*, waiting for *me*.

"I don't understand." I'm shaking again, trembling with a chill that has nothing to do with the AC inside the car. "Why would anyone want me dead? I haven't done anything, I don't know anyone, I'm just—just me."

Nikolai's expression shifts, a strange pity entering his gaze. "No, zaychik, I don't think you are."

"What?" I push against his bizarrely hard chest again—and nearly faint from the fresh explosion of pain in my arm. His face swims in front of my eyes, and I'm still fighting not to pass out when a startling realization filters in.

That hardness is a bulletproof vest.

In the next moment, however, I forget all about it because Nikolai asks, "Does the name *Tom Bransford* mean anything to you?"

The syllables don't make sense at first. "You mean… the presidential candidate?" As soon as the question leaves my lips, I realize how absurd it is. He can't possibly be talking about the California senator who's all over the news these days, the one they're comparing to JFK. I must've misheard or—

"That's the one." His eyes gleam like antique gold. "Unless there's another Tom Bransford with the resources to hire professional assassins, erase security tapes, and alter police records."

"Police records? What—"

"I've gone through all the files relating to your case," he says gently, "and there's nothing about the masked men at your mom's apartment—nor the black pickup that nearly ran you over. In fact, according to the official record, it was a neighbor who discovered your mother; you never even showed up to identify the body."

"That's not true! I went to the station and—"

"I know." His gaze darkens. "And there's more. Your emails to the journalists never reached their destination. Someone with a very specific set of skills made sure they'd be blocked or marked as spam—and they also got rid of whatever proof there was of your story, like traffic cam recordings and security tapes that would've shown you getting attacked."

I feel like a sinkhole is opening underneath me. "How do you know all this?" My voice shakes, my thoughts spinning like twigs in a tornado. I don't know what to think, what to believe, and the throbbing pain in my arm isn't helping. "How did you—"

"Because I also have resources. Including some that Bransford doesn't."

Of course. That's how he found me so fast today—and why I'm completely screwed if he intends to harm me. My heart thuds painfully, a cold sweat drenching my shirt as another wave of dizziness attacks me, making black dots dance at the corners of my vision. Blood loss, I realize dimly; that must be what's causing this. Desperately, I suck in air, but it only helps a little, and my voice sounds like it's coming from far away as I ask shakily, "Why did you come after me today? Why—" I drag in another breath. "Why are you bringing me back?"

His eyes return to their bright, savage tiger hue. "Why wouldn't I?"

Because I ran, I think woozily. *Because you're most likely a psychopath incapable of real feelings. Because none of this, especially you and me, makes any sense.*

I end up giving the only reason I can, one that weighs on me heaviest of all. "Because if you're right about Bransford, you and your family are in even greater danger." My voice wavers as another wave of lightheadedness crashes into me. Still, I persevere. "You have to let me go. Now. Before it's too late."

A dark curve touches his sensuous lips, a glimmer of wry amusement kindling in his gaze as he gently cups my cheek. "I don't know if you've picked up on it, zaychik," he says softly, "but my family and I aren't exactly strangers to danger. In fact, we're well acquainted with it."

He kisses me then, softly at first, then with increasing urgency, and despite everything, familiar heat sparks low in my core. He deepens the kiss, his tongue mating with mine in a primal dance that makes no allowance for our lack of privacy, and my head spins, my dizziness increasing until he's the only solid anchor in my world. Overwhelmed, I cling to him, clutching fistfuls of his shirt, and with my thoughts dissolving under the dark pull of desire, it doesn't matter that I've seen him take two lives today, that he may be the very definition of a monster.

Nothing matters except the two of us, and by the time he lets me come up for breath, we're already past the gate, back in his domain.

"Don't worry, zaychik," he murmurs, his thumb stroking my lower lip as a shiver racks my battered body. "We'll get to the bottom of this, I promise. I'll keep you safe." And in his eyes, I read the unspoken:

Even if you object.

SNEAK PEEKS

Thank you for reading! If you would consider leaving a review, it would be greatly appreciated. Nikolai & Chloe's story continues in *Angel's Cage*.

To be notified about my future books, including more stories featuring the Molotov family, sign up for my newsletter at annazaires.com.

Are you craving more dark, suspenseful romance? Check out my bestselling *Tormentor Mine* series, the thrilling story of a Russian assassin bent on revenge and the woman he becomes obsessed with, at annazaires.com.

Do you enjoy laugh-out-loud romantic comedy? My hubby and I cowrite raunchy, geeky romcoms under the pen name Misha Bell. Grab a copy of our debut novel *Hard Code* to meet Fanny, the quirky coder stuck with the task of quality testing sex toys, and her mysterious Russian boss, who steps in to help out, at mishabell.com.

Are you an Urban Fantasy fan? Check out *The Girl Who Sees*, written by my hubby Dima Zales, the epic tale of a stage illusionist who discovers she has very real powers and the hot alpha male mentor who helps her hone her skills, at dimazales.com.

If you like audiobooks, please visit annazaires.com to check out this series and our other books in audio.

Now, please turn the page to read excerpts from *Tormentor Mine* and *Hard Code*.

EXCERPT FROM TORMENTOR MINE
BY ANNA ZAIRES

He came to me in the night, a cruel, darkly handsome stranger from the most dangerous corners of Russia. He tormented me and destroyed me, ripping apart my world in his quest for vengeance.

Now he's back, but he's no longer after my secrets.

The man who stars in my nightmares wants me.

"Are you going to kill me?"

She's trying—and failing—to keep her voice steady. Still, I admire her attempt at composure. I approached her in public to make her feel safer, but she's too smart to fall for that. If they've told her anything about my background, she must realize I can snap her neck faster than she can scream for help.

"No," I answer, leaning closer as a louder song comes on. "I'm not going to kill you."

"Then what do you want from me?"

She's shaking in my hold, and something about that both intrigues and disturbs me. I don't want her to be afraid of me, but at the same time, I like having her at my mercy. Her fear calls to the predator within me, turning my desire for her into something darker.

She's captured prey, soft and sweet and mine to devour.

Bending my head, I bury my nose in her fragrant hair and murmur into her ear, "Meet me at the Starbucks near your house at noon tomorrow, and we'll talk there. I'll tell you whatever you want to know."

I pull back, and she stares at me, her eyes huge in her pale face. I know what she's thinking, so I lean in again, dipping my head so my mouth is next to her ear.

"If you contact the FBI, they'll try to hide you from me. Just like they tried to hide your husband and the others on my list. They'll uproot you, take you away from your parents and your career, and it will all be for nothing. I'll find you, no matter where you go, Sara… no matter what they do to keep you from me." My lips brush against the rim of her ear, and I feel her breath hitch. "Alternatively, they might want to use you as bait. If that's the case—if they set a trap for me—I'll know, and our next meeting won't be over coffee."

She shudders, and I drag in a deep breath, inhaling her delicate scent one last time before releasing her.

Stepping back, I melt into the crowd and message Anton to get the crew into positions.

I have to make sure she gets home safe and sound, unmolested by anyone but me.

Order your copy of *Tormentor Mine* today, at annazaires.com!

EXCERPT FROM HARD CODE BY
MISHA BELL

My new assignment at work: test out toys. Yup, that kind.

Well, technically, it's to test the app that controls the toys remotely.

One problem? The showgirl who's supposed to test the hardware (as in, the actual toys) joins a nunnery.

Another problem? This project is important to my Russian boss, the broody, mouthwateringly sexy Vlad, a.k.a. The Impaler.

There's only one solution: test both the software and the hardware myself... with his help.

NOTE: This is a standalone, raunchy, slow-burn romantic comedy featuring a quirky, nerdy heroine, her hot, mysterious Russian boss, and two guinea pigs who may or may not be into each other. If any of the above is not your cup of tea, run far, far away. Otherwise, buckle in for a snort-water-up-the-nose-funny, feel-good ride.

"Me?" Eyes widening, he steps back.

I'm committed now, so I barrel ahead. "It makes sense. I presume you trust yourself not to toss me into the Harbor. The privacy of the project isn't compromised. And, well"—I blush horribly—"you have the right parts for it."

Unbidden, my eyes drop to said parts, then I quickly look up.

The elevator doors open.

"Let's continue this in the car," he says, his expression turning unreadable.

Crap, crap, crap. Is he hating the idea? Hating me for even suggesting it? Ugh, how awkward is it going to be if he says no?

Am I about to get fired for coming on to my boss's boss?

We get into the limo again, sitting opposite each other this time.

He makes the partition go up. "Just to clarify: I test the male batch, acting as both giver and receiver, right? I actually already tested one of the pieces on myself after I wrote the app, so I could in theory do the same with the rest of them."

Yes! He's actually considering it. I want to jump up and down, even as the blush that had slightly receded on the walk from the elevator returns in all its glory. "That wouldn't be good end-to-end testing, and you know it. You wrote the code; that makes you biased."

His nostrils flare. "Then how?"

Even my feet are blushing at this point. "You just act as the receiver. I act as the giver, and record the testing data. It's the proper way these things are done."

His eyebrows lift. "That's stretching the definition of the word 'proper' way outside its comfort zone."

"Look." I try to mime his accent as best I can. "If you want to quit, I understand."

A slow, sensuous smile curves his lips. "I don't shy away from a challenge."

Can my panties really melt, or is that just a saying?

———

Order your copy of *Hard Code* today, at mishabell.com!

ABOUT THE AUTHOR

Anna Zaires is a *New York Times, USA Today,* and #1 international bestselling author of sci-fi romance and contemporary dark erotic romance. She fell in love with books at the age of five, when her grandmother taught her to read. Since then, she has always lived partially in a fantasy world where the only limits were those of her imagination. Currently residing in Florida, Anna is happily married to Dima Zales (a science fiction and fantasy author) and closely collaborates with him on all their works.

To learn more, please visit annazaires.com.